King Arthur and his Knights

ANTHONY MOCKLER

King Arthur
and his Knights

Illustrated by Nick Harris

Oxford University Press 1984

OXFORD TORONTO MELBOURNE

Oxford University Press, Walton Street, Oxford OX2 6DP

Oxford London
New York Toronto Melbourne Auckland
Kuala Lumpur Singapore Hong Kong Tokyo
Delhi Bombay Calcutta Madras Karachi
Nairobi Dar es Salaam Cape Town
and associated companies in
Beirut Berlin Ibadan Mexico City Nicosia

Oxford is a trade mark of Oxford University Press

Text © Anthony Mockler 1984
Illustrations © Nick Harris 1984
First published 1984

British Library Cataloguing in Publication Data
Mockler, Anthony
King Arthur and his knights.
I. Title
823'.914[J]   PZ7
ISBN 0-19-274531-X

Typeset by Rowland Phototypesetting Ltd, Bury St Edmunds, Suffolk
Printed in Hong Kong

Contents

Book Three   The Book of Doom

Colour Plates

These tales are dedicated,
with love and affection,
to the legendary lady,
the red-haired Gwendoline.

Foreword

ARTHURIAN legend is rich; and with each literary generation that passes it grows richer still. Every teller of Arthurian tales has built on his predecessors. This is the traditional practice; for there is no 'correct' or 'incorrect' version of the Arthurian legends but a myriad variations.

Sir Thomas Malory himself, on whose massive *Morte Arthur* most English writers base their tales, 'dyd take his copye oute of certeyn books of Frensshe and reduced it to Englysse'. Indeed his final book the eponymous *Most Piteous Tale of the Morte Arthur Saunz Guerdon* was largely drawn from the French romance *La Mort Le Roi Artu* – many incidents from which I have adapted for the final battle of the Great Plain.

The Welsh legends are nowadays generally believed to be the original Arthurian source material. The picture they present is of a very different society, more magical and far crueller than that of Malory's world of chivalry. From these legends I have adapted, in particular, the little-known Adventure of the Twrch Trwyth, as well as various incidents and references – for example, to the Raven Army of Sir Yvain.

Numerous romances, in Italian, Spanish and German, as well as French, English and Welsh, are centred on both Sir Gawain, my own favourite among the Knights, and Merlin. Learned essays have been written on the significance of Merlin's portrayal as the Giant Herdsman. His famous prophecies are to be found in Geoffrey of Monmouth's prose *History of the Kings of England*. This highly imaginative work, completed in 1135, three centuries before Malory, is the basis for many of the later legends; it does not, incidentally, mention Sir Lancelot – himself the invention of Chrétien de Troyes and the exotic Court of Champagne.

As regards far later 'sources', recently-grown-up readers and critics can hardly fail to notice the influence of both T. H. White and Tolkien. That of *The Sword in the Stone* is natural. I deliberately resisted the temptation to reread this marvellous book while writing the earlier chapters of mine; but nevertheless it introduced itself, of its own volition. Clearly the influence of *The Lord of the Rings* (which I also, deliberately, did not reread) is more studied; but in some ways more justified. For where did Tolkien draw his material if not from a medley of sagas and legends, ancient, modern and medieval? The hobbits can perhaps be traced back to *Wind in the Willows* land, the Riders of Rohan more directly to French medieval chronicles, Gondar to Ethiopian history, and Gandalf the Grey most certainly to the figure of Merlin. And where did the name of Mordor spring from if not from Tolkien's own memories of the evil Sir Mordred? Between them T. H. White and Tolkien will, I hope, have permanently influenced and enriched the Arthurian tales of those who come later.

One omission may startle: there is no telling here of the great legend of the Quest for the Grail. I felt I could not do justice to the full richness of the great legend and all its ramifications: the Dolorous Stroke, the evil Enchantments of Logres, the Waste Land, the Deaths of Sir Balin and Sir Balan, the Killings of King Pellinore and his kin, the Chess Game of Sir Yvain, the Return of Merlin, the Quest for the Good Knight, the Siege Perilous, and then all the adventures of the Quest for the Grail itself, culminating in the Healing of the Fisher King and the Return of the Knights. This is far too complex and too marvellous to be condensed into a few extra pages, and is really the subject of a separate book.

Victorian and Edwardian tellers of these tales used to set King Arthur and his knights before their young readers as models of behaviour. In rather a different spirit – so would I.

ANTHONY MOCKLER
Forest of Broceliande

Autumn 1982

BOOK ONE

The Book of Merlin

Prologue

THE Forest covered the land. Dark and menacing, it spread to the rivers' borders and the ocean's edge. Mountains and cold plains of barren stone broke through its surface. Here and there men had beaten out leafy tracks and planted castles or cities in the glades. But around them all grew the Forest, never ending, never tamed.

The Forest could be very cold and very frightening. But there was life in it: beasts and birds of all sorts, ranging from the gentle deer and the wild boar, both of which men hunted, to the lions and the leopards that hunted men. There were older things too that lurked in the Forest's deep green depths: rarely seen but much feared. Beasts like the basilisk and the wyvern and the deadly little cockatrice and beings that were almost human but were feared by man and beast alike: giants and dwarfs, of course, but also trolls and feys and sorcerers.

No man knew where Merlin the Sorcerer came from. Some said he was an incubus, the child of a flying fiend; yet, though all men were in awe of him and his cruel humour, he was not, they knew, wholly evil. The old women huddled the babies by the fires in the dark evenings and frightened the children with tales of Merlin. They told of how he could shift his shape whenever he wanted, how he knew the future and the past, how when anger seized him he swelled like a menacing shadow. They described him: he was dark and very hairy, with glittering eyes – and the children shuddered and looked around, afraid that Merlin might be there lurking among them in disguise or behind them in the shadows.

But for years Merlin stayed in the Forest and watched the stars that speckled the sky: for he loved the dark forest and the creatures of the night. He was watching for a sign. And at last the sign came. It seemed, as he watched the clouds scudding across the cold canopy of the night, that suddenly all the stars came together mistily beneath the crescent of the new moon to form a great shape in the sky: the shape of a dragon's head. The dragon's head hovered between earth and heaven. Merlin sighed, and, gathering his great black cloak around him, called for his night-riders. For he knew that a new time was beginning upon earth and that he would have to visit the haunts of men.

CHAPTER I

The Giant Herdsman

ONE morning at sunrise an old man, bent and crippled, came to the court of Uther the High King.

'King,' he said, 'grant me a favour.'

Broad-shouldered Uther laughed in his red beard, for he had just taken over the kingdom, and was in high good spirits.

'Old man,' said the King, 'on a fine morning like this, anything you want.'

'Answer me three questions.'

'I wish,' said the King, 'that everybody asked for favours as easy to grant.'

'My first question is this: who is the most beautiful woman in your realm?'

Then King Uther fell very quiet, and started

chewing his red beard. He looked around at all the ladies in his Great Hall – each and every one of them was hoping that the King would say that she was the most beautiful. But in fact the one the King loved was not there. 'Old man,' said the King, 'how can I answer your question? For if I say one of these ladies is the most beautiful, then all the others will be offended. That would be a fine way to begin my reign! No, ask me your next question.'

'My second question is this: what is the device of your reign?' A device was the symbol that each king had to choose when he came to the throne.

'By the hairs of my beard,' said the King, 'that's another difficult question. I haven't chosen one yet. It might be a leopard, it might be a unicorn, it might be . . . you must give me a little time to decide. After all, I have only been King for one day.' He laughed nervously. 'Let's hope your third question is easier than your first two.'

'My third question is this. How can you tell if an old man is not a sorcerer in disguise?'

'Well,' said the King, 'that's an easy one at last. Because . . .' But then he fell silent, for an icy wind seemed to fill the whole hall and there was the noise of the rushing of invisible wings. The warriors put their hands to their swords, the ladies muttered softly to each other, and the old man seemed to grow before the eyes of all to a figure tall and dark, ageless and frighteningly splendid.

There was a moment of hushed silence. Then the King rose from his throne.

'Merlin,' he said; and though he was brave, his voice trembled. And as a hundred voices echoed his, the name of 'Merlin' hissed around the walls.

'At least,' said Merlin softly, 'you seem to have found the right answer to my third question, O King. And now let me tell you the answer to my second question: the device of your reign and of your battle standard is a sky-dragon. And you yourself shall be known as Uther Pendragon, that is, Uther

Dragon's Head, for so the star lords proclaimed last night. And I, Merlin the Sorcerer, who know the past, understand the present and see the future, have come out of the Forest, Uther Pendragon, to serve you in the new age of mankind that now begins.'

Then the King and his warriors and his ladies were happy that the greatest sorcerer in the land had come not to cast a spell on them but to help them. The serfs brought out the gold flagons and the red wine; even the fierce wolf-hounds fawned and played at Merlin's feet. But at the height of the feasting King Uther Pendragon took Merlin aside a little and whispered in his ear.

'Sorcerer, you have not told me yet the answer to the first question.' Merlin turned his glittering eyes on the King, and the King's gaze dropped.

'You know the answer yourself, King, only too well. The most beautiful woman in the realm is Ygraine of Cornwall.'

The King's heart thudded. He knew Merlin was right.

'You have never seen her,' he blustered, 'she is not even here, I was not sure myself I loved her till just now, and besides . . .'

'And besides,' added Merlin silkily, finishing the sentence that the King had not dared complete, 'she is married to Gorlois of Cornwall, your sworn companion.'

'Yes,' said the King. 'So of this love, nothing but harm and evil can come.'

'Of this love,' said Merlin, and his voice now was not silky or sibilant but hard and clear as a burnished blade, 'I tell you this: there will come a greater king than you, the noblest and most courteous king of all the world. His knights will be the most famous knights in all history, his tale shall be told as long as men and children love stories, and even grey death that lies in wait for all kings shall not destroy him. That is your fate, and his fate, Uther Pendragon.'

With that, Merlin swirled his great cloak about him and vanished from the hall back into the gloom of the Forest, leaving the young King bemused and agape. For he knew now that he was part of a greater thing than he would ever be himself.

Ygraine of Cornwall could have been the sea-god's daughter, all men said, or maybe even a sea-witch herself. Her eyes were sea-blue, her golden hair was tossed and windy, her skin gleamed silvery, and she could swim like a dolphin. Uther Pendragon rode down to Cornwall to see her: for, ever since talking to Merlin, he had been smitten with the love-madness.

'Hello, fair sire,' she said – she was an old friend of Uther's from the days before he was king, and so she could talk to him more merrily than most ladies – 'How are you and what is it like to be king? I'm sorry Gorlois isn't here to welcome you too, but he has gone sailing over the summer seas and won't be back till autumn. But come in, come into the hall, away from the wind-swept cliff. It is so long since I have seen you, Uther. Why, your beard is redder than ever. Have you been spilling wine all over it?' And so, chattering all the while, she took her king by the hand and led him into the hall where three little girls rushed forward.

'Girls,' said Ygraine, suddenly solemn. 'This is your lord the King.' The three girls stopped dead, for they had never seen a king before. 'My lord King,' she went on, 'you may remember Morgawse my eldest daughter' – she held out her hand to a girl aged nine, tall and shy with eyes as blue as her own but hair that was raven black.

'One day,' said the King, 'you will be as great a beauty as your mother.'

'This is my second daughter, Elaine.' Elaine was a plain child. The King patted her kindly on the head.

'But this one,' said Ygraine, 'you have never seen. She is my baby and she bewitches us all. So Gorlois always calls her Morgan le Fay.'

Uther looked down at a little girl of three clutching at his scabbard and playing with the jewels on it, totally unawed. Her eyes were green as emeralds, her cheeks as red as fire, and her voice curled around Uther and crept up his body like a wraith of smoke – a voice that said only one word over and over again: 'King . . . King . . . King . . .'

So Uther Pendragon feasted in Gorlois' hall. He stayed a week, and then another week, a month and then another month. Men saw that he could hardly bear to leave Ygraine's side for the love-sickness. Women said that he had eyes only for her and would have married her had she not married Gorlois first. But Ygraine loved her handsome husband, Gorlois the sea-rover; and though, when she was in the mood, she would comb the King's red beard for him, she would never allow him to brush her golden hair. But as the sunlit summer turned to autumn and Gorlois was expected to sail back into harbour any day, the King grew more and more lovesick. He spent hours sitting by himself.

One morning Uther heard screams near the hilltop where he was brooding, looking out to sea. He picked up his sword and dashed to the rescue. It was the little girl Morgan le Fay who was screaming. She was cowering away from the biggest and ugliest giant the King had ever seen.

The giant was tall, black, bristly, lean, old with a great age, and at least eighteen feet tall. His head was as big as a buffalo's, he had a hideous hump behind his spine, his mouth was large and wide as a dragon's, his thick lips always open so that his teeth showed all round – and, most hideous of all, his ears hung down to his waist like a winnowing fan. In his hands – the palms of his hands were where the backs should have been, his hands were all the wrong way round – he held an enormous club. Uther was very brave and had fought many giants but he had never seen one as dreadful as this before. Besides, he had no armour, only a sword.

'Fight him! Fight him!' cried Morgan le Fay, clapping her hands. Her green eyes gleamed with excitement. She did not seem in the least bit frightened now – though King Uther certainly was. Uther raised his sword. The giant took a mighty swipe at it, and knocked it flying out of his hands. Uther ran after it, tripped, fell, felt sure that the next blow would smash his skull to smithereens and closed his eyes. Nothing happened. He opened his eyes again. The gaint was standing over him with a horrible great smile on his face.

'Who are you?' asked Uther.

'The Giant Herdsman,' said the giant. His voice sounded like ten trumpets, and when Uther looked up, he could see to his surprise stags, bucks and harts all coming out of the Forest and gathering around the Giant Herdsman.

'Why aren't you fighting?' screamed Morgan le Fay. 'Go on, King. Go on, Giant. Fight!'

The Giant Herdsman turned towards her, rolled his eyes, and twitched his enormous ears.

'Swee, swi, swo, swirl,' he said, swirling his enormous club up over his head, 'I smell the blood of a succulent girl.'

With a scream Morgan le Fay ran away, really frightened. She knew all about what giants liked eating.

'What a little monster,' said the giant. 'Not what I would call a tasty morsel at all. In fact I rather think that an unbiased observer would judge her to be potentially more alarming even than myself.'

This was not the sort of way giants usually talked. Uther was amazed. He looked at the giant very carefully and, as he looked, the Giant Herdsman seemed to fade away and another, more familiar figure take his place.

'Merlin!' cried the King.

Merlin stood on the cliff-top, and the sun went in.

'Merlin,' said Uther sharply, 'why give me such a fright?' Merlin pulled at his long silky beard, a little embarrassed.

'It wasn't you I meant to scare, O King,' he said. 'I just thought I'd teach that little green-eyed fiend-child a lesson. Show her what a wizard can do.'

'It's monstrous!' exclaimed Uther.

'Yes,' said Merlin, rather pleased. 'I was rather, wasn't I?

But I've always had a penchant for the Wild Man of the Woods, you know. Not that I think I really scared her at all,' he added with regret.

'Merlin,' said Uther pitifully, 'kings are more important than little girls. Hear *my* worries now. I love Ygraine the sea-witch, as you told me I did, but she loves only Gorlois the Handsome, her husband. Why, she will not even let me brush out her hair. Unless I can have Ygraine, I will be dead of love. But she will on no account have me. Your prophecy about her was all wrong, sorcerer.'

Merlin's eyes flashed. He did not care to be called 'sorcerer' or told he was wrong, even by a king.

'Tonight,' he said, 'Ygraine the Beautiful will love you.'

'Rubbish,' said the King moodily.

The next thing Uther knew was that the cliff in front of him had fallen away with a great roar and he was teetering on the edge of a sheer drop of several hundred feet.

'Never say "rubbish" to a sorcerer, O King,' said Merlin savagely. 'Otherwise I might forget who you are. Tonight, I say.'

And swirling his cloak around him, he seemed to float away into the sea mists.

That evening in the Great Hall Ygraine appeared more beautiful than ever to the besotted King. The bard sang on his harp the story of how Gorlois and Uther together had burnt their enemy Vortigern in his stronghold before Uther became King; and of how the two had ever since been sword-companions. King Uther drank deeply. When he held his goblet out for the seventh time to be refilled, he was rather drunk: but not so drunk that he did not notice that the drink he was pouring down his throat tasted black and sticky, not sweet and red. He turned round to the cup-bearer to complain: it seemed to him that the cup-bearer leaned over and murmured in his ear: 'Bat's wings, toad's blood, owl's pellets, marsh mud, dragon's brains, cow's cud.'

'What?' said Uther, highly alarmed.

But the cup-bearer, who had seemed for a moment tall and hairy with an evil grin, was just an ordinary cup-bearer again and simply poured out another goblet of good red wine.

'Go to bed, Uther,' said Ygraine a little later. 'Go to bed and sleep it off, poor King.' She smiled a little sadly and ran her cool hand through his tumbled hair.

So Uther, escorted by his squires, stumbled up to his chamber and flopped down on his bed. As he dreamt, Merlin appeared to him.

'Awake, King Uther Pendragon,' he said. 'Now has come the hour. Go to her now.'

Hardly knowing what he was doing, the King rose to his feet and made his way to Ygraine's chamber.

'Who is it?' cried Ygraine, waking up as he bent over her. To his amazement Uther heard himself say in a voice that was not his own: 'Gorlois your husband.' As he felt Ygraine's soft arms around his neck and her cheek touching his, he realized with a start that he had no beard.

'Gorlois,' she murmured. 'Back at last! Gorlois, my heart!' and pulled him gently down beside her.

Sure enough, when the sun rose, there were the ships of Gorlois riding at anchor beneath the cliffs. King Uther awoke in his own chamber and greeted his sword-companion Gorlois with great joy, all the greater because he had had his love with Ygraine that one night thanks to the magic potion of Merlin which had changed him for a few hours into the image of Gorlois the Handsome. Ygraine never knew she had loved the King instead of her dear husband.

Long afterwards King Uther asked Merlin casually: 'Was it really toad's blood and bat's wings and all the rest of it?'

'All that and much more,' he said. 'After all, it needed a really mighty potion to make a man like you look and smell

and taste like the handsome Gorlois, even in the dark. You may be a king, sire, but you are not exactly good-looking.'

Nine months later the beautiful Ygraine gave birth to a baby boy. She and Gorlois were overjoyed to have a son at last. But Uther Pendragon when he heard the news was even more overjoyed, for he knew the son was really his. 'Little Boar of Cornwall' Gorlois called him, because he was a bold and savage baby. But his real name was Arthur.

Of them all Merlin alone knew that he would be the most famous knight in all the world.

CHAPTER 2

Merlin and Sir Hector

WHILE Arthur was still a tiny baby Merlin took him away from dangerous Cornwall to a castle in the Fenland, far from the Forest and far from the wild Celtic Sea. The owner of the castle was a small bad-tempered knight called Sir Hector who was a great friend of Merlin's.

'What's this baby *for*?' said Sir Hector. 'Castle's full of blasted babies already. I've got quite enough of my own, can't even remember all of their names as it is. Besides, he isn't even a beautiful baby. He's got a nasty gleam in his eye. No, Merlin, I don't want him and I won't have him.'

'Hector,' said Merlin calmly, 'stop hectoring.'

'I won't have him, wizard,' repeated Sir Hector,

'and that's that. You're always trying to foist something on me: babies in the bathroom, bats in the belfry, dooms in the dungeon, get rid of them all, I say.'

'Hector,' said Merlin a little less calmly. 'Did you say the baby's got a nasty gleam in its little eye? If you think that, have a look in my eye and tell me what you see there.'

Sir Hector looked up at Merlin who was growing very tall and menacing as he always did when he was about to lose his temper. Merlin had two *very* nasty gleams, one in each eye.

'Don't think you can frighten me, you blasted wizard,' said Sir Hector. 'Yap. Yap, yap, yap. Yap, yap. Yap.'

Sir Hector suddenly realized he was yapping, not hectoring. He also realized he was squatting, not standing. He looked at his hands and to his horror saw they were paws. He looked behind him and to his horror he saw he was wagging a small pudgy tail. He suddenly stopped yapping and licked Merlin's feet with a little red tongue.

'That's better,' said the wizard; and a moment or two later Sir Hector was back full-size – which still wasn't very large – again. 'It's a beautiful baby, isn't it?'

'Yes,' said Sir Hector humbly.

'And you'll bring it up like one of your own babies.'

'If you say so,' said Sir Hector.

'And you won't yap at it.'

'Well I can't change my character, can I?' muttered Sir Hector indignantly.

'No,' said Merlin affectionately – for he really liked Sir Hector as he was – 'it would need more than my magic to change your character. Even I couldn't change you into any sort of dog I wanted. You wouldn't have done as a spaniel, for instance, all soft and cuddly.'

'Bah!' said Sir Hector, at the thought of being soft and cuddly. 'What was I anyway?' he added.

'You were a pug.'

'Never heard of a dog called a pug in my life,' said Sir Hector indignantly, 'and I know all about dogs.'

'It comes from China.'

'Never heard of a place called China in my life,' said Sir Hector, 'no such place!'

'Ah,' sighed Merlin, 'I keep forgetting how ignorant you knights of the realm of Logres are. Didn't you ever learn any geography or history or zoology or biology?'

'Certainly not,' said Sir Hector. 'I studied archery and heraldry, chivalry and horsemanship, that's what I studied.'

'Reading and writing?'

'Ugh!' cried Sir Hector with real indignation. 'That's for clerks, not knights and squires. And let me tell you this, wizard, if I have to have this baby, he'll learn what I've learnt, and that's all, and he's not going to ruin his eyesight with reading and writing and arithmetic and all that rubbish.'

'Well,' said Merlin, 'so be it. Bring him up to be a good squire as you always do in the Fenland. But take care of him — don't let him go wandering off into the Forest or into the Sea. For he is a very precious little baby.'

'Who is he?' said Sir Hector, looking at the baby for the first time with real curiosity.

'That, I'm afraid,' said Merlin, 'is a secret. Always let him think he's your own son. I'll be back from time to time to see how he's getting on.' He lent over the baby and ran a finger down its plump little cheeks. 'Goodbye, Little Boar of Cornwall. You'll be happy here.'

Then he swirled his great cloak around him.

'Oy!' cried Sir Hector, as Merlin was disappearing. 'Oy!'

'What is it?' said Merlin, unfolding himself again.

'You haven't told me the brat's name.'

'Nor I have,' said Merlin. 'I must be getting old and forgetful. A few centuries ago I had everything pat. His name is Arthur.'

'Arthur,' said Sir Hector when Merlin had disappeared properly. 'Arthur. Pretty silly name, Arthur. Never heard of it before. Don't suppose anybody will ever hear of it again.'

But that was where Sir Hector was very wrong.

So Arthur grew up in Sir Hector's castle in the Fenland, thinking he was Sir Hector's own son. He learnt archery and heraldry, chivalry and horsemanship; and from time to time Merlin came and taught him special things.

'I don't like wizards,' said Kay – Kay was Sir Hector's eldest son. 'One day I'm going to be a knight and lord of this castle and the Fenland, and then I won't allow any wizards here at all. But you can stay if you like, little Arthur. You can be my squire.'

'I want to be a knight errant,' said Arthur.

'Well, you can't be,' said Kay who was tall and rather arrogant. 'You must be my squire and wait on me at table and lace up my helmet and hand me my lance at jousts. If you're lucky I'll let you ride into battle beside me. But if you're clumsy I'll beat you.'

'I am going to be a knight errant,' said Arthur, 'whether you want me to or not.'

'Oh you are, are you?' said Kay. 'We'll see about that' – and proceeded to beat him. Arthur fought back but though he was wiry, he was much smaller than Kay. Their scuffle brought Sir Hector stumping out of the tilt-yard.

'What's all this?' he said, giving them both a tap with the flat of his sword. 'What's all this row?'

'I want to be a knight errant when I grow up,' cried Arthur.

'He can't,' shouted Kay. 'He's got to be my squire and look after me because I'm the oldest and I'll be lord of the castle when you're dead.'

'I'm not dead yet, you little blighter,' growled Sir Hector, giving Kay a really hard blow with the flat of his battle-axe that made his eldest son squeal. 'Now go and polish the lances – all of them. I want them gleaming by tea-time, else it's a night in the dungeons for you. Go! As for you, Arthur, what's all this nonsense?'

'It's not nonsense, father,' said Arthur, trembling as he always did when he was excited. 'I want to ride out on quests through the realms of Logres and Lyonesse and the Seven

Kingdoms, I want to know the Forest and the Sea, I want to have my own war-horse and my own hound, my own shield and my own spear and my own marvellous sword – I'm going to give them each a name – and I want to do great deeds and win knightly renown.'

'And no doubt,' said Sir Hector, 'win a princess too.'

'Yes,' said Arthur, 'I'm going to save the most beautiful princess from the most dreadful dragon in the whole realm.'

'All a pack of nonsense,' said Sir Hector. 'Now you listen to me, boy. Out there, in the Forest and over the Sea, there are horrors you've never dreamed of. Here in the Fenland we have happy, quiet lives. How old are you now?'

'Ten, father,' said Arthur.

'And you've been happy?' asked Sir Hector, who was very fond of this strange son of his, even though he wasn't his own child.

'Yes, father.'

'Well,' said Sir Hector, 'if you want to stay happy, stay in the Fenland. It's your home. No wars here, no marauding kings, no trolls, orcs, giants, elf-witches, no dragons, no monsters. If you want a battle or two, we'll arrange a battle when Kay becomes a knight and you become a squire.'

'When will that be?' said Arthur eagerly.

'Well, not for a few years yet,' said Sir Hector. 'Kay's twelve, isn't he? Well, he can't become a knight till he's seventeen and you can't become a squire till you're fifteen – so that's . . . Dammit, Arthur, how many years is that? I was never much good at arithmetic.'

'Five, father.'

'Well,' said Sir Hector doubtfully, 'I suppose it's quite useful in a way Merlin coming and teaching you all this adding and subtracting. What else does he teach you?'

'Runes,' said Arthur, 'and a little sorcery.'

'Don't like that,' said Sir Hector, 'don't like that at all.' He was silent for a moment. 'Hasn't taught you how to change anyone into anything, has he?'

'Oh no,' said Arthur, 'not spells. Just elementary sorcery. How to understand birds and animals and fishes and foreigners, that sort of thing. What he calls modern languages and mysticism.'

'That's all right, then,' said Sir Hector, much relieved. He didn't fancy being changed into something awful by his own son. 'What was I saying? Oh, yes. Now look here, Arthur. Kay's quite right, you know. Some day I'm going to grow old and die, and Kay's going to be Sir Kay and lord of this castle. Then you must be his squire and help him. He'll be a good knight and you'll be a good squire. Don't be jealous of him – he won't marry a princess either! We're not rich or powerful, you know, just plain honest Fenland knights, and that's how it should be. Of course I agree there aren't many adventures in Fenland nowadays. But I won't forget about the battle,' he added hastily, not to disappoint Arthur. 'I'll go and see Sir Grummore Grummorson in the autumn and we'll fix it up. He'll be the enemy and we'll go and besiege his castle and then he'll come and besiege our castle, and in the end we'll have a pitched battle.'

Sir Hector glanced at Arthur to see how he was taking it. Arthur's eyes were wide-open, glowing with excitement.

'Good boy!' said Sir Hector, well pleased. 'Now run along and practise your archery. Archery, jousting, hand-to-hand combat, scaling ladders in full armour – you and Kay must practise and practise and practise so as you don't disgrace me in the battle. Oh, there'll be blood flowing and damsels fainting! We might even manage a bit of loot and pillage if we storm Sir Grummore's castle. We'll swop off the heads of a few peasants. Dammit, I'm quite looking forward to it myself. Long time since I've enjoyed a good battle.'

As the years passed, Merlin's visits to Sir Hector's castle became rarer and rarer till they almost ceased. Then one day, in mid-winter, Merlin appeared again, looking very gloomy.

'Have a glass of hot mead, old friend,' said Sir Hector 'and cheer up. There's a blazing fire in your bedroom at the top of the tower' – Merlin always slept at the top of towers – 'and clean green rushes for you to sleep on.'

'Haven't you heard the news?' said Merlin.

'What news?' asked Sir Hector.

'King Uther Pendragon is dead,' said the wizard.

'Oh, that,' said Sir Hector, 'yes I heard something about that. Poisoned, wasn't he?'

'He and a hundred warriors with him. I buried them inside the Giant's Ring.'

'Yes, well, very sad,' said Sir Hector. 'He was a friend of yours, wasn't he? But to tell the truth, Merlin, here in the Fenland we don't worry too much about marauding kings – wars and deaths and murders and all sorts of horrors. No, they don't bother us and we don't bother them.'

'Foolish man,' said Merlin angrily. 'You will have to begin to worry now. For a shower of blood will fall, and death will lay hands on the people. The seeds shall be rooted up and the children slain. The island will be sodden with the tears of the night-time. The Ravens will swoop down upon the land and the Worms will puff forth fire. The tail of Scorpio shall generate lightning and Cancer will fight with the Sun.'

'Well, yes,' said Sir Hector who always got upset when Merlin started prophesying, 'doesn't sound too rosy, does it? But of course, we can't let all that interfere with our little battle here. Just keep the Worms and the Ravens and Scorpions away, will you Merlin, please, at least till that's over. The boys will be too disappointed, otherwise.'

'The Boar of Cornwall shall arise and trample their necks beneath its feet,' went on Merlin, paying no attention to Sir Hector. 'The Islands of the Ocean shall be given unto the power of the Boar. The House of Romulus shall dread the Boar's savagery, and the end of the Boar will be shrouded in mystery.' He paused. 'What's all this about a battle?' He glared fiercely at Sir Hector. Obviously the wizard was in a very bad mood indeed, liable, Sir Hector realized, to start changing anyone into anything at the drop of a helmet.

'Oh, it's just to amuse the boys,' explained Sir Hector hastily. 'It's been fixed for years. You see, Kay's seventeen now and he's receiving the Order of Knighthood next Wednesday – actually he's fasting in the chapel all this week to prepare for it – and so of course we had to arrange a little battle to celebrate. Nothing very spectacular. No real danger for armoured knights and squires, though blood will have to be shed of course. But it's time they were blooded, you know.'

'They?' asked Merlin.

'Well, Kay and Arthur. Arthur's going to be his squire, of course. He's a good lad, and I've specially ordered a new suit of armour for him. Cost me a fortune.'

'You must call the battle off.'

'I can't,' said Sir Hector indignantly. 'Not now. Besides, I don't want to. I've been looking forward to it myself, almost as much as the boys. Years since we've had a proper battle here.'

'Do as I say,' said Merlin. 'There'll be battles enough soon enough to satisfy all you bloodthirsty knights. Call it off.'

'No, I won't, wizard. It's all fixed between me and Sir Grummore.'

'Worm,' said Merlin meditatively.

'What?'

'Worm, I said. Yes, a worm, I think.'

'Now wait a minute, Merlin. Now wait a minute,' said Sir Hector looking down worriedly at his feet to make sure they hadn't turned into a slimy tail. 'Don't be hasty. Please. With all these birds about it's not a joke.'

Falcons and peregrines, goshawks, sparrowhawks, kites and buzzards, his great hall was full of birds of prey that were only half-tame and always hungry.

'You deserve to squirm a little,' said Merlin.

Sir Hector felt himself shrinking and turning pale pink.

'Battle's off!' he cried hastily while he still had a tongue. His normal size and shape and colour returned. 'But the boys will never forgive me. They're my sons, Merlin, not yours. Why the devil should you interfere?'

'One of them,' said Merlin, 'is not your son.'

'Well, I suppose not,' said Sir Hector grumpily. 'Not technically. But he thinks he is and I've always treated him like a son. Anyway I don't see what that's got to do with the battle.'

'I cannot risk having Arthur killed in some wretched little skirmish,' said Merlin. 'He is too important.'

'Oh, so you want to train him to be a wretched wizard, do you? Too important to be a knight, is he? I always knew it.'

'On the contrary,' said Merlin. 'On the contrary, my dear Sir Hector.' He helped himself to another glass of hot mead. 'He is far too important not to be a knight.' Sir Hector only looked puzzled. 'But I tell you what I'll do', added Merlin, 'to make up for the disappointment. Tell the boys I'll arrange a special adventure for both of them.'

'What's the adventure called?' asked Sir Hector.

'It's called the Sword in the Stone,' replied Merlin, 'and it is going to be one of the most famous adventures in the whole world.'

'Don't believe a word of it', said Sir Hector. 'Rubbish. It's all a . . . eey-ore. No, wait, you wily wizard. Not a . . . eey-ore. Eey-ore, eey-ore. Eeey-ore.'

'Donkey,' said Merlin affectionately, pulling one of Sir Hector's long ears.

CHAPTER 3

The Sword in the Stone

KING Uther Pendragon was dead and the whole realm of Logres was in confusion. For each of the Seven Kings who ruled the Seven Kingdoms wished to be King of Logres in his place.

King Lot of Orkeney, a very fierce king from the North, was married to the dark and beautiful Morgawse, Arthur's eldest sister. King Nentres of Garlot was married to Elaine, Arthur's in-between sister. King Urien from the magical land of Gore was married to Morgan le Fay, Arthur's youngest sister, the one with the green eyes whom Merlin had once called a little monster. She was grown-up now and she had a son of her own, Yvain.

Who were the other four Kings? King Anguish of

Ireland, King Leodegrance of Camelard, the King with the Hundred Knights, and the wild and hairy King Royance of the Isles. People found all these marauding kings confusing and simple knights like Sir Hector were very glad to live far away from all their wars in the Fenlands.

None of the Kings of the Seven Kingdoms was powerful enough to conquer all the others. So it seemed impossible that Logres should ever have a High King again, and all the people were in despair. Then on the morning of the great feast of Michaelmas a marvel happened in the churchyard of the great castle of Camelot. Men, women, and children first rubbed their eyes with disbelief, then ran to tell their whole family and friends. For overnight a huge four-square marble stone had appeared in the churchyard and in the stone a great glittering sword was sticking. Underneath the sword and along the top of the stone there were runes, which said in the old language:

Whoso Pulleth Out This Swerd of This Stone
Is Rightwys Kynge Borne of All the Realme.

A few daring men and a few cheeky boys tried to pull the sword out, without success. But the Seven Kings soon put a stop to that when they heard about the Sword in the Stone. They came riding into Camelot, one after another, and the first thing they did was to set a guard of two knights in the churchyard with orders to let no one except themselves touch the sword or even the stone. They were afraid of trickery.

Then all seven of them rode into the churchyard, eyeing each other suspiciously. They were sure that one of the seven was going to pull the sword out, and the only question was which one it would be. The people were allowed to watch them, and made bets. Nobody bet on King Nentres of Garlot, whose arm was paralysed from a battle wound. They all hated King Anguish of Ireland; and they all hoped that the King with the Hundred Knights would not pull out the sword, for his hundred knights were known as bullies. They would have liked King Urien of Gore to be High King, though they were a little afraid of his wife, Queen Morgan le Fay; many preferred the courteous and gentle King Leodegrance of Camelard. He had a well-loved daughter called Guinevere, but he was, everybody admitted, rather old. That left the two strongest and roughest of the Seven Kings, King Lot of Orkeney and King Royance of the Isles.

Sure enough, the first five Kings tried and failed. Then King Lot glared at King Royance and grasped the sword with both his mighty hands. But though he tugged and grunted for over five minutes till you could have heard his back creaking, he could not shift the sword a single inch.

King Royance roared with laughter.

'What's happened, Lot?' he jeered. 'Muscles all gone? Getting old? Too much namby-pamby with your women?' He dug his elbow in Lot's ribs, and leered at Lot's wife, the dark and silent Queen Morgawse. Then his mood changed.

'Down on your knees, all of you,' he bellowed. 'You've all failed. Only I am left and so I must be High King of Logres. On your knees and do me homage!'

The six Kings looked at each other uncertainly, and King Nentres of Garlot went down on both his knees.

'First,' said Queen Morgan le Fay, King Urien's wife, 'I think we might remind our dear friend the high and mighty King Royance that there is one little thing he has forgotten to do.'

'What's that?' grunted King Royance. Like all the other Kings, he knew Queen Morgan le Fay's reputation as an enchantress and always felt uneasy when she turned her green eyes on him.

'A very simple little thing,' said Morgan le Fay silkily. 'A nothing for such a mighty warrior. Just a tiny gesture. Pull the sword out of the stone.'

King Royance glared at her angrily.

'Quite right, Morgan,' said King Lot. 'Why didn't we all think of that? Come on, Royance. Let's see you do it.'

King Nentres of Garlot scrambled shamefacedly to his feet again. King Royance laid his hand on the sword, and pulled casually as if he expected it to come out easily. It did not budge. He put both hands to it. It did not budge. He heaved with all his might. It did not budge. He went red in the face and kicked at the stone with his armoured foot. It still did not budge.

'What's the matter, Royance?' jeered King Lot, delighted. 'Try using your teeth, that's my advice. It's the only chance you've got left. And I hope you break your jaw-bone, old friend.'

'Poor dear King Royance,' said Queen Morgan le Fay, half-smiling to her sister Queen Morgawse.

But though everybody was delighted that King Royance had failed, they were all dismayed because there was still no High King of Logres. 'If only Merlin was here,' the Kings said to each other, 'he would advise us.' But Merlin was nowhere to be found. Some said he was in the realm of Lyonesse, others that he had gone to the enchanted Forest of Broceliande, and others still that he was visiting the elf-kingdom of Annwen, that men call Avalon. But no one really knew.

In the end the Kings decided to let cry a great tournament at Camelot. Then, they announced they would allow the knights of most prowess in the tournament to try their hand at pulling out the sword; and they all swore that they would accept a knight of prowess, if he drew out the sword, as their rightful High King.

News of this tournament spread quickly throughout the realm, and brought knights riding in from hundreds of miles away. The news even reached the Fenland, and Sir Hector decided to take the boys. Not that he particularly wanted to joust, and of course he knew he had no chance at all of pulling the sword from the stone and becoming High King, but he wanted to make it up to them for cancelling the battle with Sir Grummore Grummorson. Kay, who had just been made a knight, was particularly excited.

'You see,' he explained to Arthur as they rode towards Camelot, 'if a new-made knight can't have a battle, the next best thing is a tournament. I'm going to joust with all those kings' sons and with luck I'll unhorse them. Then, unless they cry pity, I'll race off their helms and swop off their heads. You can be my squire, Arthur. You must keep my lance sharpened and my sword bright. If you behave yourself I may let you ride my war-horse. But of course normally you'll only have a palfrey – like a damsel.'

Arthur hoped heartily that it would be a war-horse, but looked forward to taking part in the tournament – even as Kay's squire. When they did get to the great castle of Camelot, Kay soon stopped boasting. Tall towers loomed from the high battlements, a thousand pennants floated in the wind. Rich tents spread over the meadows on all sides down to the shores of the Sea. There was jangling of armour and horses, singing of maidens, riding of knights, feasting such as the Fenland had never seen.

It was not till the seventh day of the tournament that a day was set aside for new-made knights to joust. Sir Kay was so excited when he rode into the lists that he forgot his sword; so he sent Arthur back to their lodgings to fetch it as quickly as possible. But the lodgings were all locked up.

'I must get a sword for Kay from somewhere,' said Arthur to himself. Then he remembered that he had seen a sword sticking in a huge marble stone in the churchyard. He had noticed that the churchyard was always guarded – 'No doubt that's to stop anyone stealing the sword,' he said to himself – but he thought that he would ask the guards if he could simply borrow the sword for the tournament.

To his delight there were no guards there. They had gone to watch the tournament themselves. So Arthur ran up to the stone, and pulled the sword out as easily as he would have pulled a sword out of a normal scabbard. Then he dashed to the lists.

'Kay,' he said, 'I couldn't get into the lodgings. But I've borrowed a sword for you.'

'It's rather a fine sword,' said Sir Kay examining it closely. Indeed it was. The sword was three-edged and bright with a golden hilt, a clasp of ivory and a jet-black buckle upon the clasp. Along its blade ran runes. It looked like an enchanted sword. Kay did marvels with it in the tournament, and beat three other new-made knights in single combat, much to Arthur and Sir Hector's delight. At the end of the day King Leodegrance of Camelard who was presiding over the tournament of new-made knights, called Sir Kay and his squire forward to receive the prize.

'Sir Knight,' he said courteously, 'you have shown yourself today a knight of great prowess and . . .'

Then his eyes fell on Sir Kay's sword, 'Sir Knight,' he said, 'where did you get that sword?' Kay looked round at Arthur, hoping that the sword was not some sorcerer's, such as no true knight should use.

'Sire,' said Arthur, 'from the stone in the churchyard.'

An immense hubbub and outcry followed. Damsels threw themselves at Sir Kay's feet, and knights knelt in homage to him. King Leodegrance hurried away to tell the other Kings that a new-made knight of prowess had drawn the sword from the stone. Sir Hector dashed around asking all the older knights. 'What's happening? What's my boy done?' But, as he was a little deaf, he couldn't understand the answer with all the noise. Sir Kay sat on his war-horse holding the sword, looking dazed but pleased. No one took the least notice of Arthur.

The Kings came galloping back with King Leodegrance. 'What's your name, young man?' said King Lot gruffly.

'Sir Kay, son of Sir Hector, of the Fenland,' called out Arthur. It was quite usual for squires to answer questions put to their knights, when the knights had their helmets on and could not be heard very easily.

'Where did you get the sword?'

'From the stone in the churchyard,' repeated Arthur.

'You drew it forth unaided?'

'Yes, Sire,' said Arthur.

The Kings looked at each other. 'King Kay,' said King Leodegrance uncertainly.

'To the churchyard!' bellowed King Royance. 'I'm not going down on my knees to some little boy from the Fens till I've seen him do it with my own eyes.'

At the churchyard the Seven Kings alone rode in with Sir Kay and his squire and Sir Hector.

'Put the sword back in,' they said sternly. Sir Kay did so.

'Now pull it out again.'

Arthur's heart jumped with anxiety as he saw Kay heaving and tugging and the faces of the Kings, who were beginning to think they had been tricked, growing sterner and sterner.

'Kay,' he said, 'let me help you.'

He put his hand on the sword-hilt and pulled the sword out as easily as he had done before.

'King Kay indeed!' bellowed King Royance. 'It was all a trick. Swop his head off for him!'

He whirled up his battle-axe and then, much to Kay's relief, slowly lowered it again. He was beginning to realize what he had just seen.

'The squire did it,' he muttered, 'the little Fenland squire did it. He pulled the sword out of the stone.'

'Can you read runes, boy?' said King Lot.

'Yes,' said Arthur.

'Read me these runes then.'

Arthur read out aloud 'Whoso Pulleth Out This Swerd of This Stone Is Rightwys Kynge Borne of All the Realme.'

'Who are you, boy?'

'Arthur,' said Arthur.

'King Arthur,' said old King Leodegrance, sinking down unto his knees, 'High King of Logres. Sire, I do you homage.'

Then one by one all the other Kings, even King Lot and King Royance, did Arthur homage.

Then Sir Hector knelt down in front of him, and after a moment's hesitation so did Sir Kay.

'My own dear father and brother,' said Arthur, 'why are you kneeling down to me?'

'No, no, my lord Arthur,' said Sir Hector. 'I was never your father or of your blood. Indeed you must be of a higher blood than I thought you were.'

Then Sir Hector told Arthur how Merlin had brought him to the castle as a little baby and left him there to be educated. Arthur burst into tears when he understood that Sir Hector was not his real father. In those days even grown knights would often cry with emotion, and Arthur was only fifteen.

'Sire,' said Sir Hector to Arthur, 'will you be my good and gracious lord when you are King?'

That was the moment when Arthur first properly realized what the words on the stone meant for him.

'Of course I will, father,' he cried (for he still could not realize that Sir Hector was not his real father). 'Otherwise I would be to blame, for you are the man who has done most for me in the whole world. If it is God's will that I be King, you can ask me whatever you like and I will do it for you.'

'Sire,' said Sir Hector, 'all I ask you is to make Sir Kay Seneschal of all your lands.'

Every king had a seneschal in those days who, next to him, was the person whose orders everyone except the other knights obeyed.

'That shall be done,' said Arthur, 'and by the faith of my body, nobody except Kay shall be seneschal while he and I live.'

'But who is he?' the Seven Kings asked Sir Hector. 'If he is not your son, whose son is he?'

They drove Sir Hector half-mad with their questions, and he could only say that Merlin knew.

'That dream-reader!' said King Lot, who feared no wizard.

In the end they drove Sir Hector back to his placid castle in the Fenland, just to get away from their questions. When he reached home, the first person he found there was Merlin, quietly practising spells in the tower.

'Good grief, Merlin,' he cried. 'Don't you know what's happening? Don't you know . . .'

'Of course I know,' said Merlin. 'I'm a wizard, aren't I?' I know what has happened, what is happening, and what is going to happen. Only I sometimes grow tired of it all. I need a rest in the country, like anyone else, a quiet time just to think up a few new spells. Like this one for instance . . .'

To Sir Hector's horror Merlin disappeared and a fat white sheep took his place.

'Damnation,' said Merlin, reappearing, 'That's the wrong way round.'

'Baa-baa,' Sir Hector found himself bleating. He bleated even louder when Merlin disappeared again and a wolf took his place. The wolf grinned evilly at him and licked his chops. Sir Hector was never so pleased in his life as when he was changed back into human shape again.

'This is no time for your fun and games,' he lectured the wolf. 'You must grow up. You're worse than . . .'

'Yaaaa,' growled the wolf, snapping greedily at Sir Hector's waving finger. 'Aaaaooo,' the wolf howled.

Sir Hector ran, and slammed and bolted the door. 'Who is Arthur anyway?' he yelled through the keyhole. There was no answer. When at long last Sir Hector plucked up courage to unbolt the tower door, there was no sign of either Merlin or the wolf. There were merely runes saying: 'Alrighte. But it was a Goode Newe Espell.' That was no comfort at all to Sir Hector, because he could not read runes. But, as Merlin said later, you can't expect even the best wizard in the world to remember everything.

So Merlin came to the great castle of Camelot and let it be cried that Arthur would be crowned King at the high feast of Pentecost.

'But, Merlin, who am I?' Arthur kept asking.

'I will tell you all,' said Merlin 'at the day of your coronation.'

'I'm not sure,' said Arthur, 'that the Seven Kings will let me be crowned.' The Seven Kings had been muttering that the realm of Logres should not be ruled by a fifteen-year-old boy, however good he might be at pulling swords out of stones.

The day before the coronation King Lot of Orkeney rode into the city with his wife Queen Morgawse and five hundred knights. King Anguish of Ireland rode into the city with seven hundred knights. King Urien of Gore rode into the city with his wife Queen Morgan le Fay and four hundred knights.

'I don't like the look of this at all,' said Sir Kay who as seneschal was in charge of arrangements for the coronation; and he fingered nervously the sword from the stone that Arthur had given him as a present.

Arthur also sent messengers with presents to these Kings, and to the other four Kings, but King Royance and King Lot sent the messengers back, shamefully. They wanted no present, they said, from a beardless boy. They had come to give him a present between neck and shoulders with sharp swords.

'Leave this to me,' said Merlin.

He called all the kings and queens and all their knights together. They were delighted to see him at long last, even King Lot.

'Why,' they asked, 'should this boy Arthur be made our King?'

'Sires,' said Merlin with his hands on Arthur's shoulders. 'I shall tell you why. This boy is the son of King Uther Pendragon and of Ygraine of Cornwall. Those, Arthur, were your parents. So your father was King of all this realm before you. That is why you alone could draw the sword from the stone. As for your mother, the beautiful Ygraine, she was mother to three queens here: Queen Morgawse, Queen Elaine, and Queen Morgan le Fay. They are your half-sisters.'

Everybody was so amazed, just as Merlin had planned,

that they could think of nothing but the good luck of it all. Arthur kissed his half-sisters, and they kissed him a thousand times. None was more delighted than Queen Morgan le Fay who looked very like Arthur and was only a little older than he was. It was a splendid coronation feast. Only King Royance of the Isles muttered darkly, as he ran his fingers through his own great shaggy beard, 'For all that he is only a beardless boy.'

CHAPTER 4

The Questing Beast

KING Arthur lay side by side with his sister Morgan le Fay in a sunny glade of the Forest.

'The birds are twittering,' he remarked lazily. 'They are saying that you are beautiful but dangerous.'

'So you speak to birds, do you, little brother?' said Morgan le Fay, smiling down at him.

'Not only birds,' said Arthur, 'but some beasts too. To tell the truth, I don't exactly speak to them. I just understand what they say. Merlin taught me.'

'I speak to all the beasts of Forest and Sea,' said Morgan le Fay dreamily. 'That is because I am Queen of the magical land of Gore. Listen a moment.'

Arthur listened. He was fascinated by this newly-found sister of his, even though she called him 'little brother' when she was only four years older.

All the birds fell silent; then started twittering again louder than ever.

'They are saying,' said Arthur, 'that you talked to them without talking. They say you must really be a bird disguised as a human being.'

'I transfer thoughts,' said Morgan le Fay. 'I'm not a bird, you know, I'm just an enchantress.'

'You're certainly much more enchanting than Kay ever was,' said Arthur generously. 'I never thought I'd like a sister but now I've got you I wonder how I managed all these years without you.'

'Don't worry, little brother,' whispered Morgan le Fay. 'Now I have found you, I will look after you always – in life and in death.'

Arthur did not much like the thought of death. He wondered whether his sister knew exactly what was going to happen to him now that he was King. After all, if she was an enchantress . . .

'No, I don't,' Morgan le Fay interrupted. 'I'm not a wizard like your Merlin. I can't see the past and the future and I haven't been living since the Dark Ages, like him. Compared to Merlin, I'm just a little enchantress who can cast a few simple spells – and read your thoughts of course, little brother.'

'Call me Sire,' said Arthur, getting up and brushing the grass off his armour. He did not like having his thoughts read, even by his favourite sister.

'Yes, little Sire,' said Morgan le Fay, teasing him.

The kings and queens and knights departed; and the great castle of Camelot lay still and quiet. Arthur rode out into the Forest and killed his first troll. Trolls were strong as giants and squat as dwarfs, very black and ugly indeed, with enormous jaws; all knights killed them whenever they came across them. The troll Arthur killed was called Nor, so Arthur nicknamed his lance the Nor-killer. He rode out every day with the Nor-killer, hunting in the great green Forest that surrounded Camelot. Sometimes he rode out with hounds and huntsmen and Sir Kay his Seneschal and other knights, and they all hunted white harts. Sometimes he rode out alone by himself, like a knight-errant in search of adventure. That was how he was nearly killed one day.

He was sitting by a fountain in the middle of the Forest, day-dreaming, when he heard an enormous crashing and banging, and the strangest beast he had ever seen or heard of came bursting through the Forest to the fountain to drink. It had a head like a serpent, a body like a leopard, hindquarters like a lion, feet like a hart, and a tail like a dragon. What was even more terrifying was that it was as enormous as an elephant. Its belly rumbled as if there were sixty hounds barking inside. Arthur sat stock still, not daring to move, and watched it drink. While it drank it made no noise. When it had finished gulping down the whole pool, it crashed away again through the trees, its belly rumbling and barking as before.

Arthur fell asleep. He was woken up by a big knight whom he had never seen before, shaking his shoulder very roughly.

'Sleepy knight,' said the stranger, 'did you see a strange beast pass this way?'

'I did,' said Arthur. 'It must be many miles away by now. What sort of beast was it, Sir Knight?'

'Sir, it is called the Questing Beast, because it sounds as if there are thirty couples of hounds questing away in its sto-mach. I have been chasing it for twelve months, and sooner or later I will catch up with it and kill it, or it me.'

'Sir Knight,' said King Arthur, 'let me have your adventure and I will follow the Questing Beast for the next twelve months.'

King Arthur in fact wanted to be a knight errant and ride

out on adventures. He thought he was too young to be a settled king and stay in one place. Also he missed his sister Morgan le Fay and hoped that the Questing Beast might lead him to the magical land of Gore.

'Fool,' said the stranger knight. 'The Questing Beast shall never be caught except by me or my kinsmen.'

King Arthur stood up and put his hand to his sword. He was much smaller and younger than the stranger knight; but he was a king now and no one had the right to call him a fool.

'That shall I amend,' he said very slowly and clearly.

'Then defend yourself!' cried the stranger knight. They leapt at each other with their swords drawn, hewing and slicing each other's armour till the glade in which they fought was drenched in blood. Then they rested. Then they set to again, and charged at each other like two wild boars, colliding with so great a crash that both fell backwards on the ground. But Arthur's sword broke into two pieces.

'Now you are at my mercy,' cried the stranger knight. 'Yield to me as beaten or else you shall die.'

'As for that,' cried King Arthur, 'death is welcome when it comes. But I shall never yield.'

Arthur leapt upon the stranger knight and seized him round the middle, knocked him down and raced off his helmet. But the stranger knight was the stronger man. He rolled King Arthur over and raced off King Arthur's helmet. He lifted up his sword and was about to swop off King Arthur's head when suddenly a voice called, 'Stop!'

It was Merlin. He stood there, tall and menacing, as dark as the Forest itself.

'Knight, hold your hand,' said Merlin sternly. 'If you kill that knight you put this realm in the greatest danger it was ever in.'

'Why?' asked the stranger knight. 'Who is he?'

'It is King Arthur,' said Merlin.

But the stranger knight lifted up his sword for the death-blow once again, for now he was afraid of King Arthur's anger if he let him live. Swift as a flash, Merlin cast a spell on the stranger knight. The sword fell from his fingers, and he sank to the ground as if dead.

That is how Merlin saved Arthur twice from the death-blow. But Arthur scrambled to his feet and, instead of thanking Merlin, called out: 'What have you done, Merlin? Why have you killed this good knight with your spells? I have never met so mighty a knight as he is, and I would give half my kingdom to have him alive again.'

'Do not worry,' said Merlin. 'He is only in a trance and he will wake within an hour. You are very lucky to have escaped alive yourself, Arthur. He is at the moment the strongest knight in the world, and he hates anyone interfering with his chase of the Questing Beast. But from now on he will be your good friend. His name is King Pellinore of the Outer Isles and he shall have a son called Sir Lamorak, who will be as strong a man as his father, and a good knight of yours. Yet your whole realm shall be destroyed because of the killings of King Pellinore and Sir Lamorak.'

Then Merlin took King Arthur to a hermitage where the hermit cured his wounds. But an hour later King Pellinore awoke, took his arms, mounted his horse and forgetting all about Merlin and Arthur, rode a wallop after the Questing Beast.

CHAPTER 5

Excalibur

I HAVE no sword,' said Arthur.

He had been healed of the wounds that King Pellinore had given him; but his sword had broken into two pieces early on in their battle.

'Nearby is a sword that shall be yours,' said Merlin, 'if all goes well.'

They thanked the hermit and rode out from the hermitage, the two of them alone, through one forest after another till they came to a far forest where the trees seemed to Arthur to be taller and older and stranger than anywhere else. Indeed their branches seemed to move, even when there was no wind, so that Arthur often had to duck to avoid being swept out of his saddle.

'The Ents are in a playful mood today,' said Merlin. Then the wizard made a groaning, creaking noise, as if he was all branches and tree-trunk himself.

'There,' he said, 'that should do the trick.'

Sure enough the old trees seemed stiller after Merlin had spoken to them. Arthur glanced curiously at Merlin but saw that the wizard was in no mood to answer questions.

'You will see stranger things,' was all that Merlin would say, 'before the day is out.'

Suddenly the Forest opened, and they found themselves on the shore of a great shimmering lake of clear water.

'Here we are,' said Merlin.

'I think!' added Merlin half an hour later, when nothing had happened and their horses were getting restless. Arthur saw that it would still be wrong to ask questions, and waited.

'There!' said Merlin suddenly, pointing. Arthur shaded his eyes and looked.

Out in the middle of the lake he could see an arm clothed in white samite holding a shimmering sword.

'There,' said Merlin, 'is the sword that I spoke of.'

Now a barge appeared drifting towards them.

A beautiful lady clothed all in white sat smiling in the barge.

'That is the Lady of the Lake,' said Merlin. 'She is coming to you. Speak to her courteously, that she may give you the sword.'

'King Arthur,' said the Lady, 'the sword that you see shining over the water belongs to me. If you grant me a wish, it shall be yours.'

'Lady,' said Arthur, 'I will grant you whatever you desire – provided it is not Nor-killer, my lance, or Pridwen my round shield, or,' he added with a smile, 'Merlin, my wizard.'

But Merlin looked sad. He foresaw the doom that would come from the Lake for him, though its time was not yet.

'Very well,' said the Lady. 'Row out in this barge and take the sword. I will ask for my gift when my time comes.'

So King Arthur and Merlin dismounted and tied their horses to two trees; then they rowed out in the barge. When they came to the sword King Arthur took it by the handle, and the arm and the hand that had been holding it sank down under the water.

This was the way the sword was made. It was gold-hilted, and its blade was of gold, bearing a cross of inlaid gold of the hue of lightning. Two serpents in precious stones were set in the hilt of the sword. When it was drawn from its scabbard, it seemed as if two flames of fire burst from the jaws of the serpents and then, so glittering was the sword, it was hard for anyone to look upon it.

'What is this sword?' Arthur asked Merlin.

'It is the sword of Logres,' said Merlin solemnly. 'It was forged in the Isle of Avalon, that the elfin race call Annwen, and to Avalon it must return, else the realm of Logres shall be doomed for ever. Remember this, O King, on the Day of Destiny.'

'I will remember,' said Arthur. 'But how shall I return it?'

'By the way the sword came, by the same way shall the sword go,' said Merlin.

'What is the sword called?'

'The sword is called Excalibur. It shall be the most famous sword of all the world.'

CHAPTER 6

The Land of Gore

ARTHUR called for his war-horse and his armour. He slung Pridwen, his round shield, over his back, girt Excalibur his new sword round his waist, and grasped Nor-killer his lance in his right hand.

'Where do you think you are going?' asked Merlin.

'I am riding out to the land of Gore to visit Morgan le Fay,' said Arthur defiantly.

'That little sorceress!' said Merlin, growing tall and angry.

'May I remind you,' said Arthur, 'that she is my sister and a queen? Whereas you are merely the court wizard.'

'Great Sire,' said Merlin bowing low. 'Shall I

turn you into a toad-stool – or merely a toad? What is your command?'

Arthur trembled.

'Very well,' said Merlin forgivingly. 'Off you go and visit your queenly little sister. I remember her when she was a baby. Do you know what her first words were? "I like Kings, Kings, Kings." She's certainly succeeded. First she casts a spell on Urien her husband; now it seems she's ensorcelled you too.' Merlin stroked his long silky beard. 'It's time I arranged for you to be married.'

'Don't be silly,' said Arthur, 'I'm far too young to have a wife, and besides I don't see what that's got to do with my sister. It seems to me, Merlin, that you're a little jealous of her.'

'Bah!' cried Merlin. 'Wizards are never jealous! Wizards are a superior form of being, only just short of angels! Wizards don't give a hoot for green-eyed little – little – little enchantresses, if that's the word she prefers.'

'You're clearly over-tired, Merlin,' said Arthur, patting the wizard sympathetically on his back. 'You've been sampling too many magic potions, I dare say. Perhaps you should have a rest.'

'I shall,' said Merlin, 'while you are in Gore I will go to the enchanted Forest of Broceliande, a far more wonderful place. But I warn you, nothing good will come of this visit of yours, Arthur, nothing good at all.'

The ravens, black sentinels of the land of Gore, informed Queen Morgan le Fay that her brother was entering the kingdom. Her green eyes flashed with pleasure. She told her husband, King Urien, who always did exactly what she said, to prepare a great feast for Arthur. The tables groaned with fish and fruit, pike and perch, salmon and trout, pears both cooked and raw, peaches, pomegranates, grapes and mangoes. There were no meat or birds, though, for in the land of

Gore all winged and hoofed beasts lived in peace with men, and even the fierce flesh-eating animals turned their teeth and claws only on serpents and each other. Gore was a land of plenty, its high plains surrounded by the great White Mountains that no enemy could pass.

Queen Morgan le Fay rode out to welcome her brother with a hundred knights, all clad in gold and green. When they met, they kissed each other a thousand times, for that was the custom.

'Little brother, fair Sire,' said Morgan le Fay, 'welcome to Gore.' She snapped her fingers, and a boy aged four all in gold and green, with gold hair and green eyes, rode up on a golden pony with a velvet green saddle. 'Here is my son Yvain. Yvain, this is your uncle Arthur, our High King. When you are older you will go to his great castle of Camelot and there, if you behave, he will make you a knight.'

King Arthur was delighted with his little nephew Yvain, who was bold and merry and handsome. He was delighted with the feast, he was delighted with the land of Gore, he was delighted with King Urien who was much older than he was, but treated him with great respect and gave him gold, copper, and diamonds that the dwarfs of Gore had mined and the ravens collected. But he was most delighted of all with his green-eyed sister Morgan le Fay. Every day they rode out together; every evening they feasted together; and every night King Arthur kissed his little nephew Yvain and promised that he would look after him like his own son.

'Indeed,' said Morgan le Fay, 'you might adopt him as your own son if you don't get married.'

'Then,' said Arthur, patting the little boy's golden hair, 'he could be High King after me.'

'Yes,' said Morgan, 'yes, I suppose he could.' She said it very casually but in fact she was thinking about it the whole time. She hoped Arthur would never get married; she even put magic potions in his wine so that he would love her more than any other woman and so that even when he was far away she could find out what he was thinking. Yes, she bewitched him, so that he became less like a proper knight and a king, and more like a fawning lap-dog who followed her everywhere.

'This is not right,' said King Urien, her husband. 'You are making Arthur a mouse, not a man. He won't remain High King long unless he goes to battle or rides out on a quest. Kings and knights are for fighting, you know.'

'Be quiet, Urien,' said Morgan le Fay sharply. 'I could not bear to see Arthur hurt. It's all very well for old-fashioned kings like you whose ugly bodies are covered with scars and wounds. But times are changing. This is a new age, an age of peace.'

'That's what you think,' growled King Urien; and went off to the North, to visit his fierce brother-in-law King Lot and enjoy a few sea-fights in the Orkeneys. There the wild and hairy King Royance of the Isles joined them.

'Urien,' said Royance one day – the three kings were washing their battle-axes in the waves after having killed several hundred sea-rovers – 'Urien, is that boy still beard-less?'

'Almost,' said Urien.

'Well, when he finally grows a beard let me know,' bellowed Royance.

'Why?'

'So as I can add it to my collection!'

At this King Lot and King Royance slapped each other on the back and rolled around the shore roaring with laughter.

Merlin was in the Forest of Broceliande, by the Magic Fountain that flowed with nectar, when he heard a clumping and a crashing and the roaring of thirty couples of hounds. Sure enough, it was the Questing Beast and sure enough King Pellinore was only a few miles behind. Merlin had been relaxing in the shape of an Ent, that is to say a tall green living and moving tree. When King Pellinore rode by underneath him, he bent one of his branches down and swept King Pellinore off his saddle onto the ground.

'Creepy Ent!' gasped King Pellinore, drawing his sword and swiping at the branch. Merlin was too slow to pull it back in time – Ents are much slower-moving than animals. He cried out in pain, and at once changed back into his normal shape. When King Pellinore saw the wizard towering above him, sucking white blood from his finger, and clearly about to change him into something unpleasant, he was extremely frightened.

'The wizard!' he cried.

'Weasel!' hissed Merlin.

'No,' said King Pellinore hastily, 'Merlin, I have news I must tell you. Don't do it. Don't change me into a wretched little weasel! I thought you were an Ent. That's the trouble with this enchanted Forest, full of Ents shifting their roots and knocking knights off horses.'

Merlin looked a little ashamed.

'How am I ever going to catch the Questing Beast if infantile Ents and witless wizards keep getting in my way?' grumbled King Pellinore. 'No, I'm sorry, Merlin, I didn't mean that. I spoke hastily. I apologize for swiping your branch – your finger, I mean. When I said witless wizards, I meant other wizards of course, not the great white-blooded Merlin.'

'It's the nectar that does it,' said Merlin. 'White corpuscles dominate, unlike your ordinary human blood. Interesting, but beside the point. What's your news? Quick, or I might change my mind again.'

'Well,' said King Pellinore, 'you know that I'm only King of the Outer Isles, and King Royance of All the Isles is my liege lord.'

'Yes, yes,' said Merlin impatiently. 'What of it?'

'Well, King Royance has summoned me and all the rulers of the inner isles to gather our warriors. There is to be a war.'

'Hmmmm,' said Merlin, stroking his beard thoughtfully.

'King Lot of the Orkeneys has summoned his chieftains

too; so has King Anguish of Ireland and King Urien and the King with the Hundred Knights.'

'Hmmm,' said Merlin, 'it certainly sounds like a great war looming.'

'There's one further thing,' said King Pellinore. 'You've heard of King Royance's famous cloak that is decorated with other kings' beards?'

'Yes.'

'Apparently he has been saying there is room for one beard more.'

'Now whose beard do you think that could be?' said Merlin, stroking his own silky beard very attentively indeed.

'Not yours, wizard,' said King Pellinore.

'Why not?' snapped Merlin.

'Not that there's anything wrong with your beard at all,' said King Pellinore hurriedly, 'it would make a very fine fringe for anyone's cloak, I'm sure. Only King Royance said that this particular beard hadn't grown yet.'

Before nightfall that evening Merlin was in the land of Gore.

'Arthur,' he said, 'saddle your horse. We ride for Camelot.'

Queen Morgan le Fay, who had been lying back lazily on a green sofa embroidered with golden stars, raised herself up on one elbow.

'How very masterful you are, Merlin,' she said softly. 'Do this, do that, do the other. Such bad manners wizards have nowadays!'

'Sire,' said Merlin, looking angrily at Morgan le Fay, 'I apologize if I was abrupt – but while your sister feasts you here in Gore, your enemies are gathering their armies.'

'Enemies, enemies?' said Morgan le Fay lazily. 'My Arthur has no enemies. Wizards always exaggerate.'

'Lady,' said Merlin sharply, 'your own husband King Urien is away at the moment, I believe, gathering his forces.'

'What of it,' said Morgan.

'And who do you think he is planning to attack?'

'He didn't tell me,' said Morgan. 'But you can't mean . . .? No, he would never attack King Arthur. That would be treason.'

She and Merlin stared into one another's eyes, as if they understood each other at last.

'Wait,' she said and hurried out of the chamber.

'Arthur,' said Merlin, 'I may – I just may – have misjudged your sister. Even wizards make mistakes sometimes. I must say,' he added, stroking his silky beard thoughtfully, 'she has the most remarkable green eyes I have seen in several millenia.'

They waited in silence till Queen Morgan le Fay came back. 'Arthur,' she said, 'I think the sooner you return to your great castle at Camelot and start behaving like a real king the better. I was wrong to keep you here. The age of peace has not yet come to Logres. But one day I think we will know it, long long hereafter, you and I together. Go now, leave me, fight your battles and win your wars. But take this ointment I have prepared for you – I am not a wizard like Merlin but I do know the magic art of healing. If you are wounded, put this ointment on your wound once a day for a week, and the wound will be completely healed on the seventh day.'

She turned her gleaming green eyes onto Merlin. 'Always remember this, wizard. You know the past, you can foretell the future. All I can do is cast a few simple spells, I am nothing compared to you. But I love my little brother more than anyone else in the whole world, and I always will.'

Merlin cleared his throat.

'Arthur, Sire,' he said, 'take the ointment and ride forth. I have changed my mind. My place is here for the moment. The next battle must be all yours. You must fight it without my help. Remember, only draw the sword Excalibur when you are sure you must fight.'

Arthur looked first at Merlin, then at his sister Morgan le

Fay, then at Merlin again. He was puzzled that Merlin had changed his mind so quickly, and was worried at the thought of having to be king without him.

'Go, little brother,' said Morgan le Fay gently, 'Merlin has much to teach me here and I have much to learn from all his wisdom.' She ran her hand affectionately over Arthur's chin. 'You must be a man now, little brother, as well as a king. I liked you clean shaven before but now I think that you should grow a beard.'

So Arthur rode back to Camelot. In the weeks that followed he took his sister's advice, and let his beard grow.

CHAPTER 7

The War with the Kings

AH-HA,' said King Royance, 'the boy has grown a beard. Where's that cloak of mine?'

His trolls scurried around his sea-girt castle and brought him his great cloak of black velvet spotted with white drops of wizard blood. On its collar around the King's bull-like neck eleven beards of different colours were sewn onto the cloak, like a fringe of fur. These were the beards of the eleven Kings whom Royance had killed or conquered.

'Room for just one more!' chuckled King Royance. 'Just room for little King Arthur's.'

So King Royance sent one of his trolls to Camelot to demand King Arthur's beard.

'My master said shave it off and give it to me,'

said the troll. 'Else he will come himself with all his warriors and never leave your land till he has your beard and your hair off your head as well.'

'Troll,' said King Arthur, 'you have spoken your message, and shameful it is. Tell your king that my beard is still too young and too fresh on my chin to decorate his cloak. Tell him also this' – here Arthur leant forward – 'that by the faith of my body he shall do me homage on both his knees, as I am the rightful ruler of the realm.'

The troll came back to the Isles with King Arthur's message.

'By the blood of Behemoth,' swore King Royance, 'the boy defies me! Trolls, summon my chieftains from all the Isles, my warriors and my allies. We will march on Camelot and pluck this Arthur's beard out hair by hair from his chin!'

The King with the Hundred Knights brought five thousand warriors on horseback. King Anguish of Ireland brought another five thousand, and King Urien of Gore would have collected five thousand more had his wife Queen Morgan le Fay not kept him at home by her enchantments. As for King Lot of Orkeney, he swore that he would bring ten thousand men on foot. Then Merlin visited him.

'You would do better to hold your hand,' he told King Lot. 'Even if you were ten times as many, you would not prevail.'

'Wizard's tosh,' said King Lot uneasily. But his warships did not sail.

With his own warriors and trolls and the other Kings, King Royance had an enormous host. Together they moved down through Logres till they came to Castle Terrible.

Meanwhile King Arthur was not looking forward to a real war. He had never fought in a battle, still less in a war. He hardly knew what to do without Merlin to advise him.

'Kay,' he said, 'we had better send for Sir Hector.'

'It's a long time since father's fought any proper battles,' said Sir Kay doubtfully.

'Never mind,' said King Arthur, 'at least he'll remember

how to fight a battle better than you or me. We've no idea at all.'

Sir Hector rode in from the Fenland, in high spirits.

'I've brought Sir Grummore Grummorson with me, Sire,' he said, 'and about three hundred archers.'

'Three hundred?' said Arthur in dismay. 'There are thirty thousand of them!'

'Every one Fenland archer is worth a hundred of these wild Northerners,' said Sir Hector stoutly. 'They'll get an arrow between their eyes before they can so much as say "swing your battle-axes". Eh, Grummore?'

'Quite so, Hector,' said Sir Grummore. 'Quite so.'

But fortunately for King Arthur he did not have to rely on Sir Hector and Sir Grummore alone. King Pellinore turned up to give a hand, because he had lost the trail of the Questing Beast — and also because Merlin sent orders for him to come. As he was the strongest knight then alive, that was a great help. On his advice they sent for King Ban of Benwick, whose son was one day to be King Arthur's most famous knight, Sir Lancelot. King Ban came with five hundred knights from Gaule. Then many other knights came riding in too on their own. And finally two of the Seven Kings, King Nentres of Garlot and King Leodegrance of Camelard, decided to join King Arthur instead of the other Kings. When he heard about this, King Royance was wild with rage.

'I'll start a new cloak,' he snarled. 'I'll start it with Nentres' and Leodegrance's beards; and if they don't hurry, I'll have Lot's and Urien's too!' Even so his army was by far the larger of the two.

King Arthur advanced on Castle Terrible and, at long last, sure that he was going to the wars, drew his sword Excalibur. It was a fearsome battle. 'Come on, Grummore,' shouted Sir Hector in great excitement. 'Let's take that wild marauding King over there.'

It was the King with the Hundred Knights. Sir Hector clove off one of his arms and Sir Grummore the other. But

then the Hundred Knights, seeing their king dying, surrounded them. 'Well, Grummore,' said Sir Hector, 'it was a
dashed good last battle.'

Those were his last words.

'Quite so, Hector,' said Sir Grummore, 'quite so,' as the
Hundred Knights closed in on them.

When Arthur saw that his dear foster-father had been
killed, he ran amok, and so did Sir Kay. By the time they had
finished with them, only one of the Hundred Knights was left
alive to tell the tale of that fearful day.

King Pellinore did marvels in the battle, and routed trolls
on every side. King Ban of Benwick unhorsed scores of enemy
knights. But the most glorious deeds of all were done by two
brothers, Sir Balin, the Knight with Two Swords, and Sir
Balan. All that saw them said that they were either angels from
heaven or devils from hell. First they slew forty chieftains of
King Royance, then they surrounded King Royance himself
and were about to kill him too.

'Mercy!' cried King Royance, 'I yield me.'

'Swop off his head, Balin,' said Balan, 'that's what he
would have done to us if we'd cried mercy.'

Sir Balin raised his two swords, as if unsure which one to
use.

'Wait!' cried King Royance, when he saw the death blow
coming. 'If you kill me there will be no ransom money. Besides
King Arthur does not like useless killing.'

'That's true, Balin,' said Sir Balan.

So Sir Balin, reluctantly, because he would have loved to
swop King Royance's ugly head off with a quick double-
stroke, put down both his swords; and they took King
Royance to King Arthur.

'Sir King,' said King Arthur courteously, 'by the beard that
is still on my chin and the hair that is still on my head, you are
welcome.'

King Royance fell on both his knees and did homage, all
his boasts forgotten.

'By what adventure are you here?' asked King Arthur.

'Sire,' said King Royance, 'by a hard adventure.'

'Who won you?'

'Sire, these two knights here, the Knight with the Two Swords and his brother.'

'I do not know them,' said King Arthur.

'My lord Arthur,' said Sir Kay, 'this is Sir Balin and this is Sir Balan. There are not two better knights alive. Because they have overcome King Royance, the battle is won. It is time to stop the killing, Sire, and bury the dead.'

So it was done.

But news came to King Urien in Gore and to King Lot in the Orkeneys that while they delayed, King Royance and King Anguish of Ireland and all their warriors had been beaten, and the King with the Hundred Knights killed.

'By the Orkeneys,' swore King Lot, 'I am ashamed. If I and my warriors had been there, no host under heaven could have overcome us.'

Merlin knew this was true. He knew that if King Lot had been at the battle, King Arthur and all his people would have been slain. For one of those two Kings was doomed to die if they fought together. So Merlin had kept King Lot quiet in the Orkeneys. He had prophesied that if they stayed quiet the King would one day become the great Emperor of Rome and Queen Morgawse his wife the great Empress. This had enchanted them both, for the Orkeneys were poor and bleak but Rome was rich and golden.

'What shall I do now?' said King Lot. 'Shall I make peace with Arthur?'

'Make peace,' advised Merlin.

'Lord King,' said one of the fierce Orkeney earls, 'take no notice of this false wizard. Join King Urien at once, and set on Arthur together. They are weary with battle, and we are fresh.'

'To ship, then!' cried King Lot. 'May every warrior do his part as I will do mine.'

Queen Morgawse could not hold him back, though she was King Arthur's eldest sister. She brought their four little sons to the sea shore to wave their father goodbye. Queen Morgan le Fay could not hold back her husband King Urien either. For once he paid no attention to her charms.

So both the Kings attacked Camelot, King Urien by land and King Lot by sea. King Lot was always in the forefront and did marvellous feats of arms. But his fate was to die. King Pellinore, the strongest knight then alive, struck him a great stroke through the helmet and skull right to his eyebrows and killed him.

All the warriors of Orkeney fled at the death of King Lot. King Urien yielded. His heart had not been in the fight; he had come because he had promised his old friend and brother-in-law King Lot that he would. He swore to be loyal to King Arthur evermore; and so did all the other kings left alive.

King Arthur buried the dead with great honour. Queen Morgawse came, sadly, to the burial with her four sons, Gawain the eldest, the twin brothers, Agravaine and Gaheris, and her little baby Gareth. Merlin by his enchantments set up a great wax candle above King Lot's tomb that burnt day and night without melting down.

There was one thing more. King Pellinore, the hero of the battle, departed from Camelot to go on with his chase of the Questing Beast. But little Gawain, though he was only eleven, swore when he saw King Pellinore leaving that one day he would revenge the death of his father King Lot on him.

CHAPTER 8

The Lady of the Lake

THE Lady of the Lake rode into the great castle of Camelot, enchanting them all with her beauty and gaiety.

'Greetings, great young King,' she said. 'I come for the gift you promised me when I gave you the sword Excalibur.'

'Welcome, Lady,' said King Arthur, 'ask what you will, and you shall have it if it lies in my power to give it – even my own great castle of Camelot. For Excalibur is the finest sword and the best gift in the whole world.'

'I ask for the head of that knight,' she said loudly and clearly. Everyone fell silent and craned their necks to see who she meant. She raised her lily-white arm very slowly and pointed at Sir Balin.

King Arthur had no idea what to say. He had expected the Lady of the Lake to ask for gold or silver, not for the head of the knight who had defeated King Royance for him.

'Truly,' said King Arthur, 'I cannot give you his head and keep my honour. For he is one of the knights to whom I owe most in the world. Ask anything else, and I will give it to you, anything else at all.'

'I want nothing else,' said the Lady of the Lake, 'only that knight's head.'

'But why?' asked King Arthur, bewildered.

'He does not deserve to live,' said the Lady of the Lake sternly. 'He is a savage discourteous knight. He has stolen the sword that is like Excalibur, that was forged in our island of Annwen, that was not for him. Yet I ask for his head more for your sake than mine. For if he lives, he will bring ruin and desolation to Logres.'

All men stared at Sir Balin in silence, wondering.

'You did promise me whatever I desired, O King,' said the Lady of the Lake solemnly. 'If you do not keep that promise, it is you who will lose your honour.'

King Arthur wondered what he should do. He wished Merlin was there to give him advice but Merlin was far away.

Then Sir Balin le Sauvage stepped forward. He drew the sword that he had had from the elf-princess and went straight up to the Lady of the Lake.

'This is your evil hour. You would have my head, so' – he raised the magic sword and brought it swiftly flashing down – 'you will lose yours instead.'

The head of the Lady of the Lake flew off her shoulders and fell at King Arthur's feet. It all happened so quickly that she had not time even to scream.

'What have you done?' cried Arthur, horrified.

'Sire,' said Sir Balin, 'this lady was the sister of a sorceress who once loved me but now hates me. She was a sorceress herself too, an elfin sorceress from Annwen, and hated all good fierce knights. She wanted revenge on me but instead I have taken revenge on her. Hah! They said that with this sword I would kill my best friend and the person I loved most in the world. Instead, I have killed the person who hated me most in the world, and the worst enemy of all good fierce knights. You should thank me and reward me, O King.'

'Whatever your reason,' said King Arthur sternly, 'this lady was a lady I owed much to. She came here under my protection. Therefore I shall never forgive you this dishonour. You must leave my court at once.'

Then Sir Balin picked up the head of the Lady of the Lake and rode North with it to show it his brother Sir Balan.

'You are greatly to blame,' said Sir Balan, 'for displeasing King Arthur.'

'As to that,' said Sir Balin, 'we defeated and captured King Royance of the Isles for him, so King Arthur ought to be our good friend whatever we do.'

But Merlin, when he came back to Camelot, told Arthur that he ought to have cut off Sir Balin's head himself, at once.

'I have never heard of any court that suffered so great a shame,' he said. 'You must not allow these fierce knights to kill and slay as they please, especially in Camelot and in your presence.'

King Arthur, Merlin, and all the court made great sorrow and mourning for the Lady of the Lake and buried her richly. Merlin was particularly sad.

'She forgot,' he said, 'that Sir Balin had two swords. If he had tried to swop off her head with his ordinary knight's sword, it would have shivered to pieces in his hand. But he used his magic sword that, like Excalibur, can wound and kill even elves and warlocks. Her death makes me very gloomy.'

'Why?' asked King Arthur.

'Because the next Lady of the Lake is destined to ensorcel me, I think. Yes, even I can be ensorcelled, even an old grey wizard like me,' said Merlin sadly.

CHAPTER 9

The King Adventurous

A MESSENGER came from Camelard to appeal for help against invaders.

'Of course I will go,' said Arthur fiercely. 'What is more I am going to fight this stranger King of the invaders hand to hand and kill him if I can.'

He glared at Merlin and Morgan le Fay. They were all standing in the topmost tower of Camelot where Merlin always stayed; and Queen Morgan le Fay, Arthur's sister, always stayed there too since she had begun to study sorcery with the wizard.

'This stranger King is far, far mightier than you, little brother,' said Morgan le Fay softly. 'Send King Pellinore. He is the strongest knight alive.'

'No,' said Arthur. 'When I was in danger, King

Leodegrance of Camelard came to my help in the War with the Kings. Now King Leodegrance is in danger, and I must go to his aid. It is as simple as that.'

'It is not quite as simple as that,' said Merlin. 'I foresee another danger.'

'What?' said Arthur.

'A woman,' replied Merlin darkly. And Morgan le Fay smiled.

Arthur rode out from Camelot with thirty-five knights. He took with him as his squire his nephew Gawain, King Lot's son of Orkeney, of whom he was very fond and as his page his other nephew Yvain, Queen Morgan le Fay's son. The two boys were first cousins and they were already great friends. Gawain, the elder, was big and strong and red-haired; Yvain was slim and rather slight, always smiling, always dressed in gold and green.

When they reached Camelard, they found the city besieged by an enormous host of invaders.

'There aren't very many of us, are there?' whispered Yvain to Gawain.

'Don't worry, cousin,' laughed Gawain. 'Our uncle King Arthur is going to challenge the stranger King to single combat. It is a fight to the death, without quarter. So there won't be any fighting for the rest of us unless the stranger King refuses. I don't suppose he will, though. It would be an unknightly thing to do. Look, here he comes now. His name is King Floires of Gaule.'

'He looks enormous,' whispered Yvain, even more nervously. 'What if he kills our uncle?'

'Of course he won't,' said Gawain, but his voice trembled. For King Floires was larger than King Arthur by a head in full helm.

The two kings rode out onto an island side by side, and then wheeled round and charged each other at a great pace.

They struck each other with their lances in the middle of their shields so severely that the lances splintered, the fragments flew in the air, and they knocked each other from their horses to the ground. Arthur leaped first to his feet and drew Excalibur. But King Floires leaped up too, very bold and confident, and drew his sword most fiercely. Both sides held their breath as they watched.

King Floires struck first. He held his sword in his right hand and struck Arthur with it in the middle of the shield so that it split it and cut whatever it reached. The stroke, which was made with great power, drove downwards and broke off three hundred rings from Arthur's hauberk. The blade came down across Arthur's thigh and cut away a full hand's breadth of flesh. The blade descended with great violence and cut the spur away within three inches of Arthur's foot; and the blade drove inches deep into the earth.

King Arthur was half stunned by the blow, and King Floires charged him with his shoulder so that he almost fell to the earth. Yvain cried out in horror, and even Gawain groaned; for King Floires was so mighty that it looked as if he had already won the battle. But when Arthur saw his nephews trembling for him, he felt deep shame. In his right hand he held Excalibur and with it he struck King Floires with such fierce rage that it split and rent his shield as far as the boss and sheared off whatever it reached. The stroke descended on the helm and cut away a great part of King Floires' scalp and more than a fistful of King Floires' hair. And thereupon the helmet flew from King Floires' head because all the laces were broken. King Floires was filled with great anger and struck King Arthur upon his helm but could not harm him. Then the blood started pouring down across his eyes and over his face so that he could not even see King Arthur. His heart failed him and he fell downwards in the middle of the meadow. When King Arthur saw this he ran towards him, and raising Excalibur, stooped down, and cut off his head.

Yvain cheered, and Gawain ran over to King Arthur and

helped him to disarm as a squire should. The invaders fled, and King Leodegrance came down from the walls of Camelard to thank King Arthur for rescuing him.

'Ha, Guinevere,' he called to his daughter, 'Guinevere, come and welcome the King.'

'What a beautiful lady,' whispered Yvain to Gawain when Guinevere appeared. 'She's just like my mother.' Yvain was almost right. Guinevere's hair was golden and her smile was warm. Even Gawain was impressed, though normally he only admired women who were like his own mother Queen Morgawse, dark and silent. Guinevere certainly was not silent. She bubbled with talk. 'Hail, King,' she said, sinking down on one knee as well-trained princesses always did to kings in those days. 'Come into the castle and my handmaidens will bring warm water and fair basins of silver; then I will wash all the blood off you and clothe you in the richest robes in the palace for the victory feast. Is that right, father?'

King Leodegrance, who was rather old, smiled.

'Quite right, Guinevere,' he said.

'The only thing is,' said Arthur, smiling too but tottering, 'I need a doctor even more than a bath. This is not just King Floires' blood, you know.'

Then Arthur fainted. Guinevere gave a little cry when she saw the great wound in his leg but she did not faint herself. They carried Arthur into the castle and laid him out in her chamber.

'Lady,' said Gawain, 'I am Arthur's squire, and here is some ointment that will heal him, which it is my duty to put on his wounds.'

'My mother gave it to him,' added Yvain, 'she's his sister. She's called Queen Morgan le Fay. It's called a healing potion.'

'You're a fine page,' said Guinevere affectionately, 'and you are a fine squire, Gawain. How lucky Arthur is to have nephews like you. Now leave me the potion and I'll put it on.'

So for seven days and seven nights Arthur lay in Guine-

vere's chamber, half-conscious. Every day Guinevere without
flinching put the ointment on his wounds, and on the seventh
day, as Queen Morgan le Fay had promised, they were healed
again.

'Thanks to your wonderful sister, King,' said Guinevere.

'King, King, King,' teased Arthur. 'I have a name, young
lady.' Guinevere blushed.

'Arthur,' she said, very low.

'I'd like to save you from the most dreadful dragon in the
world,' said Arthur, taking her hand.

'You have done even better,' laughed Guinevere, 'you
have saved me from King Floires who wanted to marry me.'

Then her handmaidens brought in bowls of silver with
warm water, and towels of linen, some green and some white,
and fine rich robes. First Guinevere washed King Arthur's
head. Then she opened a wooden casket and drew out a razor
whose haft was of ivory, whose edges were rivets of gold. She
shaved his beard, then she dried his head, and his face, and his
throat very gently with the towel. Then she dressed him in a
robe and a surcoat of yellow satin with a broad gold band
upon the mantle, and led him to the victory feast. There he sat
on cushions of red linen, and they placed a harp in his hands
after they had all feasted.

'Three things are proper for a man to have in his home,'
Arthur sang, 'A virtuous wife, his cushion in his chair, and his
harp in tune.'

'He means,' whispered Gawain to Yvain, 'that he wants to
marry the Princess Guinevere.'

Then they all applauded, Gawain, Yvain, King Leodegrance and all the knights and maidens at the feast. Guinevere
sat still and smiled and smiled; and Arthur smiled too.

Arthur galloped back to Camelot with great joy. 'Merlin,' he
said, 'what will men call me now? In the War with the Kings
I killed none of the enemy kings with my own hands. But now

I have challenged and beaten a mighty King and cut off his head. Also I love the fairest lady now living, Guinevere the King's daughter of the land of Camelard. What will men call me now?'

'Sire,' said Merlin, 'you were born by adventure, and you were brought up by adventure. You won the realm by adventure, and now you have found a wife by adventure. Know that all these wonderful adventures have not come to you by chance. Therefore I say to you that men will now call you the King Adventurous and your realm the Kingdom of Adventures. Yet know that as adventures have given you the realm, so adventures will take it from you in the end.'

'The King Adventurous,' said Arthur happily.

'As for Guinevere,' said Merlin, 'as to her beauty and goodness she is one of the fairest ladies alive. But if your heart were not set on her, I should find you a damsel even more beautiful and good than she. It is not wholesome for you to marry her.'

'Not wholesome?' said Arthur. 'Not wholesome? What on earth do you mean by not wholesome?'

But Merlin would not explain.

'When a man's heart is set on a woman,' he said, 'nothing will change it.'

'That,' said Arthur happily, 'is true. Now where is my sister Queen Morgan le Fay? I must tell her the good news.'

CHAPTER 10

The Round Table

MUCH to Arthur's surprise, Queen Morgan le Fay was far from delighted when she heard that her brother was going to be married.

'I have heard of this Guinevere,' she said, 'I have heard she is saucy and silly and slavish.'

'On the contrary,' said Arthur, 'she's just like you. Just as beautiful except that she has cornflower blue eyes. Of course she's younger than you are, so she may be a little less educated. I am sure you will love her almost as much as I do, if not more.'

'I doubt that,' said Morgan le Fay drily. 'In any case I will not be here to love her. King Urien has sent for me, and I must go back to the land of Gore.'

'But the wedding,' cried Arthur. 'You must

stay for the wedding. You are my best-loved sister, you know.'

Morgan le Fay only shook her head.

'At least leave little Yvain,' pleaded Arthur. 'He loves Guinevere already and we have arranged for him to be page at our wedding.'

Morgan le Fay put her slim hand on the shoulder of her gold-green son.

'Yvain,' she said. 'Who do you love more, this cornflower Guinevere or your own mother?'

'You of course, mother,' said Yvain.

'Then you will come with me to Gore, and I will teach you the lore of the Forest and of the Sea, of the beasts and of the fishes. We have stayed too long in dreary Camelot.' Her eyes filled with tears. 'You will never be King here now,' she murmured under her breath. She was sure that once Guinevere was married to Arthur they would have many sons who would inherit the Kingdom.

So Queen Morgan le Fay and Yvain rode away from Camelot. But young Gawain stayed, though he was sorry to see his cousin Yvain go.

'Sire,' he said to his uncle King Arthur, 'I ask you in the name of God to give me a gift.'

'Ask, fair nephew,' said the King, 'and I shall grant it to you.'

'Sire,' said Gawain, 'do you know what I am going to ask? I want you to make me a knight the same day you marry the beautiful Guinevere.'

'I will do so willingly,' said King Arthur, 'and I will do you all the worship I can because you are my nephew, my sister's son.' He patted Gawain on the shoulder. 'Indeed,' he added a little sadly, 'you are the only sister's son I now have left in dreary Camelot.'

Merlin also disappeared. Before he left Camelot he told King Arthur that he would certainly be back for the wedding; and that he would bring back with him the finest wedding present in the world. And so Arthur waited and wondered what the present could be: golden armour perhaps, or a magical ship, or new weapons. Guinevere when she reached Camelot was almost as excited as Arthur.

At last the day before the wedding feast Merlin returned.

'Clear the Great Hall of Camelot,' he said. 'Seal the doors and the windows. Let nothing remain inside.'

They all knew then that whatever Merlin's present was it would fill the Great Hall: and that no one must attempt to see it for fear of being spell-bound.

Next morning King Arthur was married to Queen Guinevere with great solemnity. As soon as that ceremony was over, Gawain was led forward dressed in white samite. As he knelt before King Arthur to be knighted, a poor man pushed his way through the crowd.

'King Arthur,' he cried, 'flower of all Kings, it was told me that at the time of your marriage you would give any man the gift he would ask you.'

'That is true,' said King Arthur.

The poor man ran forward and kissed King Arthur's feet.

'Sire,' he said, 'there is my son behind me. Make him a knight and gird him with a knight's sword at the same time as your nephew Gawain.'

The King smiled and raised him up.

'Who gave you this idea?' he asked. 'The order of knighthood is a high thing for a poor man to ask for.'

'Sire, it is my son's idea, not mine. He forced me to come here and ask you, whether I wanted to or not. I have thirteen sons and all the rest are hard workers. But this son of mine will not do any work at all whatever my wife and I say. He spends his time shooting bows and throwing sharpened sticks, going off to watch battles and gawk at knights. He says he will be a knight or nothing.'

Then everyone there burst out laughing. But King Arthur told the poor man to fetch all his sons.

He lined them up in a row, all thirteen, with their mother too. Twelve of them looked just like the poor man in shape and face; but one was different, better shaped and better looking.

'Which is the son that wants to be made a knight?' asked King Arthur.

'Sire,' said the son who looked different, 'it is I. My name is Tor. There is nothing I desire so much in the world as to be made a knight at your hands.'

King Arthur turned to Merlin. 'Will this young man make a good knight?' he asked.

'He will be a knight of prowess,' said Merlin, 'for he has come of as good a kindred as any man now living. He is of king's blood.'

Tor looked amazed. The poor man looked angrily at his wife, and she looked angrily at Merlin.

'Yes, yes, it's quite true,' said Merlin. 'And it's rather dangerous to look at a wizard like that. No time to explain now, though. The ceremony must go on.'

So King Arthur called for robes and arms and armour to be brought forward. Then he took Excalibur, and dubbed first Tor and then Gawain on the neck; and knighted them.

'Arise,' he said, 'Sir Tor. Arise, Sir Gawain. Be you worthy knights all your lives and good companions to one another.'

Then the whole company went to the Great Hall. Merlin threw the doors open to display his gift. All the knights and ladies stood open-mouthed, expecting to see something wonderful.

'Oh,' said Queen Guinevere, 'it is only a table!' She peered at it more closely. 'Just a wooden table,' she added with great disappointment.

Merlin looked furious. He rumbled into his beard. He grew tall and menacing. 'It is a very fine table,' said King Arthur hastily. 'A very big table.' He looked at it more carefully. 'A very round table.'

'It is perfectly round,' said Merlin proudly. 'I carved it myself, with the help of the guild of master-dwarfs, in the enchanted Forest of Broceliande. By oak, by ash and by elm is all evil banished. It is not just *a* very round table, my lord King Arthur. It is *the* Round Table. Look at it more closely, O King and all you knights,' proclaimed Merlin loudly, 'for henceforth you will be known as the Knights of the Round Table.'

Then all the knights looked at the Round Table much more closely. They saw that there were a hundred and fifty seats in all.

'There are many hundreds of knights here, Merlin,' said King Arthur, 'how shall there be room for all of them at the Round Table?'

'King,' said Merlin, 'only the best knights in the world, of high blood and great prowess, may sit at the Round Table. For if any others sit there, knights of low blood or little prowess, they will dishonour the whole fellowship.'

Arthur reflected a moment.

'Merlin,' he said, 'you know better than anyone else the good knights and the bad. You must choose those who are worthy to sit at the Round Table.'

Then Merlin began to cry out the names of the Knights of the Round Table. And as each knight was named, his name appeared by magic in letters of gold above his seat. So the knights ran to and fro in great excitement till each found his name and his own seat.

'This is a marvellous thing,' they cried, 'and great renown will come to the realm of Logres because of this Table.' All their previous disappointment was totally forgotten, they were so excited at seeing their own names in letters of gold. Even Queen Guinevere was impressed.

When all the seats but one were filled, Merlin spoke out to the whole company of seated knights.

'From now on,' he said, 'you must help each other and hold each other as dear as brothers. The Round Table will bring you such great joy that you will forget your wives and your children and prefer to be with one another, sharing fame and adventures together.'

King Arthur took Guinevere by the hand and together they

received the homage of the Knights of the Round Table who came up, one by one, to kneel before them, and swear fealty. First came King Pellinore, whose seat was next to the one empty seat (that was called the Siege Perilous), as he was the strongest of all knights then living.

'Wait a while,' said Merlin; and put him on one side. Last came Sir Tor, who was the youngest of all the knights there.

'Wait a while,' said Merlin, and put him on the other side. Then he called forward the poor man and his wife.

'I will tell you,' he said, 'who is the real father of Sir Tor. He is a knight who is very close to you now.'

'I do not believe it,' said the poor man, looking around worriedly.

'You dishonour my mother,' cried young Sir Tor angrily.

But the poor man's wife who was very womanly hushed them both up. She told the King and Merlin that when she was a maid and went to milk her cows, 'a very stern knight came up and half by force took away my maidenhood. Then he took away my greyhound that I had with me and said he would keep the greyhound for my love.'

'Is the greyhound here?' asked King Arthur.

The wife pointed at the greyhound who was always with King Pellinore and who always followed the scent of the Questing Beast. The greyhound barked with delight when it saw her, and hurtled over to lick her face. Everyone laughed with delight.

'You have lost a greyhound,' said Merlin to King Pellinore, 'but you have gained a son!'

Then King Pellinore kissed first his new-found son, Sir Tor, who indeed looked very like him and then, after a moment of hesitation, Sir Tor's mother.

'Not so stern now, am I?' he growled; and she smiled like a womanly woman should. He even shook hands with the poor man and congratulated them both on having twelve other sons. Everyone was happy – except for one person.

Sir Gawain scowled.

'That King Pellinore,' he muttered to his brother Gaheris, 'killed our father King Lot. I swore an oath at our father's funeral that one day I would kill him too in revenge. And so I shall, with a trenchant blade.'

'But, Gawain,' said Gaheris, 'you are now both Knights of this new Round Table and Merlin has said you must hold each other dear as brothers. Also you have just been made a knight with Sir Tor who is King Pellinore's son, and our uncle the King has told you to be good companions to one another all your lives.'

Sir Gawain was baffled. He did not know which was more important – his oath to his dead father or his new fellowship of the Round Table.

'In any case,' said Gaheris, 'don't kill him now. Wait till I am a knight too, so that I can help you. As he is the strongest knight now alive, you'll need my help.'

Gaheris, though only a squire, was already as big as Gawain.

'I'm not afraid of him,' said Sir Gawain, 'but I'll wait. I don't want to trouble the high feast.'

So with all joy the great wedding-feast proceeded.

CHAPTER II

Guinevere's Gift

QUEEN Morgan le Fay did not come to the great wedding feast at Camelot. But when she heard that Gawain had been made a Knight of the Round Table, she sent her son Yvain back to Camelot to be made a knight too, as her brother had promised. Gawain was delighted to see him again. So was King Arthur and he at once made him a Knight of the Round Table.

'My mother has sent a wedding present for Queen Guinevere,' said Yvain.

'I am very glad,' said King Arthur. 'I thought your mother was perhaps a little jealous of my new Queen, but now that she has sent her a wedding present, I am sure that they will both love each other as much as they each love me. Shall we see this present?'

So Sir Yvain laughed with pleasure and ordered the damsel who had come with him to unpack the present. She brought out the richest mantle ever seen at Camelot, covered with precious stones, rubies, emeralds, diamonds, and amethysts from the deep mines of Gore.

When Queen Guinevere saw it, she was overjoyed.

'Lady,' said the damsel, 'my mistress Queen Morgan le Fay sends you this mantle as a sign of her great love and asks you only this: that you wear it yourself, you alone, none other than you. For it is a gift fit for a Queen.'

'It must be the most marvellous mantle in the realm,' cried Queen Guinevere, her cornflower eyes opening wide with excitement. 'I have never seen stones so rich. Tell your mistress I love her like my own sister, and I will wear the mantle at the next high feast.'

The damsel smiled.

Merlin did not smile when he heard the news. He scowled and bit his lip till the white blood ran. This, as King Arthur knew, was a sign that he was very worried.

'But there is nothing to worry about now, Merlin,' said King Arthur. 'You know how much my sister loves me.'

'That is exactly what is worrying me,' replied Merlin darkly.

'Indeed,' said King Arthur paying no attention, 'you know her now almost better than I know her myself.'

'Yes,' said Merlin. 'Yes,' he said heavily. 'I am afraid that I do.'

He went down to Queen Guinevere's chamber to see the mantle. He looked at it, he touched it, he smelt it and – much to Guinevere's annoyance – he even licked it. She absolutely forbade him to try it on.

'No,' said Guinevere, 'it is for myself alone to wear it. Morgan le Fay has made it specially for me.'

'I wish,' said Merlin to himself, 'that I had never taught her half of what she now knows.'

The day of the next high feast came round. Queen Morgan le Fay's damsel would not let Guinevere put the mantle on in her chamber.

'My mistress especially wanted you to put it on in front of your husband the King and all his knights,' she said.

So Guinevere went into the Great Hall. The damsel followed her, carrying the mantle. All the knights were amazed at its great beauty and richness.

'Damsel,' said King Arthur, 'now put my sister's beautiful mantle on my beautiful Queen.'

The damsel curtsied.

'One moment,' said Merlin. 'Sir King, first let the damsel try on this beautiful mantle herself.'

'Sire,' said the damsel, 'it is not right for me to wear a queen's robes.'

King Arthur looked at Merlin. He knew the wizard never asked for anything without a good reason.

'By my head, damsel,' said the King, 'you shall wear it before my Queen does or any other woman.'

He got up himself, and threw the mantle around her shoulders. To the horror of everyone watching, the mantle suddenly seemed to shoot flames. With a horrible scream the damsel shrivelled up and was burnt to cinders before their very eyes. Queen Guinevere was the most horrified of all because she realized how close she had been to the most painful death. King Arthur was stunned.

'Merlin,' he said at last, 'what does this mean?'

'It is my fault,' said Merlin heavily. 'Your sister Queen Morgan le Fay ensorcelled me with her green eyes, and I taught her spells and sorcery that she would never have learnt without my help. She is no longer just an enchantress, she is a true sorceress now.'

'But why should she want to kill Guinevere?' asked the King.

'If you do not know that, King,' said Merlin, 'then you are more brainless than I thought.'

All the Knights of the Round Table rose in a great hubbub shouting at Merlin and demanding that he apologize to the King. Merlin rose in his turn, tall and menacing, and waited for the outcry to die down.

'Brainless dolts, all of you,' he said disdainfully. 'I should turn you all into flies, and serve you to the fishes. Have you forgotten who I am?' All the knights sat very still and quiet like terrified children. 'I can see,' said Merlin more calmly but still very loftily,' that decent wizards are not wanted at Camelot. I ask myself why I am wasting my time here when I might be with more civilized and cultured beings than you could ever imagine, in China for instance, where it must be about the Ming Dynasty now. Or possibly the Sung. In any case in the company of delicate and refined minds, most unlike yours. So, Knights' – he bowed sardonically – 'farewell.'

And with a swirl of his great cloak Merlin disappeared. But Arthur sat for a long time, alone and sorrowful in the Great Hall, looking at the pile of ashes that might have been Queen Guinevere, and thinking about his sister.

CHAPTER 12

The Valley of Stones

THE more King Arthur thought about the burning cloak, the more angry he grew till he was almost mad with anger at the thought that his beloved Guinevere could so easily have died.

He summoned Sir Yvain before him. 'As for you, Yvain,' he said, 'I hold you suspect too.'

'My lord,' said Sir Yvain, 'I swear to you that I knew nothing of the burning cloak nor of the damsel who brought it. I love your Queen, the beautiful Guinevere. Indeed I think I now love her more than my own recreant mother.'

'I hold you suspect,' repeated King Arthur, 'the treacherous son of a treacherous mother.'

'Sire, uncle,' cried Sir Gawain, 'you are wrong.

Everyone knows Yvain here is the most courteous young knight that ever was. He is always joyful and pleasant. He knows no sorcery.'

'For all that,' said King Arthur sternly, 'he must leave Camelot.'

'If he goes,' said Sir Gawain who was always hot-headed and loyal, 'I will go too. For whoever banishes my cousin banishes me.' And so Sir Gawain and Sir Yvain rode away from Camelot as knights errant.

'Now,' said Gaheris, Sir Gawain's brother, 'we have lost two good knights for the love of one.'

Even when Yvain was gone, King Arthur could not forgive or forget the treachery of his sister Queen Morgan le Fay. He began to hate her now as much as he once loved her before. Whenever he saw his beautiful Queen Guinevere he imagined her black and burnt to cinders as she would have been if she had put on the rich mantle.

'I will be avenged upon my sister!' cried Arthur. 'God knows I have honoured her and trusted her more than my other sisters, and now I will have revenge on that sorceress for her false crafts.'

He called for his swiftest horse and rode out into the great Forest. He remembered that he had learnt the language of the birds when he was a boy, and so he rode and rode till he found the Eagle of Ablek, the oldest animal in the world and the one that could see furthest.

'Where is my traitor sister Morgan le Fay?' he asked the Eagle.

The Eagle scanned all the horizons of the world. 'She is not in the land of Gore,' it said, 'she is not in the Isles, she is not in the realm of Logres, she is not in Lyonesse.'

'Look further,' said King Arthur.

'Ah,' said the Eagle after a long time, 'I have seen her. She is in Annwen, the Kingdom of the Elves, that you men call Avalon.'

'How can I get there?' asked King Arthur.

'No mortal man can set foot in Avalon,' said the Eagle.

'Then I will have to lay an ambush for her on the way back,' said Arthur to himself.

For six months, day and night, King Arthur lay hidden in ambush at the Gates of Gore, waiting for his sister to return from the elf-kingdom. He stayed awake watching day and night, and Cabal, his wolf-hound, watched with him. But when six months had passed, both he and Cabal fell asleep and slept for a week. That was when Queen Morgan le Fay returned. She found her brother lying there asleep with the sword Excalibur naked in his right hand, and Cabal asleep at his feet.

'I must have this sword,' she said to herself, 'else Arthur will kill me with it for vengeance' sake.'

Very, very gently she drew it from his hand, hardly daring to breathe, for fear she might wake him, or Cabal the wolf-hound. Then, once she had it, she rode hastily on her way.

When Arthur did wake up and found Excalibur gone, it would be hard to describe his rage. He still had his lance the Nor-killer with him: so he put Cabal hunting onto the trail and soon they had a sight of Morgan le Fay.

'Ah, traitress,' cried King Arthur, 'you will not escape me now,' and he chased her as fast as he might.

Morgan le Fay rode into a valley where there were many great stones. There, when she saw she could not escape King Arthur, she turned herself, horse and all, into a stone statue by sorcery. The hound Cabal lost her scent, and King Arthur lost all sight of her. There were hundreds of stone statues in that valley and he had no way of hurting a statue even if he found the right one. So he rode home wearily to Camelot. Queen Morgan le Fay sent a dwarf after him with a proud message:

'Tell Arthur,' she said, 'that I am not afraid of him while I can change me and mine into the likeness of stones, and let him know that I can do much more when I see my time.' She was not afraid of her brother for all his rage and power.

In the Isle of Annwen Queen Morgan le Fay had fallen in love with Guiomar, King of the Elves and Guardian of the Glass City. Now that she was back safely in the land of Gore she intended to kill her husband King Urien. It was all Merlin's fault in a way. If he had not taught her sorcery, she could never have set foot in Annwen. If she had not set foot in Annwen, she would never have met Guiomar Elf-King and fallen in love with him. If she had not fallen so madly in love with him, she would never have plotted to kill her husband King Urien with Excalibur. Love sometimes makes women mad. But Morgan le Fay still loved her brother Arthur more than anyone else in the world, or out of it. Otherwise she would have killed him with Excalibur when he lay asleep; she could easily have done so.

She waited till one day she saw King Urien asleep on his bed. Then she called one of her damsels.

'Go, and fetch the sword Excalibur,' she said, 'for I never saw a better time to kill the King than now.'

'Ah, Lady,' said the damsel, 'if you slay my lord the King, you will never escape.'

She said this because she knew Sir Yvain had returned from his adventures to Gore.

'This is no worry of yours,' said Morgan le Fay. 'I see my time is best to do it now, so hurry fast and fetch me the sword.'

The damsel departed and found Sir Yvain sleeping on another bed in another chamber. So she went over to him, woke him up and bade him, 'Arise, and hurry to my Lady, your mother, for she is going to kill the King your father asleep on his bed and has sent me to fetch the sword.'

'Fetch it then,' said Sir Yvain, 'and leave it to me.'

Sir Yvain, after all his adventures since leaving Camelot, was now a bold young knight.

The damsel brought the Queen the sword with shaking hands. Morgan le Fay drew Excalibur softly out, went boldly over to the bed, and looked down at King Urien, planning how and where she might best strike him. As she heaved up

Excalibur to smite, Sir Yvain leapt upon his mother and caught her by the hand.

'Fiend,' he cried, 'what were you going to do? If you were not my mother, I would swop off your head with this very sword. Ah,' said Sir Yvain, 'they say that Merlin's father was a demon but I say my own mother is an earthly demon.'

Until then Morgan le Fay had always been able to make her son Yvain obey her. Now she saw that he was a grown man and a noble knight, who was no longer dazzled by her green eyes.

'Fair sweet son, spare me!' she cried, 'I was tempted by the Elf-King who ensorcelled me. Do not tell your father of this.'

'Very well,' said Sir Yvain, 'I will forgive you if you promise never to do such a deed again, and if you promise to make peace with Queen Guinevere and with my uncle King Arthur.'

'Fair son,' said Queen Morgan le Fay, 'I make you that promise. Also I give you the sword Excalibur to take back to my brother. Yet I fear that King Arthur will never forgive me and will never receive me in his own land though I love him better than your father, better than the Elf-King, better even than you, fair son.'

Then Queen Morgan le Fay sobbed bitterly and wept for seven days and seven nights. But Sir Yvain took Excalibur and rode back to Camelot. King Arthur was so overjoyed to have his own sword back again that he welcomed Sir Yvain like his own son: and so did Queen Guinevere. But as for Queen Morgan le Fay, King Arthur swore that, though he would not try to seek her out and kill her, he would never allow her to set foot in Camelot again because of the gift of the burning mantle. Queen Guinevere was delighted.

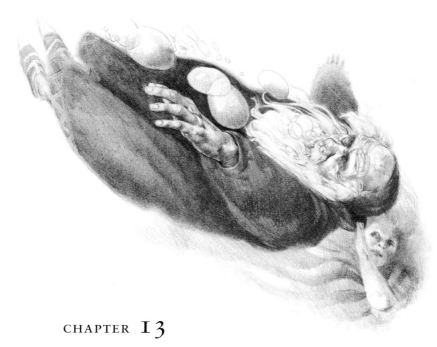

CHAPTER 13

The Underwater Castle

MERLIN was ashamed of having been ensorcelled by the green-eyed Morgan le Fay and was even a little frightened of her, now that she knew almost as much sorcery as he did himself. But all the same he had other things to think about besides the realm of Logres. He never reached the Empire of China, though. There were troubles in Lyonesse when Tristram was born, who was to be the biggest Knight of the Round Table. Merlin saved his father from a dungeon and Tristram himself from being poisoned. There were troubles in Cornwall and Cardu.

And there was trouble in Benwick. King Ban of Benwick's son had been left beside a river as a baby and had been stolen away. King Ban begged Merlin to find him.

Merlin searched high and low, and could find no trace of the boy, till he came to the Great Salmon of Loch Lore, the fish who travelled furthest in the world.

'I have heard of this vanishing baby,' said the Great Salmon. 'Swim with me, wizard, and we will see if we can find him.'

So Merlin swam for many leagues side by side with the Great Salmon till they came to an underwater castle made of shimmering glass. The castle could only be seen by fish swimming underwater; from the land above it seemed to be just the shimmering surface of a great lake.

'Therein is the son of King Ban,' said the Great Salmon. 'Good hunting, wizard. I hope you like what you find – but I am not sure if you will!' It swished its tail, and left Merlin there.

Inside the shimmering castle Merlin found the most handsome young man he had ever seen in the world.

'Who are you?' said the young man, startled.

'I am Merlin.'

'No,' said another voice, soft and silvery. 'No, I do not think that is your real name.'

Merlin looked around startled. At first he could see nothing. Then a shimmering shape slowly took form as he gazed, fascinated. It was that of a beautiful nymph, far more beautiful than Queen Guinevere or even than Queen Morgan le Fay. Her eyes were all the colours of the rainbow; they sparkled now like ice diamonds, now like rich rubies. Merlin was afraid that she would ensorcel him more than he had ever been ensorcelled before. Hurriedly he shed the fish scales he had been travelling in, and resumed his own shape, a most distinguished wizard. The nymph looked closely and steadily at him.

'I knew you,' she said softly, 'in another Age, wizard, and under another name.'

'I forget,' said Merlin, confused. 'It is all so long ago and I have seen so much. So much. What do they call you, Lady?'

'They call me Nimiane.'

Merlin looked back into the deep past.

'I can see no one by that name,' he said.

'In the Third Age they called me Galadriel.'

'Elfin Queen!' exclaimed Merlin.

'Lady of the Forest then,' said Nimiane. 'Lady of the Lake now.'

'Ah,' said Merlin. 'Elf Queen and now Lady of the Lake. The successor.'

Both were silent a long time, as they searched for the Past and the Future. But for the moment their doom lay hidden.

'Is this King Ban's son of Benwick?' asked Merlin at last.

'It is,' said Nimiane.

'I have come for him,' said Merlin. 'It is time he went to the upper earth.'

'I know,' said Nimiane. 'He has been trained. He is ready. He will be the flower of all knights. He will never be matched by any earthly knight's hand. He will be the most courteous knight that ever bore shield, the gentlest that ever ate in hall among ladies, the truest lover that ever loved woman, the sternest knight to his mortal foes that ever put spear in rest, and the kindest man that ever struck with sword.'

'What is his name?' asked Merlin.

'His name is Lancelot,' said Nimiane.

'Men shall call him Lancelot du Lac,' said the Wizard, bowing, 'that is to say, Lancelot of the Lake because he was taken and trained by the Lady of the Lake, by Nimiane. Come, let us go.'

They all three rose and left that underwater castle. Lancelot went first to his father King Ban, who welcomed him with great joy and then sent him to King Arthur's court. There King Arthur made him a Knight of the Round Table. Then Sir Lancelot vowed himself to Queen Guinevere and served her all his life.

But Nimiane, the Lady of the Lake, took Merlin to the

enchanted Forest of Broceliande. There she ensorcelled him with magic love, as the wizard knew she would; and Merlin came no more to Camelot.

HERE ENDS THE BOOK OF MERLIN

BOOK TWO

The Book of the Knights

Prologue

KNIGHTS of the Round Table never forgot they were the followers of the King Adventurous. To begin with, they were a very wild fellowship. They would ride a wallop through the Great Forest chasing trolls or giants; or else they would set out on a long quest and never return until they had achieved it. They would defy stranger knights and joust with them, usually at bridges or fords or fountains, and they were always swopping off their enemies' heads without mercy or pity. Indeed in the Adventure of the White Hart, which was the first adventure Sir Gawain and Sir Gaheris (who had just been made a knight) went on together, Sir Gawain swopped off the head of a damsel, and his brother Gaheris swopped off the head of a knight who cried pity. Queen Guinevere was so shocked at Sir Gawain (though he had not meant to swop off the damsel's head) that she made him take an oath on the Four Evangels that as long as he lived he would never again do harm to any woman. He never did. After that he was always very courteous, and they called him the Knight with the Golden Tongue.

King Arthur called all the Knights of the Round Table together at the high feast of Pentecost. He was more upset by the behaviour of his nephew Sir Gaheris than by the accident of Sir Gawain. He ordered all his knights in future always to show mercy to stranger knights that asked for mercy, never to do outrage or murder, never to battle in a wrongful quarrel for love or for worldly goods, and always to give help to ladies and damsels. All Knights of the Round Table, young and old, were sworn to obey these laws; and every year at the high feast of Pentecost they came together and swore these oaths again. Then the whole world knew that here was the flower of chivalry and a fellowship that should never be broken.

Each Knight of the Round Table had his own shield with his own device upon it. That was how they recognized each other when they rode out on quests, and that was how they made sure they did not do battle with each other, but only with a stranger knight. Sometimes, though, a knight would take a strange shield, particularly at tournaments where he did not want to be recognized. Sir Lancelot du Lac was always doing this, because otherwise at tournaments nobody would joust with him. As soon as they saw by his shield that it was Sir Lancelot, they knew they would be beaten, for he was by far the best knight at joustings and tournaments.

Sir Lancelot was as good a knight in battle as he was in the tournament. Indeed he was one of the three Knights of Battle of the Round Table. They were called Knights of Battle because they would never retreat from battle, neither for spear nor for arrow nor for sword. The other two were Sir Yvain and Sir Cador of Cornwall. King Arthur never had shame in battle the day he saw their faces there.

Here are the names of the most famous Knights of the Round Table. Sir Lancelot du Lac, and his kinsmen, all of the lineage of King Ban: Sir Bors, Sir Lionel, Sir Ector, Sir Blamor, and Sir Bleoberis. Sir Kay the Seneschal, who was brought up with Arthur; Sir Bedevere the One-Armed and Sir Lucan, who were both with King Arthur at the end of the Day of Destiny; Sir Sagremor the Desirous who bore the King's Dragon Standard that same day; Sir Yvain, the son of Queen Morgan le Fay, who was always clad in green and gold; and King Arthur's other nephews, the sons of King Lot of Orkeney and Queen Morgawse, Sir Gawain, Sir Gareth, and the twin brothers Sir Gaheris and Sir Agravaine, also Sir Mordred; the mighty Sir Marholt; King Pellinore, who was the only other King besides Arthur himself to be a Knight of the Round Table, and his two sons Sir Tor and Sir Lamorak, whom Sir Lancelot loved; Sir Tristram of Lyonesse, the biggest knight of them all; Sir Balin le Sauvage and his brother Sir Balan; they swore the Pentecost oaths but were too fierce to keep them; Sir Dinadan, who was known as the Cowardly Knight; Sir Palomides the Saracen, Sir Mador de le Porte, Sir Galehalt the Haute Prince, and Sir Perceval.

There were many, many others too; for whenever one knight was dead, another knight took his place so that, though every Pentecost there were many empty places to be seen, by the time the high feast was over King Arthur had filled them all again.

It would need many books to tell of the adventures and quests of all these knights, so there will only be a few, very few, told here. But be assured that this was the greatest fellowship of knights, and the noblest, that the world has ever seen.

CHAPTER I

The Adventure of Joyous Garde

TWO fearsome knights hated the Knights of the Round Table. They were brothers. One was Sir Caradoc of the Dolorous Tower and the other was Sir Tarquin of Dolorous Garde. Dolorous Garde was a castle, and there Sir Tarquin guarded his prisoners in his dolorous dungeons. No man had ever escaped from Dolorous Garde alive.

Both Sir Caradoc and Sir Tarquin had the habit of tying up Knights of the Round Table when they had conquered them in battle and slinging them across their horses in front of the saddle, shamefully, before carrying them off into captivity. That was how one day Sir Lancelot saw Sir Gawain: slung across the war-horse of Sir Caradoc, bumping up and down in a very uncomfortable manner.

'Gawain,' cried Sir Lancelot, 'how are things with you?'

That was a strange question as it was obvious that things were very bad indeed with Sir Gawain. But Sir Lancelot was so surprised to find that a knight as strong and famous as Sir Gawain had been beaten and had yielded that he shouted the first thing that came into his head. In fact Sir Gawain had not yielded. Sir Caradoc, who was more like a giant than a man, had given him such a blow with his mace on the head that he had stunned Sir Gawain, and then pulled him out of his saddle by his collar.

'Help me!' cried Sir Gawain. 'For if God won't help me, I don't know anyone else who can.'

Sir Lancelot spurred his war-horse forward till it blocked Sir Caradoc's path.

'Put that knight down and fight with me,' he said sternly.

'Fool!' was all Sir Caradoc said in reply.

'Why do you call me fool?'

'Because,' mocked Sir Caradoc, 'when I have finished with you I will truss you up in just the same way and add you to the pile.'

'As for that,' said Sir Lancelot grimly, 'have no pity on me, for, I warn you, I will have none on you.'

So Sir Caradoc carefully tied Sir Gawain's hands and feet together, then heaved him off his war-horse, so that he fell with a great crash to the ground, where he lay stunned, unable to move. Then he took his spear from his squire and hurtled down on Sir Lancelot.

It was Sir Lancelot's first great fight. He was very big and strong, but Sir Caradoc was even bigger and much more experienced. Sir Caradoc struck Lancelot on the shield, so that he pierced and split it and made the head pass through Lancelot's left armpit, and if it had caught him it would have killed him. Then they crashed together with their bodies and heads and shields. The reins and shield straps flew from their fists, and each bore the other down to earth so violently that you could have walked a mile and back before anything else

Nick Harris Aug 1982

happened. They lay there dazed. They had no idea what was happening.

But when they came to their senses they leapt up and grasped the shields by their straps. Sir Lancelot drew his sword, but Sir Caradoc attacked him with his flailing mace in a terrible fury. Lancelot put his shield forward but Caradoc's mace shattered it with one blow. The mace came downwards with such strength that if it had hit Sir Lancelot it would have shattered his armour too. Fortunately it missed him and hit the ground, sending flowers and stones and earth flying. When Sir Lancelot saw the blow had missed, his own strength and courage grew in him. He felt great anger and hatred, raised his sword high and drove it down through the middle of Sir Caradoc's helm, so that he split him in two right down to the waist. Then he untied Sir Gawain.

When the story of this great fight was told, Sir Lancelot gained great honour. Sir Gawain praised him and told the story to everyone, so that all men began to say that Sir Lancelot was the knight of most prowess among all the Knights of the Round Table. Queen Guinevere favoured him above all other knights, and he loved her above all other ladies all his life long, and for her did many noble deeds of chivalry.

Sir Ector de Marys was Sir Lancelot's younger brother. He was not as big or strong as Sir Lancelot but he was a brave knight for all that, and was always ready for a new adventure. One day he had been riding for a long time through the Forest when he came across a man who seemed to be a forester.

'Fair fellow,' said Sir Ector – that was the courteous way knights used to address ordinary men on foot – 'do you know of any adventure to be had here in the woods?'

'Fair Sir,' said the forester, who was in fact a troll in disguise and loved mocking knights, 'a mile further on the left hand side there is a fair ford and over the fair ford grows a fair tree, and on the fair tree hang many fair shields.'

'Fellow,' said Sir Ector, who realized the forester was being too polite with all those 'fairs', 'whose shields are they?'

'Shields that once coward knights wielded,' said the troll, who especially hated knights that came from King Arthur's court and so would not tell him that they were all shields of the Knights of the Round Table.

'But why are those shields hanging on the tree?' asked Sir Ector, who was rather slow-witted.

'If you want to know that,' said the troll, smiling slyly, 'this is what you must do. You must strike three times with the butt of your spear on a great gong of copper and brass that is hanging at the foot of the tree.'

'And then?'

'Then,' said the troll, 'you will have news of some adventure.' And as Sir Ector rode off after thanking him courteously, he muttered to himself: 'Or, if you don't, you will be the luckiest knight to have ridden through this Forest in many years!'

So Sir Ector de Marys rode on, and found the ford and the tree. On the branches of the tree many shields were hanging: one that he recognized at once had the device on it of his cousin Sir Lionel. Then he looked at all the others more closely and he saw that they were all shields that belonged to the Knights of the Round Table who had disappeared. He was a little frightened by this time, but all the same he turned his spear round and beat the gong three times. Three times it boomed. Nothing happened. So he let his war-horse have a drink of water at the ford.

When a thirsty war-horse gulps down water, it makes a lot of noise; so Sir Ector did not hear a knight ride up behind him. It gave him a great shock when he turned round and saw the knight, a very big, strong knight, a giant of a knight, just sitting there waiting, with his lance already feutred, ready to fight. So Sir Ector feutred his own lance, set spurs to his war-horse, galloped down upon him, and struck him such a brave blow on his shield that it spun the knight and his war-horse round and round again.

'Well done,' said the giant knight, 'that was a good stroke for a small man.'

Then he set spurs to his own war-horse but, instead of striking a blow at Sir Ector, he just leant across, caught him under his right arm, and lifted him clean out of his saddle. Then he galloped away with Sir Ector slung across the saddle-bow to his own castle and threw him down in the courtyard with a great thump and clanging.

'You did better against me,' he said, 'than any knight has done for twelve years. So I will spare your life, if you swear to be my true prisoner.'

'No,' said Sir Ector who was lying on his back on the ground, looking up at the giant knight. 'I will never swear that. I will always try and escape whenever I can, and will never be your true prisoner.'

'The worse for you,' said the giant knight grimly, and he stripped Sir Ector of his armour, beat him with thorns when he was all naked, and hurled him, bleeding and freezing, into a deep dungeon. Sir Ector looked around him and saw lots more naked, bloody men. One of them tottered over to him.

'Lionel?' said Sir Ector, 'is that you, Lionel?'

The prisoner nodded. He was so sad and shameful he could hardly speak. Ector looked around at all the prisoners and began to recognize them too, though they were thin and covered with long hair and beards. They were all Knights of the Round Table, sixty or more of them, all those whose shields had been hanging on the branches of the tree by the ford. Among them was Sir Kay, who hung his head for shame.

'How long have you been here?' asked Ector to his cousin.

Sir Lionel held up three fingers.

'Three days? Three weeks? Three months?'

Sir Lionel shook his head sadly.

'Three years?' asked Sir Ector unbelievingly.

Sir Lionel nodded his head even more sadly.

Then, bold though Sir Ector de Marys was, his heart began to fail within him. He turned to Sir Kay the Seneschal.

'Yes,' said Sir Kay, who was quite unlike his usual bouncy self. 'You have guessed right. This is Dolorous Garde, and no prisoner has ever escaped from here alive.'

Of course it was very foolish of the prisoner-knights to forget Sir Lancelot. There was some excuse for the other knights, who did not then know him too well, some excuse even for his cousin Sir Lionel who had been in prison for three years without Sir Lancelot even trying to rescue him. But there was no excuse for Sir Ector de Marys. He ought to have known that his own brother would soon be coming on a quest to find him.

Sure enough, not many weeks had passed before Sir Lancelot was at the ford, under the tree and striking the great brass and copper gong with the butt of his spear. Nobody came at all, so he struck again, and then in his mighty rage again and again, till the bottom fell out. Still nobody came, but Sir Lancelot had no intention of giving up. He had recognized Sir Ector's shield that was now hanging up there beside all the other shields of the Knights of the Round Table, sixty-one of them in all, and so he knew that Sir Ector could not be far away – if he was still alive, that is. So he followed the trail that went from the foot of the tree deep into the Forest. He rode for a mile or two and then he suddenly saw a giant knight riding one war-horse and driving another in front of him. Across the war-horse the body of a big armed knight was slung, trussed like a sack. Sir Lancelot rode up close and saw the trussed knight's face as it bounced up and down. It was all bloody with wounds; the knight was Sir Gaheris, Sir Gawain's brother.

By this time the giant knight had seen Sir Lancelot. At once they both feutred their spears.

'Now, fair knight,' said Sir Lancelot with his usual courtesy, 'put that wounded knight down from that horse, and let him rest awhile. For he is a Knight of the Round Table, and my fellow companion.'

'I defy you and all your foul fellowships!' roared the giant knight.

'That is uncourteously said, fair knight,' said Sir Lancelot mildly. But the giant knight only roared with fearsome laughter.

Then they both set spurs to their war-horses and came together as fast as they could. Each smote the other hard and fierce in the middle of their shields, so that both their horses' backs broke with a dreadful crack. The two knights fell to the ground, stunned. Then they heaved themselves up, drew their swords, raised their shields, and hewed and smote at each other like two wild boars. For over two hours they hewed and smote and gave each other many grim wounds till the ground over which they were fighting was bespeckled with their blood. Then they both stood apart a little, because they were out of breath, and leant on their swords.

'Now, fellow,' said the giant knight, 'hold your hand for a moment and tell me what I ask of you.'

'Say on,' said Sir Lancelot.

Then the giant knight said: 'You are the biggest man I ever came up against, and the best-breathed, and for all your soft words the fiercest fighter. If you are not the one knight I hate above all other knights, I will make peace with you and set free all the prisoners I have. Then you and I will be companions, and always be loyal to one another for as long as we live.'

'I agree,' said Sir Lancelot, 'and I would much like to have your friendship. But who is the knight whom you hate more than anyone else in the world?'

'I will tell you,' said the giant knight. 'His name is Sir Lancelot. He killed my brother Sir Caradoc of the Dolorous Tower, one of the best knights who ever lived. So because of Sir Lancelot I have killed many knights and flayed others so that they are totally maimed, and left others in my dungeons where many have died. But sixty-one are still alive and all shall be set free, if only you tell me your name and if only your name is not Sir Lancelot.'

'Now, sir knight,' said Sir Lancelot, 'I see by this that you must be Sir Tarquin of Dolorous Garde. And since it is not right that I should know your name but you not know mine, I will tell you my name, as you have asked. Know then,' he said proudly, 'that I am Sir Lancelot du Lac, King Ban's son of Benwick and true Knight of the Round Table.'

'Ah,' said Sir Tarquin with a grim laugh, 'I am more pleased to see you here than any other knight that might be! Here I take my oath that one of us two shall meet his end.'

'Now I defy you,' said Sir Lancelot fiercely, 'and do your best!'

Then they hurtled together like two wild bulls, rushing and lashing with their shields and swords. The Forest rang with the clash of arms, even the birds fell silent for fear, the ground grew all damp and slippery with their blood. Sir Lancelot struck Sir Tarquin upon the helm; but it was so hard-forged that he could not hurt it. Then Sir Tarquin attacked him so sharply that he first drove Sir Lancelot backwards step by step, then struck him with his sword a great blow on the helm, so that he cut through it and wounded him on the left side of the head, then sent him staggering backwards in a rush; and he would have killed Sir Lancelot there and then if the sword had not turned in his hand. But Sir Lancelot lost his temper then, caught up his shield, and leapt upon his enemy hewing and smiting and drawing blood, till at the last Sir Tarquin for all his giant might was almost fainting for the loss of blood. He took a step or two backwards, and then let his shield fall, he was so weary. Sir Lancelot saw him drop his guard, rushed at him, seized him by the face-guard and his helmet, pulled him down upon his knees, raced off his helm, raised his sword high, and with a great stroke cut off his head. Then he staggered over to Sir Gaheris and cut him loose.

'Fair knight,' said Sir Gaheris, 'you must be the best knight in the world, for you have slain under my eyes the mightiest man and the best knight, except yourself, that I ever saw. What is your name?'

'Sir Gaheris,' said Sir Lancelot, opening his visor, 'I am Sir Lancelot du Lac. It was my duty to help you for King Arthur's sake and especially for your brother's sake, my lord Sir Gawain. Now I will rest awhile but, as you are fresh, you must ride ahead to the castle of this dead knight, for I am sure you will find there many of the Knights of the Round Table. I have seen their shields hanging on a tree some way back. Ride now, I pray you.'

First Sir Gaheris went on his knees, and kissed Sir Lancelot's hand, and swore always to be his man in life and in death because he had rescued him from a shameful beating and imprisonment. Then he rode a wallop to Dolorous Garde. He threw down the gatekeeper at the gates and took his keys from him. He opened the dungeons and let all the prisoners out. When they saw Sir Gaheris, they all went down on their knees and thanked him, for they thought he must have killed Sir Tarquin himself.

'Not so,' said Sir Gaheris, 'it was Sir Lancelot that slew him worshipfully with his own hands, and he greets you all well.'

No sooner was Sir Kay free than he prepared a feast. 'For,' he said, 'it is many a day since we have had anything to eat at all, except the rats and mice and beetles of the dungeons!'

Then they all laughed, and roasted and baked the venison; and when Sir Lancelot rode in that evening, they greeted him with great cheer.

'Here,' said Sir Kay, 'let us drink a toast to this castle. For I assure you all, I who am the King's foster brother and know his mind, that King Arthur will give this castle to Sir Lancelot as a reward for having rescued us all.'

'It is a very fine castle,' said Sir Lancelot.

Indeed it was. It was set between two rivers, one of the strongest castles in the world, and no army could ever capture it if it were properly defended.

'But we cannot drink a toast to a castle with a gloomy name like Dolorous Garde,' cried the knights.

'Then let us rechristen it,' said Sir Gaheris, who was always quick-witted. 'Let us call it no longer Dolorous Garde but Joyous Garde.'

Then all the knights shouted together as they clashed their drinking horns and let the red wine flow. 'Joyous Garde!' they cried.

Joyous Garde was the name of that castle ever after; and, as Sir Kay had said, King Arthur gave it to Sir Lancelot, and it was Sir Lancelot's own castle in the realm of Logres.

HERE ENDS AN ADVENTURE OF SIR LANCELOT

CHAPTER **2**

The Adventure of the Falcon

ONE day Sir Lancelot, who was by now a famous knight, was riding past a small castle when he heard bells ringing up in the air. He looked up and saw a falcon swooping over his head, with long leather jesses, dangling from her legs; and on each of the jesses was a little bell. The falcon flew towards a high elm tree and there she perched on a bough. But when she tried to take flight again, she could not, for the jesses were tangled up with the bough and so the falcon was pulled short in her flight and dangled upside down by her legs.

Sir Lancelot was sorry for the fair falcon, for he saw that she would destroy herself. But it was no business of his, so he rode on.

Then a fair lady came out of the castle and called to him: 'Ah, Lancelot, Lancelot, you who are the flower of all knights, help me get my falcon back. I was holding her and she slipped out of my hand. If my lord my husband finds out, he is so hot-tempered that he will kill me for it.'

'Well, fair lady,' said Sir Lancelot, 'since you know my name and ask me by my knighthood to help you, I will do what I can to get your falcon.' He looked up at the elm. 'God knows, though,' he muttered to himself, 'it is a very high elm. I am a very bad climber, and there are hardly any branches to help me.'

All the same he dismounted, tied his war-horse to the elm, and asked the lady to help him off with his armour. Then he took off the rest of his clothes, except for his long shirt and his pants. It took a long time but he managed to climb up right to the top of the elm. When he reached the falcon, he tied her jesses to a bunch of leaves and threw her down, leaves and all, so that she landed softly by the lady who was waiting down below.

As soon as the lady had picked up the falcon, her husband sprang out of some nearby bushes, in full armour.

'Ah, Knight Sir Lancelot,' he called up from the foot of the elm, waving his naked sword, 'now I have you where you will never escape me!'

'Lady,' Sir Lancelot called down, 'why have you betrayed me?'

'She only did what I commanded her to,' called up the knight whose name was Sir Phelot. 'Your hour is come, Sir Lancelot and you must die.'

Sir Lancelot knew he could not fight a battle with his bare hands. He slithered half-way down the tree, all the same.

'Give me my armour,' he said. 'You are a fully-armed knight and it will be your shame if you slay a naked man.'

'Fetch it if you can,' said Sir Phelot, grinning, 'for you will get no help from me.'

Sir Lancelot knew he would be killed before he reached his armour, let alone before he could put it on.

'Take my armour away then,' he cried. 'But at least hang my sword up there on the branch below me so that I can reach it. Then do your best, and kill me if you can. You will have full armour, and I will have none.'

'No,' said Sir Phelot, 'I know you better than you think. Once you have a sword in your hand, I would be a dead man, armour or no armour. You will get no sword from me.'

'It is a pitiful thing,' muttered Sir Lancelot, 'for a noble knight to die because he has no weapon.'

He looked up, and he looked down, and then he suddenly leapt up in the air from the branch on which he was standing and grabbed at another spiky branch over his head. It broke away in his hands, and he missed his footing and came falling down, thirty feet or more. But luckily he landed so that the war-horse was between him and Sir Phelot. By the time Sir Phelot had come round the horse and was lashing at him, Sir Lancelot was up on his feet again and parrying the blows of Sir Phelot's sword with the spiky branch. Then he gave the branch a great swing and caught Sir Phelot such a blow on the side of the head that he knocked him down. Then it only took him a moment to pounce on Sir Phelot, wrestle his sword out of his hand, and swop off his head.

'Alas,' cried the lady, 'why have you killed my husband?'

'Your husband would have killed me with treachery for no reason,' said Sir Lancelot. 'Instead death has fallen on him, a recreant knight. As for you, lady' – he took a step towards her and raised his sword – 'you trapped me with your falsehoods.'

Then the lady screamed, for Sir Lancelot looked very grim standing there. For even though he wore no armour or helmet and his shirt-tails were fluttering in the breeze, she could see her husband's life-blood dripping from the sword in his hand and she was afraid that he would kill her too.

But Sir Lancelot conquered his temper.

'We do not harm ladies or damsels, even treacherous

ones,' he said, throwing the sword down, 'we who are Knights of the Round Table. Arm me now, then bury your husband.'

The lady armed him in silence. When he was armed, Sir Lancelot mounted his war-horse.

'Look up there,' he said, pointing with his lance to the top of the elm tree.

The lady looked up.

'I may be the flower of knighthood,' said Sir Lancelot grimly, 'but all the same, lady, if I should hear you have betrayed a knight ever again, I will come back here and hang you by your fine clothes from that very branch where your falcon was hanging!'

Then he rode away.

HERE ENDS AN ADVENTURE OF SIR LANCELOT

CHAPTER 3

The Adventure of
La Roche aux Pucelles

SIR Gawain and Sir Marholt rode through the Forest to a far stony land. It was a cold land too; the wind whistled round the great shapeless rocks, and all that could be heard was the howling of orcs that mingled with the wind. There were no human beings there, no animals, no trolls even.

'Dwarf-land,' said Sir Gawain, peering down into the gloomy entrance of great caves. 'Marholt, let us go back to the Forest. There is nothing for us here.'

But Sir Marholt wanted to ride on. He had a feeling, he told Sir Gawain, that they would find an adventure; and as Sir Gawain knew Sir Marholt's feelings were usually right, they rode on.

For three days and three nights more they rode deep into that barren land, all alone, Sir Gawain laughing and joking as he always did, his great red beard flying in the cold wind, and Sir Marholt, as big and broad-shouldered as Sir Gawain, riding along half-listening with a faraway look in his deep dreamy eyes. As they rode on, the stones and rocks became more and more gigantic throwing up strange shapes that cast shadows over the two riders.

'How much further, Marholt?' called Sir Gawain.

'Not much, my friend,' was all Sir Marholt would say, 'Not much.'

They camped that night in the shadow of a boulder that looked like a great stone monster towering over them.

'Far from the stones and out of the storm,'

hummed Sir Gawain as he snuggled up against the war-horse to sleep,

'Oh for a damsel to keep me warm!'

His war-horse, which was called Wing Mane, snorted.

'Never mind, Wing Mane,' said Sir Gawain, patting its neck and blowing up its nostrils, 'you're no damsel, but you're the next best thing, eh Marholt?'

But Sir Marholt was already fast asleep, dreaming.

Next morning the mists swirled around them, and even Sir Gawain was reduced to a grumpy silence. Wing Mane shied and started as every new shape loomed up out of the mists.

'Seeing dragons everywhere,' grumbled Sir Gawain, pelting the war-horse with the flat of his sword. Sir Marholt's horse was hardly any better. About midday both war-horses suddenly refused to go on. A great rock was looming out of the mist in front of them, barring their path. Sir Gawain signalled to Sir Marholt to try and go round it one way and he would try and go round it the other. So they both pelted their horses till their arms ached and at last drove them lumbering forwards. Sir Gawain rode to the left and Sir Marholt to the right. The rock seemed to curve round very smoothly; it was impossible to see how high it reached. At first the two horses neighed to each other; then as they drew further and further apart, they neighed just to keep their own spirits up. Once Sir Gawain thought he heard a tinkling laugh, but then he decided it must be just his imagination; or perhaps the clanking of Wing Mane's bit.

Half an hour later he was still riding round the rock and still had not met Sir Marholt. He rode on. He seemed to be riding round in a circle. A strange thing was that the walls of the rock were very smooth, like glass. At last one of Wing Mane's lonely neighs was answered by an echoing neigh nearby. Then through the mist Sir Marholt's war-horse came trotting up. But there was no sign of its rider.

'Marholt! Marholt!' he shouted. The mist blanketed his shouts, and there was no answer.

So Sir Gawain waited. What else could he do? There was no sign of blood or a struggle, and it is useless to ride around in a mist looking for someone. He waited with the two war-horses by the rock wall. Gradually the mist began to clear and rays of sunlight to peep through. From time to time he shouted 'Marholt!' and again he could have sworn that he heard tinkling laughter somewhere. As the mist cleared, Sir Gawain noticed the most extraordinary thing: the dark rock wall rose smooth, beautifully curved, without crags or gullies or jutting rocks, higher and higher.

'Marholt!' he called again, looking upwards, and this time he was sure he could hear an answering shout.

'Up here!'

But how could Sir Marholt have got up the rock? It seemed impossible to climb. Slowly Sir Gawain rode around the whole rock again. It took him nearly an hour; and on all sides it was smooth and impossible. He still could not see the top, for the rock was taller than ten trees. So he came back to where he had started, baffled.

Then he certainly did hear a tinkling laugh. He looked up.

'Gawain,' said a voice, a beautiful soft woman's voice that sounded almost as if it were in his ears. 'Gawain, do you want to come up?'

The war-horses laid back their ears and swished their tails angrily. Sir Gawain shuddered. He realized it must be sorcery and said nothing.

'Gawain,' said the beautiful voice again, 'up here there is food and drink, soft beds to sleep in, repose for weary knights. Gawain, do you want to come up?'

Still Sir Gawain said nothing.

'Gawain,' the voice sank softer and huskier. 'There are twelve of us up here, twelve beautiful damsels of the Rock. Sir Marholt is with us. Do you want him to enjoy all our company? Are you now the woman-hater, Gawain the Golden-Tongued?'

'But it is impossible to come up,' shouted Sir Gawain angrily, 'I have ridden all around your rock. There is no way up for an armoured knight. Even a fly would find it difficult!'

The voice chuckled. 'Leave that to us,' it said.

And a moment later the two startled war-horses shied backwards as Sir Gawain seemed to hurtle upwards through the air. Then they tossed their manes, and started grazing as all horses do as soon as they can, forgetting the marvels about them.

The high feast of Pentecost came round at Camelot; but neither Sir Gawain nor Sir Marholt rode in to take their seats at the Round Table and renew their oaths. King Arthur was dismayed, particularly at Sir Gawain's absence, for he loved Sir Gawain more than all his other nephews.

Sir Tor leapt to his feet, King Pellinore's son.

'Sire,' he cried, 'I will go on a quest for my lord Sir Gawain. It is my right. For he and I were both made knights by you on the same day, the day you married Queen Guinevere. You told us to be worthy knights all our lives and good companions to one another. Those were your very words.'

'So they were,' said King Arthur, pleased that Sir Tor remembered them so well, 'so they were. You shall have the quest, as is your right. Go now, and seek my dear nephew Sir Gawain. If he is dead, try and bring back his body and I will bury it here in splendour, or else send it to my sister Queen Morgawse of the Orkeneys for a sea-burial if she wishes. But I do not think my nephew will be dead. He is a knight who always seems to survive.

So Sir Tor rode out. He loved Sir Gawain, and only wished that Sir Gawain had chosen him as a sword-companion rather than Sir Marholt. He did not realize that Sir Gawain had taken an oath one day to kill Sir Tor's father, King Pellinore. And it was to King Pellinore that Sir Tor first rode, to ask him his advice, for he had no idea how to find Sir Gawain.

'Nor have I,' said King Pellinore, 'I have heard no news of him in the past year, though I have been up and down many lands, chasing the blasted Questing Beast. I tell you what, Tor, the one person who could probably help you is Merlin.'

'But Merlin never comes to Camelot,' said Sir Tor, dismayed, 'and nobody knows where to find him nowadays. Men say he has probably gone to that other country he loves as well as Logres, the land that is called Whina.'

'Not Whina, Tor,' said King Pellinore, 'you sons of mine are all so badly educated. It's called Thina.' He scratched his beard for a moment, deep in thought. 'At least I think it is. Something like that anyway. In any case the Questing Beast never goes there, so it's of no importance. The point is that I don't believe Merlin is there either. I was chasing the Questing Beast through the Forest of Broceliande last autumn and the rumour is that he's there.'

'But it's Pentecost now,' said Sir Tor dismayed. 'He'll probably have gone.'

King Pellinore shook his head.

'Some love affair with an elfin queen. She keeps him there. Can't understand it myself, you'd think a wizard would have more sense. I ask you, what chance would I ever have of catching the Questing Beast if I started having proper love affairs? Short and sweet, that's how it should be. Like with your mother. Ah, what a fine woman she was. Hope my greyhound's happy to be back with her. Best greyhound I ever had.'

'Best woman too,' said Sir Tor a little angrily. He thought his father should have married his mother properly.

'What?' said King Pellinore. 'Yes, yes, dear boy. Yes, of course. Well, I must be off, me on my quest, you on yours. Good luck, my son. See you next Pentecost at the high feast. Don't forget to let me know how you're getting on.'

Sir Tor rode through the enchanted Forest of Broceliande. The Ents in their age-old fashion passed word of his progress throughout the Forest and, for Merlin's sake, took him under their protection so that he met with no adventures. For the Ents were the real rulers of the Forest of Broceliande. They had been there before dwarf or elf, before troll or wizard, before beast or man; they were the Tree Lords and even orcs and dragons feared their rumbling green anger.

One day Sir Tor camped in the most marvellous open glade by a splendid fountain. It was beautiful warm weather. When he woke in the morning as the first rays of the sun were playing through the tree-tops, he could hardly believe his eyes. The glade was full of an enormous number of wild beasts, hundreds and hundreds of them, who had all come to drink at the fountain. There were white harts, wild red deer, even a unicorn; but there were also fiercer animals, herds of wildebeeste, troops of troll-like apes, wild brachets, wyverns, and the long-horned lyre cattle that could only be found in Broceliande. There they were all peaceful, all almost tame, grazing in the glade, and even round the feet of a knight in armour, totally unafraid. Sir Tor rubbed his eyes.

A giant shadow fell over him.

'Ah,' said a voice that Sir Tor recognized at once, 'King Pellinore's son.'

Sir Tor leapt to his feet and looked wildly around. But there was no one to be seen.

'No,' said Merlin's voice, 'I am afraid I am rather a shadowy figure these days. Even as a shadow I do not often manifest myself; Nimiane does not like it, you see. But I am the guardian of these beasts and when I heard that you were coming I decided to make a special effort. For after all you are in a way my special knight, are you not?'

'Of course I am, Merlin,' said Sir Tor. 'If you had not promised King Arthur I would be a knight of prowess, he would never have knighted me at his wedding feast. He will be overjoyed to hear that I have spoken to you.'

The shadow seemed to tremble.

'Say nothing to the King, or to anyone,' said Merlin anxiously. 'Nimiane would not like it. Indeed she will not allow me to stay long in any case. So, Tor, how can I help you?'

Sir Tor thought it very sad that Merlin should seem to be so frightened of this elf-queen.

'How can I help *you*, Merlin?' he said boldly.

'You cannot, Tor,' said Merlin. 'I am ensnared and ensorcelled by my own choice. Do not be sad for me. I quite enjoy it. After all, it is not every hoary old wizard who enjoys the favours of an elf-queen. No, Tor, I am afraid all your prowess will be of little help to me. A knight cannot fight against shadows. What can I do for you?'

'I am on a quest to rescue Sir Gawain.'

'Ah.'

'Do you know where he is, Merlin?'

'Not exactly. But I can foresee this, Tor: that it would be better for you if Sir Gawain were never found.'

'How can you say that, Merlin?' cried Sir Tor angrily. 'He and I swore to be good companions, and in any case the King loves him.'

'Well, well,' said Merlin. 'In any case, Tor, you will never find him. It is not your fate.'

'Is he alive?'

'Yes.'

'Then if I will not find him, tell me who will.'

'Very well,' said Merlin, 'if you insist. There is only one knight who will find him and rescue him, and that is his own brother Sir Gaheris. My sight is dimmed, but I think Sir Gaheris will find Sir Gawain and his companion at La Roche aux Pucelles.'

'What is La Roche aux Pucelles?'

'It is a very tall rock where I once imprisoned twelve dangerous sorceresses. I'm afraid it was a mistake. I thought that they would starve to death, you see, and that they must be dead by now. But Galadriel — or rather Nimiane as she is called in this Age — she tells me that they are still alive.'

'Where is La Roche aux Pucelles?'

'In the Land of Stones.'

With that the shadow over Sir Tor's head disappeared; and all the beasts in the glade looked around, startled, as if their protector had suddenly disappeared too. With a great stamping and bellowing and mooing they all galloped or ran away, leaving Sir Tor all alone.

Sir Tor took ship to the Orkeneys and found Sir Gaheris in the great gloomy castle of Rethenam. Sir Gaheris was delighted when Sir Tor told him that he and he alone could rescue Sir Gawain. But Sir Agravaine, who was Sir Gaheris' twin brother, was furious. Agravaine of the Hard Hand was a big rough knight just like Sir Gaheris, but men liked him less, and Sir Gawain had always favoured Sir Gaheris. Agravaine was jealous.

'I will ride with you on this quest,' he said to Sir Gaheris.

'I don't think you should, Agravaine,' said Sir Tor tactfully. 'You see, Merlin said even I should not go, though King Arthur gave the quest to me. He said that Gaheris alone would rescue Gawain. Madam,' said Sir Tor, turning to Queen Morgawse, 'you are the mother of Gawain and of these twins;

you are also the sister of King Arthur. What do you advise?'

Queen Morgawse was dark and usually very silent. But she liked the look of Sir Tor who was a fine handsome young knight and had better manners than Sir Gaheris and Sir Agravaine, her own twin sons.

'Gaheris,' she said, 'go.'

So Sir Gaheris armed, and took ship, and went. For his mother was a woman who never needed to speak twice to her sons. But Sir Agravaine was so jealous that he secretly followed Sir Gaheris and twice fought with him, once in the Forest and once on the edge of the Land of Stones. His plan was to unhorse Sir Gaheris, take the quest in his place, and so win Sir Gawain's love by rescuing him. But the first time Sir Gaheris unhorsed him instead, though he had no idea that the knight fighting him was his own twin brother. And the second time even though Sir Gaheris was tired and bloody from a fight with a band of trolls on the edge of the Land of Stones, he not only unhorsed Sir Agravaine, he left him stunned and with his thighbone broken.

'What would you do,' said Sir Agravaine's squire as he helped his master slowly back onto his horse, 'if you ever meet him again in battle and overcome him?'

'Though we are of the same blood,' groaned Sir Agravaine, 'nothing would stop me from cutting off his head, because I hate no man in the world so much as I do my twin brother Sir Gaheris.'

Perhaps Sir Agravaine did not quite mean what he said, and the pain of his broken leg made him exaggerate; but all the same he never forgave Sir Gaheris. They never fought again, though. Sir Gaheris never knew that he had twice overthrown his twin brother and never realized that Sir Agravaine always hated him.

Sir Gaheris rode deep into the Land of Stones for three days and three nights; and on the fourth day he came, as Sir Gawain and Sir Marholt had done, to the great rock called La Roche aux Pucelles. The difference was that he was not surprised to find it as Sir Gawain and Sir Marholt had been. He knew that he would find no way up to the top, so, unlike Sir Gawain, he made no attempt to climb or to find a way but waited till a soft beautiful voice called him. He could not have explained how he reached the top of the rock, either. One moment he was standing at the bottom, the next he was floating upwards as if he had been weightless.

When he reached the top, it was as if he were a leaf carried in by a gentle breeze. Green meadows ran round a little stream there, and on both sides of the stream were pitched gaily-coloured tents, fifteen in all. He could see for miles and miles, all across the Land of Stones, to the Forest on one side and the Sea on the other, both in the dim distance. But there was not a single living thing in sight.

He walked across to one of the tents and threw open the flap. There was a beautiful damsel there inside.

'Welcome, Gaheris,' she said, 'brother of Gawain. This is your tent. Here is food and drink, fresh garments and a soft bed.' Then she washed his face and combed his hair with a golden comb, and served him with peppered meat and honey wine.

'While you are here,' she said, 'you will forget time. There are twelve tents pitched nearby, one for myself, which is nearest, and one for each of my eleven sisters. Then there is this tent for you, a tent for your brother Gawain, and a tent for his companion Marholt.'

'Are they well?' said Gaheris.

'Of course they are well,' said the beautiful damsel. 'How could they not be well with six of us to look after each of them? But now there will only be four for each of them, for four of us will be looking after you.'

She took him by the hand to the three nearest tents and her own, so that Gaheris could see who would be looking after him, and how well. He had never seen such beautiful damsels or heard such wonderful soft voices in his life. He had to keep reminding himself that these were sorceresses, though of course he did not say that to them.

It was not till evening that Sir Gawain and Sir Marholt came out of their tents. They hardly seemed surprised to see Sir Gaheris at all. It was not till late at night that he managed to whisper secretly in their ears that he had come to rescue them.

'Rescue?' said Sir Gawain. 'Rescue did you say? But what do we want to be rescued for? We're having a marvellous time with six damsels each – well, four each, now you've come, Gaheris, not that we grudge you four – and of course we are free to go whenever we like.'

'Yes,' said Sir Marholt, 'of course we are.' He laughed. 'How could mere damsels stop a knight as mighty as Marholt?' added Sir Gawain.

'After all, we've only been here for a few days.'

That was when Sir Gaheris realized that they were both totally ensorcelled, for in fact they had been there a year and a half. But neither of them would believe him when he told them so; and he realized that they would never want to leave because they would always believe, even when they were old and grey, that they had only just arrived. Sir Gaheris realized that he would start thinking this too unless he acted swiftly.

That night he went to the tent of each of the four damsels who were looking after him. He asked each of them if he could leave when he wanted to. They each said yes. Then he told each of them that he loved only her.

'Will you come away with me?' he said. 'Now. Tonight.'

But each made some excuse; so Sir Gaheris realized that they could not leave the top of the rock but were kept there always by Merlin's spell.

The following night he invited all four to his tent.

'By the way,' he said casually, 'I came across Merlin the other day in the Forest of Broceliande.'

They all hissed a little, and their eyes gleamed like snakes. Then he was sure they were really sorceresses.

'Yes,' said Sir Gaheris mildly. 'He warned me about you, you know. He said that unless you release me and my brother and Sir Marholt, he would have to kill you.'

'Hah!' hissed the eldest and most beautiful of the twelve sorceresses, 'that weary wizard cannot kill us. He has trapped us here for ever with his spells and he thought we would die of hunger. But he did not realize that we had the power to bring food by thought. We just think of it, and even if it is a hundred miles away, it comes here in a few minutes. So we will never die. Nor will you, Sir Gaheris, nor Gawain nor Marholt. You will live with us here for ever, or at least till you die of old age. But by then we will have your sons, and in time your son's sons and in a hundred years your sons' sons' sons. And if there are too many for us then, why, we will throw them very gently over the cliff.'

Sir Gaheris thought desperately. He was quick-witted, fortunately, and quite ready to tell lies, which was why Merlin had chosen him for the quest.

'But Merlin knows all about this,' he laughed. 'He has just been playing with you. Also he never really meant to kill you, just to keep you where you can do no harm. But now unless you release us all at once, he will cast a spell that will stop your power to bring food by just thinking of it. Then what will you live on? Grass?'

The four damsels looked at one another, uncertainly.

'It is not true, sisters,' said the eldest. 'Merlin does not have that power.'

Sir Gaheris racked his brains. Then he remembered what Sir Tor had told him.

'Merlin may not,' he said. 'But do you know who Merlin's great love now is?'

'Who?' they asked.

'Nimiane, the second Lady of the Lake. She has these powers and she has promised she will use them.'

'Bah!' cried the eldest. 'We fear no water-nymph.'

'She is not a water-nymph,' said Gaheris. 'She is an elfin queen from Annwen, and her real name is Galadriel.'

Then the four sisters fell silent and went white with fear.

'From the cauldron of Annwen,' muttered the eldest, 'comes all the food and drink of the world. Galadriel is own sister to Guiomar Elf-King, sworn foe of all sorceresses of the Shadow.'

One after another they gathered up their garments and left Gaheris alone.

Next morning both Gawain and Marholt complained that they had suddenly been left alone too. The twelve beautiful damsels were nowhere to be seen. It was not till midday that they came out of their tents, and then each was in her most gorgeous clothes, satins, velvet, ermine, and gossamer. None of the knights had ever seen anything so beautiful. The peppered meats and spiced wines they served them with was such a feast as they had never had before. But instead of singing and being joyful they were weeping, weeping so bitterly that even Sir Gaheris had pity on them.

'Why are you weeping, damsels?' asked Sir Gawain.

'Because we must send you away, fair knights, and never see you again, for fear of Merlin. Ah, if only we had been able to kill that wizard in the Second Age! But instead he trapped us, and kept us here, and now he may starve us to death if we do not release you. Do not look so startled, Gawain. Do not look so shocked, Marholt. Yes, we are sorceresses. But for all that we have loved you with all our hearts and we will miss you.'

'Come with us then, beautiful ones,' cried Sir Gawain, 'for, damsel or sorceress, I never hope to meet anyone as bewitching as you ever again.'

But they only shook their heads sadly.

'Before we send you away,' they said, 'you may ask us a question. For we see the future, far more clearly even than Merlin. And it is forbidden for us to tell a lie, as he sometimes does, when we talk of this.'

Then Sir Marholt turned his far-away eyes to the ones he had loved dearest.

'There is only one question a true knight errant seeks to know,' he said. 'How shall we die? How shall the mighty Marholt die? Bravely in battle?'

'You, Sir Marholt,' they said, 'you will not die in battle but you will die of a mortal wound given you by the biggest knight alive. It will be a glorious death and by the manner of your dying you will cause, in the end, the death of the one who slays you.'

'And I?' asked Sir Gawain.

'You, Sir Gawain,' they said, 'you will die in the greatest battle of all, as befits one of the three Knights of Battle of the realm of Logres. It will be a sad death because if you had lived you would have saved the whole realm. It will be a shameful death because of the hand that strikes the blow. But your noble uncle, King Arthur, will avenge you.'

'And I?' asked Sir Gaheris.

'Do not ask,' they implored him.

'Tell me,' he insisted.

'You, Sir Gaheris, you will die in the same week as your twin brother, Sir Agravaine. You will die at the hand of the knight you have sworn to serve and who loves you best in the world. You will die without defending yourself against him.'

Then Sir Gaheris fell very silent.

'Tell us at least,' he said at last, 'which of us three will die first, since die we all must, and none of us peacefully in our beds.'

'Sir Marholt shall die first,' they said. 'Then you, Sir Gaheris, and last of all you, Sir Gawain. If you had stayed here with us, you would have died of old age, peacefully. Now go, fair knights, to your adventures and your doom. Farewell.'

So the three knights found themselves returning to the foot of the rock in the same manner as they had gone up. There they found their war-horses, who were more than pleased to see their masters. But they rode away sorrowfully, back to Camelot, each wrapped in his own thoughts, each thinking of the doom to come.

HERE ENDS AN ADVENTURE OF SIR GAWAIN,
AND HIS BROTHER SIR GAHERIS; ALSO OF
SIR MARHOLT AND SIR TOR

CHAPTER 4

The Adventure of
the Silken Tent

I T happened that Sir Lancelot had been riding through the Forest all day – a hard ride as he could find no proper path. Night was falling, and he was very weary. He saw a tent of red silk in the middle of the Forest.

'By my knighthood,' said Sir Lancelot, 'that is where I will rest tonight.'

So he dismounted, tied his horse to a nearby tree and disarmed. Inside the tent he found a beautiful feather bed with silk sheets and pillows of soft down. So he lay down and fell sound asleep.

It was very dark that night with little moon. The knight whose tent it was, Sir Belleus, rode up, dismounted and disarmed. He could see a shape in the bed, but he thought it was his lady love, so he lay down by Sir Lancelot, took him in his arms, and began to kiss him.

When Sir Lancelot felt a rough beard kissing him, he woke up at once, leapt out of bed, and dashed from the tent. Sir Belleus thought his lady love was only being playful, so he leapt up too and chased after. But when he came out of the tent, he saw in the moonlight not a fair damsel but a big grim man with a naked sword in his hand, who gave a great roar and smote him.

'Aieee!' cried Sir Belleus, falling to the ground. 'Foul fiend, you have slain me in my own tent.'

Sir Lancelot put up his sword. He was ashamed. He saw that he had wounded an unarmed knight in his night-shirt.

'Sorry,' he said. 'But I was adread of treason, for not long ago I was ensorcelled while I was asleep. Come back into your tent, and I suppose I will staunch your blood.'

Then came the knight's lady love, a fair damsel. When she saw her lord Sir Belleus bleeding badly, she wept and screamed at Sir Lancelot, though he was trying to bind up the wound.

'Peace, my lady and my love,' said Sir Belleus, 'for this knight is a good man and a knight of adventures, but I kissed him by mischance thinking it was you, and he did not like the prickling of my beard.'

'For all the prickles in the world it was unknightly of him to wound you almost to death,' sobbed the lady. 'If I had come first instead of you, and laid down beside him, and kissed him, he would never have wounded me.'

'I suppose not,' said Sir Lancelot, 'for you are a lady of great beauty, much more beautiful than any lady save only Queen Guinevere.'

Then the lady was so pleased at his courtesy that she quickly dried her tears.

'Now I know by your speech who you must be,' she said. 'Only Sir Lancelot du Lac, the most courteous knight alive to all damsels and ladies, could speak in that fashion. But for all your courtesy you have done great harm to me and my lord Sir Belleus.

'Very sorry,' said Sir Lancelot again.

'Well,' said the lady, 'for this harm when you come to King Arthur will you cause Sir Belleus to be made a Knight of the Round Table? For he is a good man of arms, and a mighty lord of lands in the Out Isles.'

Sir Lancelot promised, and so it was done. When Queen Guinevere asked him why he had pressed the King so hard to make Sir Belleus a Knight of the Round Table, 'Lady,' he told her, 'because he is the only knight who has ever kissed me as heartily as you.'

At this Queen Guinevere did not know whether to laugh, or to scold Sir Lancelot.

HERE ENDS A TALE OF SIR LANCELOT

CHAPTER 5

The Adventure of
the Fountain

King Arthur sat at Camelot, yawning. He sat upon a
seat of green rushes, over which was spread a canopy
of flame-coloured satin, and a cushion of red satin
was under his elbow.

'If you do not mind,' said King Arthur to his
household knights, 'I would like to have a sleep
before dinner. I am feeling tired. You can entertain
each other by telling stories. Ask Kay for a flagon of
wine, and some meat.'

So King Arthur fell asleep. Sir Kay went down to
the cellar and returned with a flagon of honey wine,
golden goblets, and a handful of iron skewers with
bits of meat skewered on them. They ate the meat
and began to drink the honey wine together.

'Now,' said Sir Kay, 'I have done my part. It is time for you to tell me my story.'

Sir Yvain turned to Sir Conan who was called one of the three Ardent Lovers of the realm of Logres. He loved Sir Yvain's sister, the bewitching Morvyth.

'Conan,' said Sir Yvain, 'tell Kay the story he wants.'

'Well,' said Sir Conan, 'you are older than I and a far better story-teller, and you have seen more marvellous things than I have. You should tell Kay the story we owe him.'

'I have heard all Yvain's stories,' said Sir Kay rudely. 'So tell me your story, Conan. And make sure it is true. Because with Yvain's stories you can never be sure that they are not just his imagination. He tries to ensorcel even the King with them. In that he takes after his mother, that sorceress Morgan le Fay.'

Queen Guinevere had been sitting with her damsels sewing by the window. Now she lifted her head.

'Kay,' she said, 'you have the wickedest tongue in the world. It is amazing my husband has not cut it out.' She smiled at Yvain. 'Yvain, no one can blame you for your mother's evil-doing. You are my favourite knight — you and Sir Gawain.'

What about Sir Lancelot? thought Sir Kay. But he did not say anything more, for fear that the Queen might indeed suggest something drastic to Arthur.

'Conan,' she went on sweetly, 'I would love to hear your story, though. And so would one of my damsels.' She smiled at the beautiful Morvyth, who was playing the harp beside her.

So Sir Conan told his story. It was all about a marvellous quest where in the end he had jousted with a Black Knight on a coal-black horse, and lost. The Black Knight had ridden off with Sir Conan's war-horse, leaving Sir Conan to walk all the way back to Camelot.

'Now you must admit, Kay,' said Sir Conan as he finished his tale, 'no man ever before told a tale so much to his own discredit.' He glanced with a smile at the beautiful Morvyth.

'It would certainly be a noble quest,' said Sir Yvain, 'for another Knight of the Round Table to succeed where you failed.'

'By the bones of my father,' sneered Sir Kay, 'you are always telling things you might do, Yvain. But you never seem to do them.'

Queen Guinevere frowned. Fortunately at that moment King Arthur woke up, else there might have been a serious quarrel.

'Did I doze off?' he said, rubbing his eyes.

'Yes, Lord,' answered Sir Yvain. 'You were asleep for a little while.'

'Well, well,' said King Arthur. 'I must be growing old. Is it time for us to go to dinner?'

'It is, Lord,' said Sir Yvain.

Then the horn for washing was sounded, and the King and all his household went to wash, and then sat down to eat. But when the meal was over, Sir Yvain made ready his horse and his armour. For he had been bitten by Sir Kay's taunts, and was determined to go on the quest where Sir Conan had failed.

Next day at dawn Yvain put on his famous golden armour, with the green plumes and the green shield, mounted his war-horse and rode out alone. He travelled through many lands till he came to the Forest of Broceliande and to a great glade with a mound in the centre, which Sir Conan had described in his tale. All over the glade wild animals of every sort were grazing – white harts and red deer, wildebeeste and lyre cattle, and many many more, hundreds and hundreds of them – and even one white unicorn. Sir Yvain was amazed. But he was even more amazed at the being sitting on the mound in the centre. He was black and hairy, at least eighteen feet tall, so ugly that any man would tremble at the sight, with thick lips always gaping open, a hump behind his spine, bristly black hair that hung over his eyes, and a head as large as a buffalo's. His hands were the wrong way round – the palms were where the backs should be and the backs were where the palms should be – and, most hideous of all, his ears hung down to his waist, as wide as a winnowing fan.

'Who are you?' said Sir Yvain nervously.

The being raised a great club in his hand and struck a stag a great blow so that it brayed loudly. Then all the animals in the glade came together towards the mound, pushing Sir Yvain and his war-horse along with them. There must have been a thousand or more, crowding in. Then all the thousand bowed their heads and knelt on their forefeet, and Sir Yvain's war-horse did the same, much to his surprise.

'I am the Giant Herdsman,' said the being, and his voice sounded like ten trumpets. 'I watch over the beasts of wood and forest. I live on herbs and fruits and berries and dwell in the arms of the Ents.' Then his voice changed, and sounded more like ten soft lutes.

'Bow your head too, Knight of the Round Table,' he said, 'for I am much more than that.'

Sir Yvain found that almost against his will his head was bowing.

'Now rise and graze, beasts of Broceliande,' boomed the Giant Herdsman. 'As for you, Sir Knight, follow me.'

The Giant Herdsman stepped down from the mound, and mounted the stag who had brayed. Then to Sir Yvain's amazement he seemed to shrink in size till he was little and bent, more like a dwarf than a giant, as old as the ages of mankind. Sir Yvain followed him out of the glade, and the animals made way for them both, bowing as they passed.

'You too, Sir Yvain,' grunted the Dwarf Herdsman, 'will have a special power over beasts and animals.'

Sir Yvain was amazed that the Herdsman knew his name. But he did not dare ask him any questions.

'Here I leave you,' said the Herdsman at a green cross-roads. 'Follow that path there till you come to the Fountain of Barenton where nectar flows. By the side of the fountain is a marble slab and on the slab of marble is a silver bowl. Take the bowl and throw a bowlful of water on the slab.' The Herdsman gave a short laugh.

'Then you will have as much adventure as you can stomach, my gold-green knight. And if ever you come alive out of that adventure, salute your uncle King Arthur – and tell him an old friend salutes him but cannot come to him. Yes, and salute your mother Queen Morgan le Fay too when you see her.' He noticed that Yvain looked baffled.

'Yes,' he said, 'you will see her again. In her way an entrancing woman.'

The Dwarf Herdsman seemed to grow tall and menacing, like a giant shadow.

'But not so entrancing as she who now keeps me entranced!' he muttered as he turned away.

The Forest grew dark behind him; and Sir Yvain rode on his way, wondering who was this being that seemed to know so much and could change his shape so rapidly.

Sir Yvain rode on till he found the Fountain of Barenton. He took the silver bowl and threw a bowlful of water onto the marble slab.

No sooner did the water splash on the marble than the heavens seemed to tremble with fury, mighty peals of thunder shook the sky, and hailstones showered down so fast, so cold, and so heavy that Sir Yvain only saved his life by putting his shield up over his own head and his horse's. He wondered what trap the Herdsman had led him into. But then, as suddenly as they had started, the hailstones stopped. The sky cleared from black to blue, the sun shone, and a flight of beautifully coloured cockatoos settled on the trees. They sang so sweetly that never before or after did Sir Yvain hear so sweet a song. He listened so entranced that he did not notice that the Black Knight was there. It was only when the drumming of galloping hoofs came that he looked round and saw a coal-black war-horse thundering down upon him; and a lance with a pennant of jet black velvet upon it aiming straight at his heart.

Sir Yvain only just escaped death then. If he had been lazy and slow, that lance would have caught him. But fortunately he was thin and agile, so he swerved aside and it just missed. The Black Knight went crashing by down the valley. By the time he had reined up and turned around, Sir Yvain had feutred his spear.

Sir Yvain was a Knight of Battle, a better fighter than Sir Conan had ever been. In the end after a fierce fight he struck the Black Knight a blow through his helmet and head-piece and visor, through the skin, the flesh, and the bone till it pierced the brain itself. The Black Knight felt he had received his death blow. He groaned, turned his coal-black war-horse's head, and fled.

Sir Yvain chased him. Ahead of them appeared a vast shining castle. The Black Knight galloped across the draw-bridge through the castle gate. Sir Yvain galloped after him – and then the worst thing that had happened to him that day happened. Just as he was galloping over the drawbridge, the portcullis fell with a mighty crash. Its iron spikes missed Sir Yvain, just. That was lucky for him, else he would certainly have been crushed and spiked to death. But they hit his war-horse just behind the saddle and cut the horse in two. At the same moment the inner gate was closed. So there was Sir Yvain trapped on the drawbridge between the two gates, with his war-horse split in two and dying, and he himself slipping about in its blood and trying not to fall into the castle moat. If he had fallen, he would certainly have drowned. For knights in armour could not swim; they sank like stones.

'Quick,' said a voice. He looked up and he saw the Lady Luned, who was a legendary damsel errant, stretching her hand out towards him through the inner gate.

'Take this Ring,' she said, 'and put it on your finger with the stone turned inwards. Now close your hand, with the stone inside your palm. As long as you conceal it, it will conceal you. When the townspeople come to put you to death, they will have to open the inner gate. I will wait for you by the horse-block over there. You will be able to see me, though I will not be able to see you. Twist the ring then, come through and put your hand on my shoulders, so as I will know you are there. Then follow me.'

Sir Yvain did exactly as the Lady Luned told him. The people of the castle came, but could not understand what had happened to him: one moment he was there, waiting to be killed, and the next he had disappeared, and all that remained were the head and forelegs and saddle of his warhorse inside the portcullis, and the hindquarters and tail outside.

Yvain, invisible, followed the Lady Luned to a rich chamber where she gave him water to wash in, and food and drink – never had he tasted food better cooked – and a couch to sleep on that was of scarlet and fur, satin and sendal, fit for King Arthur himself.

'Why are you doing this for me, Lady?' he asked.

'Every woman ought to help you, gold-green knight,' smiled Lady Luned, 'for I never saw knight more fitted for the service of ladies than you. But give me the Ring, for now that you are clean and clothed I want you never to be invisible again, beautiful knight. I want to feast my eyes on you.'

Sir Yvain was a little alarmed, for he thought the Lady might want to marry him, and she was not very beautiful. But what could he do? She had saved his life. He gave her the Ring.

'Do you know what this is?' said the Lady Luned. 'It is a Ring of Power, one of the nine Rings of Middle Earth, forged by the dwarfs of Avalon for the elfin lords.'

'How did you obtain it, Lady?' asked Yvain. He feared, wrongly, that she might be a sorceress.

'From the hands of the Giant Herdsman,' said Lady Luned. 'He warned me that you were coming to the Fountain from which nectar flows.'

Then Sir Yvain wondered more than ever who this Giant

Herdsman might be who seemed to have Rings of Power and knew the elfin lords.

In the middle of the night they heard a great cry.

'What is that outcry?' asked Sir Yvain, waking.

'The Black Knight, the Lord of the Castle, is dead,' said the Lady Luned. 'Now if they find you, his people will tear you limb from limb in revenge.'

At this Sir Yvain was very gloomy. At dawn the streets below were filled with wailing and clamour, trumpets and sad songs. The people of the castle were taking the body of the Black Knight for burial.

Over the coffin was a veil of white linen; on it wax candles were burning; six sad knights were carrying it on their shoulders. Behind the coffin walked a lady with yellow hair falling over her shoulders. She was beating her hands together in sorrow. No sooner had Sir Yvain cast eyes on this lady than he started trembling with love for her. He asked his companion who she was.

'My mistress,' replied Lady Luned. 'She is called the Lady of the Fountain.'

'Truly,' said Sir Yvain, 'she is the woman that I love best in the whole world.'

Lady Luned looked with pity at him.

'Do you not know who her husband is?'

Yvain shook his head.

'Her husband is – was – the Black Knight,' she said, 'the knight you killed yesterday.'

Lady Luned went up to the castle, to the chamber of her mistress. The Lady of the Fountain was so stricken with grief that she just lay on her couch, sobbing.

'Luned,' she sobbed, 'why did you not come to comfort me last night when my dear husband lay dying? Why did you not come? It was wrong of you. It was wrong of you.'

'Lady,' said Luned, 'I thought you had more sense than to

lie here sobbing. Sob as much as you like, but you will not bring back what is lost. Tears are wasted on that dead knight or on anything else you cannot have.'

'In the whole world,' sobbed the Lady, 'there is not a man as good as he was.'

'That is a stupid thing to say,' said Luned. 'For now any man who is alive is more use than a man who is dead, even an ugly one, even a brute.'

The Lady of the Fountain stopped sobbing, and sat up.

'I swear to Heaven,' she cried angrily, 'that if you were not my cousin I would have your tongue torn out for insulting my dead husband. As it is, go! I never want to see you again!'

'Very well,' said the Lady Luned haughtily. 'Banish me if you like. May Satan curse me if I seek to make it up! I did have something important to tell you. But never mind. It would have helped you. But never mind.'

With that Luned, her head held high, swept away to the door. But with her hand on the door she paused. As she had expected, the Lady began sobbing and crying to attract her attention.

'You have a wicked character, Luned,' said the Lady. 'All the same if you know something important that will help me, tell me.'

So Luned came back into her mistress' chamber.

'Very well,' she said. 'Now listen carefully, Lady. You cannot keep this castle and these lands unless you find someone to defend the Magic Fountain of Nectar from which all its riches flow. No one is brave enough now to defend the Fountain except one of those peerless knights they call the Knights of the Round Table. So here is what I will do for you. I will go to Camelot and return with a knight to guard the Fountain even better than your dead husband the Black Knight has done.'

'That will be a hard task,' said the Lady. 'But if anyone can do it, Luned, you can. For you love adventures, just as if you were a man and a knight errant.'

'That is why they call me the Damsel Errant,' said Luned proudly.

So the Lady Luned set out, on pretence of going to King Arthur's court. But in fact she went back to the chamber where she had left Sir Yvain, and hid there with him for as many weeks as it would have taken her to ride to Camelot and back. At the end of that time she dressed and went up to the Castle.

'What news?' said the Lady of the Fountain.

'The best of news,' replied Luned. 'I have done what I promised and enchieved our quest. When would you like to see the knight I have brought back with me?'

'Bring him here to visit me tomorrow at midday,' said the Lady.

So Luned went back to her chamber.

'My bold knight,' she told Yvain, 'I have done your wooing for you. Tomorrow thanks to me you will have your Lady. Tonight let us make you beautiful enough for her.'

She warmed water on a fire, brought out a towel of white linen, and placed it around Sir Yvain's neck. Then she poured the warm water into a silver basin, and washed his head. Next she took a razor. Its haft was of ivory, and its two blades were of silver. She shaved his beard carefully, then dried his head, and combed and brushed his golden hair. Next morning she dressed him in a cloak of green satin, with a broad band of gold lace. Sir Yvain then pulled two pieces of white linen over his hands.

'What are those?' asked the Lady Luned.

'They are a garment I have invented,' said Sir Yvain. 'I call them doves, because they are like a pair of white birds cooing.'

'They are very elegant,' said the Lady Luned, 'and a marvellous invention. I will make some myself. But you cannot call them doves. It is too sentimental. Call them – I don't know – goves.'

'Not goves,' said Sir Yvain. 'It's an ugly word. Perhaps loves?'

'That is even sillier than doves,' said the Lady Luned decisively.

'I know, gloves.'

And gloves they have been called ever since.

Together they went up to the castle at midday. The Lady of the Fountain was very glad to see them. But she looked long and steadily at Sir Yvain before she said a word.

'Luned,' she said, 'this knight does not have the look of a traveller.'

Luned's heart thumped. She wished she had not made Sir Yvain quite so elegant. But she knew there was no point in trying to lie to her cousin.

'What harm is there in that, Lady, as long as he is a fine bold knight?'

'The harm is,' said the Lady, 'that I am certain this was the knight, and none other, who disappeared after he had chased the soul from the body of my dead lord.'

But Luned looked her mistress boldly in the eyes.

'So much the better for you, Lady,' she cried. 'For he must be stronger than your dead lord, else he would not have been able to kill him. So he will be a better guardian of the Fountain. And he loves you, Lady. Look how beautiful you are together; like golden twins, like a pair of turtle doves.'

'Luned,' said the Lady of the Fountain, 'you are a wicked, traitorous, deceitful damsel. But it is impossible to argue with you. Very well, I will marry this knight you have saved.'

'It will be very, very well, Lady' said Luned.

So, with joyous hearts, Sir Yvain and the Lady of the Fountain were married. All her lords and knights did him homage, and for three years Sir Yvain defended the riches of the Fountain with sword and lance. No one in the whole world was more beloved by his subjects or by his wife than Sir Yvain.

HERE ENDS AN ADVENTURE OF SIR YVAIN

CHAPTER **6**

The Adventure of
the Broken Sword

ING Anguish of Ireland gnawed his beard in rage. He
sent for Sir Marholt that bold knight, sword-
companion to Sir Gawain and Knight of the Round
Table. Sir Marholt's sister was the Queen of Ireland,
his own wife.

'Fair brother, Sir Marholt,' he said, 'here are
messengers come from Cornwall. King Mark refuses
to pay our truage that by right we ought to have for
seven years past unless we send a champion to fight
his champion.'

'Sire,' said Sir Marholt, 'if you want me to be
your champion, I will. I suppose King Mark of
Cornwall will choose a Knight of the Round Table
for his champion, for the Cornish Knights are but

feeble knights. But I the mighty Sir Marholt will gladly fight even the best Knight of the Round Table, for I know all their tricks of fighting.'

Sir Marholt sailed out of Ireland with six ships, and cast anchor under the castle that is called Tintagel. For six days he lay at anchor, dreaming of damsels, and each day a messenger came down to the ships to say that King Mark had not yet found a champion to do battle with him.

'I will not stay longer,' threatened Sir Marholt, 'but the truage of seven years must be paid or else the castle of Tintagel will be burnt and sacked. And in any case for the honour of King Anguish and of Ireland, I will now only fight with a king's son or a king's brother.'

On the seventh day Sir Marholt was riding up and down a little island set in the sea under the shadow of his six ships when a barque sailed up. From the barque a young man stepped out leading a war-horse. He was very big, the biggest young man Sir Marhold had ever seen.

'Sir Knight,' called Sir Marholt, 'are you come to challenge me for the honour of Cornwall?'

The young man said that was so.

'Then tell me your name and your lineage, for I will not fight with any but a king's brother or a king's son.'

'As to that,' said the young man, 'you need have no worries. My name is Tristram of Lyonesse, son of the King of Lyonesse. My mother is called Queen Elizabeth, and she is King Mark's sister. King Mark of his great goodness yesterday gave me the order of knighthood, so that I might do battle with you. For before yesterday I was a harper, not a warrior.'

Then Sir Tristram armed and mounted, and turned to his squire.

'Take the barque,' he said, 'and commend me to my uncle King Mark. If I am killed, let him bury me as seems fit. But if I yield or flee, bid him throw my body to the fishes, shamefully. And for your life,' said Sir Tristram, 'do not come back to this island until either I have won the battle or I am overcome and slain.'

Then his squire and the boatmen went down to the barque, weeping. Even Sir Marholt felt sorry for this new-made knight, who had fought no battles ever before.

'Sweet singer, fair Sir Tristram,' he said courteously, 'what are you doing here? Your courage will not help you. For the best knights of the land have been overthrown by the mighty Sir Marholt, and for my noble deeds King Arthur made me a Knight of the Round Table. Indeed I have matched the best knights in the whole world. Go to the barque, I advise you. Go back to your harp-playing before it is too late.'

'Ah, fair knight, noble Sir Marholt,' said Sir Tristram, 'you know I cannot give up this challenge. It was to fight you that I was made a knight; and to deliver the country of Cornwall from the old truage. And know, Sir Marholt, that what gives me the greatest courage of all is that all men say you are one of the most renowned knights of the world, so it will be much to my honour to fight with you. And I hope you will find that I am not just a sweet harper but a true king's son who may yet play a merry tune on your armour.'

Sir Marholt listened quietly, almost dreamily, marvelling at the size of the young knight Sir Tristram. He was the biggest man he had ever seen, bigger by far than Sir Lancelot. But this did not frighten Sir Marholt. He knew that big knights were often slow; and the bigger they were, the clumsier they were likely to be, and the greater the target for his own lance. When Sir Tristram had finished, Sir Marholt spoke again.

'Fair young knight,' he said proudly, 'since you wish to win worship for fighting me, know this. No worship will you lose if you stand against me for three strokes. For many knights have fallen at my first stroke, and most at my second.'

Then they feutred their spears, and came so fiercely together that all crashed down, horses and knights alike. But Sir Marholt had driven the point of his lance into Sir Tristram's side, and the blood was gushing out.

For all that Sir Tristram rose to his feet and pulled out his sword, and the two knights hurtled together like rams, striking and thrusting. Sir Marholt gave Sir Tristram a great buffet that clove his shield. Then he gave Sir Tristram another great buffet that cut through his shoulder armour and his left shoulder, so that blood flowed from shoulder above and side below. But Sir Tristram fought even more fiercely and redoubled his strokes. He was so big and so well-winded. At that Sir Marholt summoned all his strength and cunning, and caught Sir Tristram a great blow sideways athwart his helm that would have felled a fresh knight and sent him grovelling to his knees. But Sir Tristram just shook his head, like one dazed, and roared with pain and anger.

Then Sir Marholt knew that he had met his match, and the young knight was mightier than he had ever been. He felt his heart fail, and his arm begin to feeble. His eyes began to swim, and Sir Tristram loomed bigger and bigger in front of them as he swayed forward, lashing at Sir Marholt again and again with his flashing sword. At the last Sir Marholt felt a horrible stroke on his helm; he felt Sir Tristram's blade pierce his steel cap, cut painfully through his skull and stick agonizingly in his brain. Then, as he sank down on his knees, he remembered dreamily the twelve damsels of La Roche aux Pucelles. What had they told him? Was it that he would meet his death at the hands of the biggest knight in the world? A great icy fear came over him.

Sir Tristram pulled at his sword but it was stuck in Sir Marholt's brain and would not come out. He pulled again, and he pulled again, and at last it came out. But the edge of the sword had broken off and was lodged in Sir Marholt's brain. Then suddenly Sir Marholt rose to his feet, grovelling and shrieking, threw away his sword and shield, and ran away crouching.

Sir Tristram was astounded.

'Sir Knight of the Round Table,' he called, 'for shame! Are you fleeing from the harper? From a young knight in his first battle? I would rather be hewn to bits piecemeal myself than run away in battle!'

Sir Marholt answered not a word, but, groaning and staggering, slumped to his ship. They carried him up, and sailed him back to Ireland. When his head was searched, they found a piece of Sir Tristram's sword embedded in it but no leechcraft could remove it.

So the mighty Sir Marholt died, the first great Knight of the Round Table to lose his life. But his sister the Queen of Ireland took that piece of the sword from his skull when he was dead, and kept it with her forever. She had loved Sir Marholt her dear brother, very dearly, as all ladies had done, and she thought that one day she would be revenged if she ever found the knight who had ended his dreams and put out the light of his eyes.

HERE ENDS THE LAST ADVENTURE OF
SIR MARHOLT; AND THE FIRST ADVENTURE OF
SIR TRISTRAM

CHAPTER 7

The Adventure of the Apple Tree

S IR Lancelot summoned his cousin Sir Bors de
Gaunes to ride out with him. 'We must seek adventures,' he said, and Sir Bors was his sword companion. So they armed, mounted their horses, rode
through the deep Forest, and so into a golden
plain.

It was midday, the weather was hot, the flies
buzzed, and the bees bumbled. Then Sir Bors saw an
apple tree by a hedge.

'Fair cousin,' he said, 'here is shade. We can rest
ourselves and our horses.' ·

'That is a good idea,' said Sir Lancelot, 'for, do
you know, I have never felt so sleepy as I do now, not
for seven years.'

So they dismounted, tied up their horses, and Sir Lancelot lay down under the apple tree, with his helmet under his head. He fell fast asleep while Sir Bors kept guard. While he kept guard, he saw three knights come riding by at a great wallop, and one knight followed after, chasing them, all three. When Sir Bors saw him, he thought he had never seen so well-armed and well-riding a knight. He had a mind to challenge him. So he took his horse quietly so as not to wake Sir Lancelot, mounted and rode away after the three knights and the well-armed knight, chasing them. So Sir Bors rode far away on his own quest.

Four queens came riding by on four white mules; four knights rode beside them, carrying a canopy of green silk on four spears stretched over the heads of the queens to shade them from the heat. As they rode by, they heard a war-horse grimly neigh. So they turned aside, and looked and saw a knight sleeping under an apple tree, all in armour except for his face that was uncovered.

'That is the most handsome knight I have ever seen,' said one of the queens, 'as big and as strong as my own husband was when he was young.' She was the Queen of the Outer Isles, and her husband was King Pellinore.

'He is far too handsome for you,' said another queen. She was the Queen of Estland, and very merry. 'I think he would rather prefer me.'

'I am sure,' said the third queen, the Queen of North Galys, 'that I would be his choice. Certainly he would be mine, for such a fine knight as this one I have never seen. And I am a fine woman, who has seen many fine knights.'

The fourth queen smiled. Her green eyes glittered.

'It is too hot to argue,' she said. 'We are all beautiful in our own way. So let this knight choose between us. I will put an enchantment on him, so that he will not wake up for seven hours. We will take him to my castle and put him safely in the dungeon. Then I shall take the enchantment off him, and let him say for himself which one of us he loves best.'

The three other queens did not argue. For they were a little afraid of the fourth queen. They knew she was a sorceress, and they knew, in their heart of hearts, that she was the most beautiful of them all. So the enchantment was cast, Sir Lancelot was lifted onto his shield, and carried by two knights on horseback to Castle Chariot. They put him in a cheerless dungeon and at night they sent a damsel up with his supper. By then the enchantment was past.

'What cheer?' said the damsel.

'I cannot say, fair damsel,' said Sir Lancelot, 'for I do not know where I am, or how I came here or why, unless I am still asleep and dreaming.'

'Sir,' she said, 'you must make good cheer. For you came here by enchantment.'

But Sir Lancelot made very bad cheer all that night, and slept very little. So in the morning he was cold and in a bad temper.

The first queen to visit him was the Queen of the Outer Isles.

'Fair knight,' she said, 'how do you find me?'

'Fair Queen,' he said, 'too old.'

'You are a most discourteous knight,' she said, 'and if I had my way I would throw you to the Questing Beast for its supper!'

Then Sir Lancelot guessed that she was the wife of King Pellinore. He told the Queen of Estland that she was too thin; and the Queen of North Galys that she was too bad. But when the fourth queen came in, Sir Lancelot could find no word to say against her, she was so bewitching.

'You do not find me too fat?' she smiled.

Sir Lancelot shook his head.

'Too thin perhaps?'

Sir Lancelot shook his head again.

'Too evil?'

Sir Lancelot shook his head more vehemently.

'Too beautiful?'

At this Sir Lancelot nodded even more vehemently than ever.

'Well, Sir Knight,' said the Lady, still smiling. 'Do you know what I find you? Too tongue-tied. But you must loosen your tongue, Sir Knight, you must say aloud which of us four queens you choose.'

Sir Lancelot looked puzzled.

'You must choose one of us, you see' – and here her smile seemed suddenly to grow cruel – 'or else you will die here in this castle.'

At this Sir Lancelot found his tongue at once.

'Lady,' he said, 'this is a hard saying. Yet know that of the four queens here you are by far the most beautiful, and I would willingly choose you and be your knight, if I was not vowed to another queen. But as it is, I would rather die with worship if I must.'

'Who is this other queen?'

'It is Queen Guinevere, the truest lady to her lord living, and the only lady who shall ever have my love.'

'Guinevere! Guinevere!' cried the fourth queen angrily. 'That silly empty-headed Guinevere. Guinevere who is always in my way! Guinevere who turned Arthur against me! Guinevere who enchanted my own son! Well, Guinevere, you will lose your lover and, knight, you shall lose your head!'

She stormed out, and slammed the dungeon door. When the damsel came with his food, Sir Lancelot asked her who this queen was.

'Why?' said the damsel. 'Do you not know? It is Queen Morgan le Fay, queen in this world and queen in the other world, the sister of King Arthur, the Lady of Avalon, the Lady of Gore, the mother of Sir Yvain. But since King Arthur and then Sir Yvain quarrelled with her, she has lived here, in her great secret castle. It is called Castle Chariot.'

'Ah,' said Sir Lancelot, 'I have heard of her.'

He remembered the story of how Queen Morgan le Fay had sent Queen Guinevere a cloak to burn her to ashes, and he was very afraid. He remembered too that he had heard that King Arthur had chased her, but she escaped him by turning herself and her horse into stone. If she could turn herself into stone, perhaps she would turn him into stone too? Or would she simply burn him to ashes? But that afternoon when Queen Morgan le Fay came back to see him, she seemed to be in a better temper.

'Well, Sir Knight,' she said, 'at least I am not like the other queens. They are all three begging me for your head on a platter, they say they have never been so insulted in their whole lives. But what do I care for their whinings? I think I will keep you alive here, all for myself, as a reward for saying that I was so beautiful. I will give you a chamber, Sir Knight, and there you can live till you come to love me. For you are very, very handsome. Castle Chariot is enchanted by the way, and if you try to escape, you will blow up.'

Sir Lancelot turned pale. He had no idea what 'blowing up' meant, but it sounded horrible.

'So do not try to escape. What is your name, Sir Knight?'

'Lancelot du Lac.'

'A pretty name, Sir Lancelot. That little blue-eyed hussy Guinevere is lucky indeed.'

So Queen Morgan le Fay gave Sir Lancelot a large chamber to live in and a small chamber to sleep in; and left him there for three months. When she came back she found he had painted all the walls of the great chamber with all his knightly adventures.

'Very fine, my pretty knight,' she said, 'very fine.'

But then though Sir Lancelot tried to stop her, she went into the small chamber where he slept. There were more paintings there, great golden apples all over the walls, and at first she thought they were fine too. But when she looked more closely, she saw that inside each of the apples was painted a scene of love between Lancelot and Guinevere.

'By the bones of Behemoth,' cursed Queen Morgan le Fay, 'Enough is enough! Go back to my besotted brother and my simpleton of a son! Each of you is as bad as the other. First cooings for Guinevere, then weddings for Guinevere, and now, to cap it all, paintings for Guinevere. Apples for Guinevere! Go away, you are free! You may be handsome but you have a pea-brain. Give me a wily wizard or an erotic elf-king any day rather than a nincompoop knight! Get out before I change my mind – and change you into a puffed toad, as you deserve! Out, I say; out!'

When Sir Lancelot finally encountered Sir Bors again, he told him that he had never met anyone so terrifying as King Arthur's sister, and had never felt so pleased to escape from any danger.

'It is an amazing adventure, fair cousin,' said Bors. 'The flower of knighthood captured under an apple tree and spending his time painting instead of escaping.'

'There was this blowing-up spell,' said Lancelot sulkily.

'I don't believe a word of it,' said Sir Bors. 'It was just a trick to keep you there. Wait till I tell Lionel and Ector!'

'Don't you dare,' said Sir Lancelot fiercely. 'Don't you dare, fair cousin. Not a word to your brother or mine, and above all not a word to King Arthur or Queen Guinevere. I swear you to secrecy. No one must ever know about the adventure of the apple tree.'

HERE ENDS AN ADVENTURE OF SIR LANCELOT

CHAPTER 8

The Adventure of
the Damsel Sauvage

A T the high feast of Pentecost when all the Knights
of the Round Table assembled, it was King Arthur's
custom never to go into dinner till he had seen or
heard a great marvel.

One Pentecost Sir Gawain looked out of the
window a little before midday. He turned to his
uncle King Arthur.

'Lord, go to your meal,' he said, 'for here at hand
come strange adventures.'

The horn sounded for washing; the King and the
hundred and fifty knights took their seats at the
Round Table. Then three wild men came into the
great hall. The one in the middle was leaning on the
shoulders of the other two as he could not walk

properly himself. But when they reached the King, he stood up straight. He was tall and big, but what the knights all noticed was that he had one strange thing about him: his left arm was much longer than his right.

'Give me three gifts, King,' he cried. 'The first I will ask now and the other two I will ask in twelve months' time at the next high feast of Pentecost.'

'Ask,' said King Arthur, making no promises.

'Give me meat and drink for twelve months in your castle.'

King Arthur looked him up and he looked him down. Despite his wild hair and his ragged clothes he was strong and broad-shouldered. Perhaps he was of noble blood, thought the King.

'What is your name and lineage?'

'King, I cannot tell you.'

The King turned to his Seneschal.

'Kay,' he said, 'give this young man meat and drink for twelve months. Also clothes and equipment, as if he were a lord's son.'

'There is no need to waste money on him,' said Sir Kay severely. 'If he had been a lord's son, he would have asked for horse and armour, not food and drink. He is clearly a low-born oaf, and as for fine clothes and equipment, he would only spoil them. Look at his gangling arms! As he has no name, I will call him Beaumains – beautiful hands.'

'At any rate, Kay,' said King Arthur, losing interest, 'give him what he has asked for.'

'Very well, Sire,' said Sir Kay. 'I'll take him down to the kitchens, there he can work for his living and stuff himself day and night, till at the end of twelve months he will be as fat as a hog.'

Then Sir Kay turned to Sir Gawain, 'Is this your strange adventure, Gawain?' he mocked. 'To find me another kitchen knave? Can you do no better than that?'

'Mock away, Kay,' muttered Sir Gawain angrily. 'Who knows? One day this kitchen knave may mock you!'

'Go with the Seneschal,' said King Arthur to the young man, 'and obey him in everything for a twelve months.'

So Beaumains was put in the kitchen, and slept with the kitchen boys. He worked hard in the kitchen and politely obeyed the Seneschal as King Arthur had commanded. Both Sir Lancelot and Sir Gawain had pity on him, and of their great courtesy invited him to their own chambers for meat and drink. But Beaumains refused them, though Sir Kay never stopped mocking and taunting him for his clumsiness.

So twelve months passed till the high feast of Pentecost came round again.

'Sire,' said Sir Lancelot, 'we may go in to our feast, for I have seen a damsel coming with some strange adventures.'

Beaumains was hard at work in the kitchens for that great feast, basting and carving, sweating and scurrying, greasing and scouring. As he was so strong, Sir Kay sent him up to carry the great boar's head in to the King. When he reached the hall, he saw a damsel standing proudly in front of King Arthur.

'As for the recreant knight who is besieging my sister,' she was saying, 'he is called the Red Knight of the Red Lands.'

'Lord,' said Sir Gawain excitedly, 'that is one of the most dangerous knights in the whole world. Men say he has seven men's strength, and I would like to ride out and encounter him.'

'Fair nephew,' said the King, 'none of the Knights of the Round Table, not even you, shall ride out without my permission. But I will never give my permission till this damsel tells us her name and lineage.'

'That I will not,' said the damsel. 'But you may call me the Damsel Sauvage.'

Then Beaumains went on his knees before the King and served him with the boar's head. But he did not get up from his knees, though the King was astonished and urged him to rise.

'Sir King,' he said, 'I ask you for the two other gifts you promised me.'

Then the King remembered who this kitchen boy was.

'Ask on,' said the King.

'Sir, grant me this adventure of the Damsel Sauvage. For like me, she will not say her name or lineage.'

'I grant it you,' said the King.

'Fie on you, Sir King,' said the damsel angrily. 'Have you nothing better to offer me than a kitchen knave? Keep him! I will go elsewhere.'

She turned and stormed out of the Great Hall. Beaumains seemed not to notice.

'Sire,' he said, 'the other gift I ask is that Sir Lancelot du Lac shall make me a knight. When I ride out, order him to follow me and make me a knight if he finds me worthy.'

King Arthur looked across at Sir Lancelot, who nodded and smiled.

'I grant you this too,' said the King. 'But hurry, or you will lose your quest.'

Beaumains armed, and rode off. He armed richly, in cloth of gold that a dwarf brought him, so that all the knights marvelled. But Sir Kay leapt up angrily.

'I will see if my kitchen boy still knows who his master is,' he cried.

Both Sir Lancelot and Sir Gawain begged him to stay and feast on; but they knew that when Sir Kay lost his temper, there was no holding him back, for he was such a proud knight. So they shrugged their shoulders and drank their honey wine as they watched him arm and ride out from Camelot.

Sir Kay caught up with Beaumains, just as Beaumains caught up with the Damsel Sauvage.

'Beaumains,' he cried, 'back to the kitchens, kitchen boy.'

'Well said, Sir Knight!' said the Damsel Sauvage. 'Take him back to his greasy pans, for I have no use for him.'

Beaumains turned his horse and saw it was Sir Kay.

'Seneschal,' he said, 'King Arthur ordered me to obey you for twelve months, and so I did, though you mocked me shamefully. But now the twelve months are over. Order me no orders now, Seneschal.'

Sir Kay in a fury galloped straight down upon Beaumains. But though Beaumains had only a sword, he turned Sir Kay's lance with it and gave him a great thrust in the side, so that Sir Kay fell to the earth as though dead.

At this moment Sir Lancelot rode up.

'Kay would have done better to take my advice and Gawain's,' he said, 'for he has paid dearly for his mocking.'

Then Beaumains took Sir Kay's spear and offered to joust with Sir Lancelot.

'Willingly,' said Sir Lancelot.

Beaumains was delighted, for it did great honour to a kitchen boy to joust with the flower of knighthood.

So they rushed together like two wild boars, and fought for nearly an hour. Sir Lancelot was amazed at Beaumains' size and strength, and was almost afraid he would be beaten.

'Beaumains,' he cried at last, 'do not fight so fiercely! We have no quarrel with one another.'

'That is true,' said Beaumains, 'but it did me good to feel your might. Yet, my lord, I could have done even more if I had tried my hardest.'

'In God's name,' said Sir Lancelot, 'I promise you by the faith of my body that you need fear no earthly knight.'

'Then, I pray you, give me the order of knighthood.'

'Sir, first you must tell me your true name and lineage.'

'That I will do,' said Beaumains, 'but you must keep it secret.'

Then he whispered his true name and lineage to Sir Lancelot.

'I knew you were of noble blood,' said Sir Lancelot happily, 'and did not come to Camelot just for the meat and the drink.'

So he joyfully gave him the order of knighthood, and then went back to Camelot, taking Sir Kay with him, who was carried on his shield, so badly wounded that he barely lived.

Then all men mocked Sir Kay for being beaten by his own kitchen boy, especially Sir Gawain.

'What did I say, Sir Kay?' chuckled Sir Gawain. 'Now you know what it feels like to be skewered!'

Sir Kay could only groan in reply.

Beaumains rode on till he caught up with the Damsel Sauvage. When she saw him again, she was not pleased.

'What are you doing here?' she cried. 'Go home, you stinking, filthy kitchen knave. I came to Camelot for a true knight, a beautiful knight and a king's son, like the one whose life I saved, the gold-green hero.' For in fact the Damsel Sauvage was the Lady Luned; and she only liked elegant and very clean, well-washed, well-barbered knights like Sir Yvain.

'And what do I get?' she went on scornfully. 'A long-haired sluggard, an oafish spit-turner, a greasy dish-washer!'

'Damsel,' said Sir Beaumains, 'say what you like, I will never leave you whatever you say, for I have promised King Arthur to enchieve your adventure, and so I will finish it, or die.'

'Die, I hope,' said the Lady Luned nastily.

But the first to die were six robbers: Sir Beaumains smote one to death, then another, and at the third stroke he killed the third. The other three fled; but Sir Beaumains chased and killed them all. Then he rode back to the Damsel Sauvage.

'Ride further away, knave,' she cried, 'for now you stink of blood as well as grease. What do you think? That I admire you for killing this rabble of thieves? Soon you will see a sight that will make you turn home again, a real knight to strike terror into your heart.'

They rode on till at last they came to a black land, and there was a black hawthorn tree on which hung a banner on the one side and on the other a black shield. By it stood a black spear, tall and heavy, and a great black horse covered with silk. There was a black stone nearby, and on it sat a knight all armed in black harness. His name was the Black Knight of the Black Lands.

'Damsel,' said the Black Knight sternly, 'have you brought this knight from the court of King Arthur to be your champion?'

'No, fair knight,' said the Lady Luned, 'this is just a kitchen knave who will not leave me alone but keeps following me, whatever I say. I pray you rid me of him. Slay him.'

'Well,' said the Black Knight. 'as he is a kitchen knave, it were not to my honour to kill him. So I will let him go free on foot. But he must leave his horse and harness for me.'

'You make very free with my horse and harness,' said Sir Beaumains mildly, 'but I tell you this, Sir Knight. You will only have my horse and harness if you win them with your hands. So let us see what you can do.'

'What? Is that how you dare answer me?' said the Black Knight astonished. 'For that you will lose your life.'

In great anger they mounted their horses and clashed together like thunder. The Black Knight's spear broke, but Sir Beaumains thrust his own spear deep into the Black Knight's body, so that its point broke off inside his body. Nevertheless the Black Knight drew his sword, and smote many mighty strokes and wounded Sir Beaumains badly. But in the end he fainted, fell from his horse, and died.

Sir Beaumains saw how well-horsed he was, and how well armed, so he dismounted and armed himself in the Black Knight's armour and took his great black horse in place of his own. He rode on and caught up with the Damsel Sauvage again.

'Cursed be the day,' she cried, 'that a wretch like you should slay so good a knight! It was just luck. For if his spear had not broken, he would have killed you easily. But your luck will not last, kitchen knave. My advice to you is to ride back to Camelot before you are killed, as now you will surely be.'

'I may be killed,' said Sir Beaumains, 'or I may not. But I warn you, fair damsel, that I will ride with you all the way and never leave you. So do not rebuke me all day long, for what is the good of it?'

As they rode along, they saw a knight come galloping towards them, all in green, both horse and harness. He reined up in front of the Damsel Sauvage.

'Is that my brother the Black Knight that you have brought with you?'

'No, no,' cried the Lady Luned, 'this wretched kitchen knave has killed your brother treacherously.'

'Traitor!' said the Green Knight to Sir Beaumains. 'You shall die for the slaying of my brother.'

Then the Green Knight rode to a green horn hanging upon a green thorn tree. He blew three blasts on it, and two damsels came to fasten his armour. Then he took a great war-horse, and armed himself with a green shield and a green spear. He and Sir Beaumains galloped together with all their might and broke their spears in their hands.

Then they drew their swords and gave each other great strokes and many wounds, till at last Sir Beaumains drove his horse sideways into the Green Knight's horse and sent horse and rider crashing to the ground. The Green Knight leapt to his feet and Sir Beaumains leapt off his horse. They hurtled together like two mighty boars, thrusting forwards and backwards, slashing and cutting, till the blood flowed.

'For shame, noble Green Knight,' cried the Damsel Sauvage. 'Shame that you were ever made a knight to stand so long fighting with a kitchen knave. Think of all the worship you have ever won, and smite him down!'

At her reproaches the Green Knight lost his temper and doubled his strokes, wounding Sir Beaumains so badly that the blood ran down his armour to the ground. But Beaumains also lost his temper too at the shameful words of the Damsel Sauvage, and gave the Green Knight such a buffet upon the helm that he fell to his knees. Then Beaumains struck him to the earth, grovelling, and raised his sword to kill him.

'Mercy, noble knight,' cried the Green Knight, 'do not slay

me. I will yield to you with the fifty knights in my service, and forgive you the death of my brother the Black Knight and all our disputes.'

'All is in vain,' said Sir Beaumains, 'you will die unless my damsel who has come with me begs for your life.'

Then he unlaced the Green Knight's helm.

'Not so savage, you wretched knave,' cried the Damsel Sauvage.

Beaumains raised his sword as if to swop off his head.

'Do not let me die, lady, for a fair word spoken,' begged the Green Knight.

Then at last Lady Luned gave in.

'Let him be, Beaumains,' she said, 'do not kill him, for he was a noble knight – at least till he yielded to you.'

Then the Green Knight of the Green Lands did homage to Sir Beaumains, and his fifty knights with him.

'I thank you,' said Sir Beaumains, 'but I call upon you to ride to my lord Arthur, and yield yourselves rather to him. Tell him you were overcome by Beaumains.'

'Sir,' said the Green Knight, 'this we will do.'

'In the devil's name,' swore the Lady Luned, 'why should a kitchen knave like you deserve to win fifty knights' service?'

As Sir Beaumains rode on with her, she chided him and rebuked him in the foulest manner she could, told him he had beaten the Green Knight only by good fortune, and warned him that he would surely be killed in the next encounter.

'Damsel,' said Beaumains at last, 'you are always threatening me that I shall be beaten or killed by the knights we meet, but, whatever the reason may be, it seems that I escape and they all lie in the dust or the mire. So wait, I pray you, till you actually see me beaten or yielding, and then you may bid me to go from you and rebuke me as shamefully as you like.'

But Lady Luned was as pitiless as ever.

'I gave you a last warning, kitchen knave,' she said. 'Throw away your shield and spear, and run. For we are now near to Castle Perilous where my sister is besieged. Even if you were a knight of such prowess and lineage as Sir Lancelot or Sir Tristram or the good knight, Sir Lamorak, you would not come out alive. For the knight who besieges her is the most perilous knight now living, the Red Knight of the Red Lands. He is a man without mercy, and has seven men's strength. So get you gone, Beaumains, while you can!'

Then Sir Beaumains smiled, because he thought that perhaps the Damsel Sauvage was really worried for his life.

'I would be worse than a fool to leave you now,' he said, 'when at your side I win such worship. For if I match this Red Knight of the Red Lands, I will be called the fourth knight of the world, after Sir Lancelot du Lac, Sir Tristram de Lyonesse, and Sir Lamorak de Galys.'

'You stink now alive,' said the Lady Luned abruptly, 'but think of this: your body will stink even more when you are dead.'

They rode through the fair forest till they came to a plain, at the end of which they could see a great castle with all around it tents and smoke and noise. But Sir Beaumains had no eyes for the castle. He was staring with horror at the tall trees on the edge of the forest. There were forty trees, and from each tree a dead knight was dangling. Their shields were tied around their necks and their swords were hanging from their waists. Their armour clanged and clanked grimly as their bodies swung to and fro in the breeze.

'What does this mean?' asked Sir Beaumains hoarsely.

'All these noble knights came here to rescue my sister,' said Lady Luned, 'but the Red Knight of the Red Lands overcame them all, and put them to this shameful death without mercy or pity. He will hang you up there too, wretched Beaumains, unless you flee now, before it is too late.'

'God defend me from such a villain's death,' was all that Sir Beaumains replied.

He rode on slowly towards the Castle till he came to a

sycamore tree. On it was a great horn hanging, made of an elephant's tusk, the greatest that was ever seen.

'If you blow that horn,' said the Lady Luned, 'you will see why my sister's castle is called Castle Perilous. For you will face the greatest peril ever any kitchen knave faced in the world.'

Beaumains had had enough of the Lady Luned's tongue; and at long last he showed it.

'Say no more to me, Damsel Sauvage,' said Sir Beaumains, 'for you are rightly called sauvage and he would be a fool who called you fair! I will either win worship and save your sister or die like a brave knight in the field. That is what I will do. What you will do is hold your tongue.'

Then the Lady Luned fell silent at last. But Sir Beaumains spurred his horse to the sycamore tree, and blew the great horn such a blast that all the country and the castle rung with the sound.

The Red Knight of the Red Lands armed himself. Two barons set spurs on his heels, and an earl buckled his helm. All was blood-red, his armour, his spear, his sword, his shield, and his great war-horse.

'Sir,' said the Lady Luned, 'there is your dreadly enemy, and over there at the window in the castle my sister is watching, the Lady Lynette.'

'Where?' asked Sir Beaumains.

'There,' said the Lady Luned, pointing with her finger.

Then Sir Beaumains saw the Lady Lynette, and she smiled and waved to him gladly.

'Leave your looking, Sir Knight,' bellowed the Red Knight as he rode up. 'You should do better to look at the knights hanging on the trees behind you. For that is where I will hang you too, and the carrion crows will pluck out your eyes.'

'No lady could ever love you, evil knight,' said Sir Beaumains, 'for you shame yourself and all knighthood. Do you think the sight of even a hundred knights' bodies shamefully hanged would frighten me? I defy you!'

Then they both feutred their spears in great anger and came together with such force that the girths and cruppers and saddles of their war-horses all broke, and they both crashed to earth. All who were watching from the castle or the siege thought that they had broken their necks.

'The stranger knight is a big man and a noble jouster,' they said, amazed, 'for never till now did we see any knight who could match the Red Knight of the Red Lands.'

Then both knights sprang to their feet and ran together like fierce lions. Each gave the other such a buffet that they reeled backwards two paces. Then they recovered and hewed great chunks of each other's armour and shields till the ground was littered with chunks of iron. At times they hurtled together like two rams; at times they fell grovelling to earth, at times they were so dazed they snatched up each other's swords. They fought on and on till evening, and no man who watched could tell which was likely to win the battle. Their armour was so hewn that men could see their naked flesh. The Red Knight was a wily fighter, much more than the Black Knight or the Green Knight, and seven times mightier too. But Beaumains learnt to know his manner of fighting, though not before he had been wounded again and again.

At last they tottered apart, staggering, bleeding and panting, so that all who watched them wept for pity's sake. Then they both sat down by common consent on two molehills, and undid their helms, and let the cold wind blow. Sir Beaumains looked up. He saw the Lady Lynette gazing down at him from the castle window, smiling. So his heart felt light, and he laced his helmet on again. But so did the Red Knight of the Red Lands, grimly.

Then the Red Knight caught Sir Beaumains so fierce a stroke sideways that he knocked the sword flying from his hand, and Sir Beaumains stood there weaponless.

'Now die!' roared the Red Knight grimly. He smote a great buffet over the helm, and Beaumains fell grovelling to the earth. The Red Knight hurled himself on him to pin him

down and unlace his helm. Then all watching knew that the battle was over and that the Red Knight of the Red Lands had proved his mastery again. Sir Beaumains' body would soon be swinging from a tall tree, there was no help.

'Ah God!' cried the Lady Luned, 'God help us all. My lady, my sister, is shrieking and weeping, my own heart is heavy. Ah, Sir Beaumains, where has all your great courage gone?'

When Beaumains heard the Damsel Sauvage call him Sir Beaumains and praise him for the first time, his strength came back to him. He hurled the Red Knight off his body, clambered to his feet, and seized his own sword again in his left hand, which was the longer arm, so the Red Knight was baffled and could not reach him. He doubled his strokes and smote so thick and so fast that the Red Knight fell to earth. This time it was Sir Beaumains who hurled himself upon him, and unlaced his helm.

'Noble Knight,' said the Red Knight, 'I yield to your mercy.'

But Sir Beaumains thought of the knights hanged so shamefully.

'This I grant you,' he said, 'that I will not put you to so shameful a death as you did to so many other good knights. But I cannot for honour's sake let you live.'

With that he raised his sword and brought it flashing down so fast that the Red Knight's head flew apart from his body, right to the foot of the sycamore tree.

Then the Lady Luned ran to him, and helped him off with his armour and bound his great wounds.

'Fair Beaumains,' she cried, 'forgive me all I have ever said or done against you.'

'With all my will,' said Beaumains courteously. 'For the more you rebuked me, the more you angered me. And the more you angered me, the more I wreaked my wrath on my enemies. Therefore I hope that every knight may have a damsel sauvage with him, to prick him on when he goes into battle. But now the battles are done I would rather like a damsel gentle, with a soft voice and a sweet tongue.'

'You will have one,' said Lady Luned laughing, and had him carried on a shield to her sister Lady Lynette.

'Jesu, sister!' said the Lady Luned to the Lady Lynette, 'I marvel what manner of a man he may be, for never did any woman revile a knight so shamefully and foully and so often as I did this Sir Beaumains. Yet, he was always courteous to me, spoke boldly, acted bravely, fought best of all.'

'A man like that must be of noble blood,' said the Lady Lynette hopefully.

'If he is,' said the Lady Luned, 'marry him, fair sister. If he is not, I may marry him myself, though I am sworn to be a damsel errant and to have no home, for he is certainly the bravest boldest finest knave that ever came out of a kitchen! And by now I am even quite fond of his smell.'

HERE ENDS AN ADVENTURE OF SIR BEAUMAINS

CHAPTER 9

The Adventure of
the Wild-Haired Baby

THE Green Knight of the Green Lands rode into
Camelot with his fifty knights.

'Welcome, Sir Knight,' said the King. 'Why have
you come to Camelot?'

'On the orders of a mighty young knight to do
you homage,' said the Green Knight, 'for he overcame me but granted me mercy of my life on this
condition. He said to tell you that Beaumains sent
me.'

'Ah,' said Sir Lancelot, delighted, 'I knew he
would overthrow any knight in the world.'

'He overthrew my brother the Black Knight of
the Black Lands and killed him at the Black Thorn,'
said the Green Knight sadly. 'But I think that he will

be dead himself by now, for he went riding on to fight my other brother the Red Knight of the Red Lands, who has the strength of seven knights and is a knight without pity.'

'Does his strength increase at noon?' asked Sir Gawain curiously.

The Green Knight nodded.

'Then I must fight him,' said Sir Gawain, whose strength also increased at noon, 'and avenge the death of poor Beaumains.'

'Fair nephew,' said King Arthur, 'we will ride out with you, and the Green Knight of the Green Lands shall guide us.'

Then there was great jangling of armour and mounting of war-horses in Camelot as all the knights of the household made ready to ride out on this quest to Castle Perilous.

So they rode out on a summer's day, and as they wended their way through the great Forest, behold, a press of wild knights from the North rode down upon them. Then they all halted, and laid their hands on their swords for fear of treachery. In the midst of the wild knights rode a dark Queen on a snow-white pony. Sir Gawain looked at Sir Gaheris, and Sir Gaheris looked at Sir Agravaine; and with one accord the three brothers beat a path to her feet, jumped off their horses, and kissed her hands and her feet. For this was their mother Queen Morgawse of Orkeney, and they had not seen her for seven years.

'My sons,' she said proudly, laying her cool hands on their heads. Then she looked around fiercely. 'But where is Gareth? Where is my youngest son, my joy and my delight? Gawain, Gaheris, Agravaine, what have you done with your brother Gareth?'

Up rode King Arthur and greeted his elder sister as a king should greet a queen. If it was seven years since her sons had seen her, it was fourteen years since he had.

'But, fair brother,' she said, 'where is my baby Gareth? It is twelve months and more since I sent him to your court.'

King Arthur was as baffled as Sir Gawain and the twins. But being a king had made him wise and quick-witted.

'Ah, yes,' he said. 'The baby Gareth. Would he by any chance be a wild-haired little baby, sweet sister? And in fact the biggest, strongest baby that has ever come to Camelot?'

'He is certainly by far the biggest and strongest of all my sons,' said Queen Morgawse proudly, 'though I think it discourteous of you, my sweet brother, to call his hair wild. I would say it is in the Northern style.'

'His arms,' said Sir Gawain. 'Of course! We should have remembered. Gareth always had one arm longer than the other. It must be Beaumains!'

'Beaumains?' asked Queen Morgawse.

Then they had to tell their mother the whole story, and explain that they had not recognized their own brother because last time they had seen him he had been a little boy.

'Ah, brother,' said Queen Morgawse sternly to King Arthur, 'you did yourself great shame when you kept my fair son, your own nephew, in the kitchen and treated him like a knave.'

'Fair sister,' said King Arthur, 'you might have warned us that he was coming. But he came leaning on two men's shoulders, as though he were half-witted and played the game with us for a year to see who would treat him as a courteous knight should, and who not. But enough of this talk. We will ride together, and find him if he is still alive. In any case dead or alive, he is proved to be a man of worship, and that is my great joy.'

Then King Arthur and Queen Morgawse and all their company journeyed through the Black Lands and the Green Lands and the Red Lands till they rode into Castle Perilous. And there were even greater rejoicings when they found Sir Gareth alive, except for the Green Knight of the Green Lands who was sorry his mighty brother was dead, for all his shamefulness.

Then the Lady Lynette married Sir Gareth as he was so

noble and a king's son, though she and Lady Luned always called him Beaumains when they were alone together. Sir Gawain and his twin brothers, Sir Gaheris and Sir Agravaine, gave them great gifts. And what great cheer Sir Lancelot made of Sir Gareth and he of him! For there was no knight Sir Gareth loved so well as Sir Lancelot who had made him a knight, and it was ever afterwards a question whether he or Sir Gaheris loved Sir Lancelot better.

HERE ENDS AN ADVENTURE OF SIR GARETH, WHO WAS CALLED SIR BEAUMAINS

CHAPTER 10

The Adventure of the Lion

S IR Yvain was sitting at his meat in Arthur's hall,
when a lady rode in on a bay horse covered in foam.
Her face was hidden under a veil of yellow satin, so
nobody could see who she was.

She rode straight up to Sir Yvain, seized his hand
and pulled the wedding ring off his finger.

'That is how the deceiver, the traitor, the faithless, the disgraced should be treated!' she said.

With that she turned her horse's head and rode
straight out again. All the knights there looked at Sir
Yvain who sat open-mouthed in astonishment and
anger.

'There is only one woman in the whole world
who would mock a knight like that,' jeered Sir Kay.

'And there is one knight here who should know her voice well.'

'Who is that, Kay?' asked Sir Gawain.

'Your own brother, Sir Gareth of Orkeney, whom I christened Beaumains. For she mocked him for a stinking kitchen knave from here to the Red Lands.'

'That were best forgotten, Kay,' said Sir Lancelot courteously, 'else men will not forget how I found you almost dead on the ground after Sir Beaumains' first joust. Your boy of the kitchen came near to carving you up, Sir Seneschal.'

Then all the knights laughed at Sir Kay; but Sir Lancelot smiled at Sir Gareth, the big young man whom he loved even more than his own kindred.

'But tell us, Gareth,' added Lancelot, 'was that indeed the Lady Luned? For Kay is right in this at least, you certainly more than anyone should recognize her voice when she speaks in scorn.'

'That was her,' said Sir Gareth easily, 'oh yes, that was certainly Luned.'

Then Sir Yvain remembered how he had betrayed his wife, the Lady of the Fountain. For after three years of marriage he had left her to visit his uncle King Arthur. But he had stayed at Arthur's court for three years, though he had promised his wife that he would stay for three months only. He knew the Lady Luned was right to call him a faithless recreant.

In his sorrow and grief Sir Yvain rose from the Round Table and went out into the Forest all alone. He wandered to the distant parts of the earth till all his clothes were worn out, he whose clothes had been the most elegant of all the knights at Camelot. His body wasted away, his hair grew long, he kept company with the wild beasts of the Forest, and fed with them, more like a wild man of the woods himself than a king's son. That was when he first learnt the language of the eagles, and the ravens. The birds of the air, who travelled furthest, knew that his mother was Morgan le Fay: for them she was the witch-queen of the Half World who could take their shape

when she wished, and they protected her son and fed him
mice and young rabbits that they had killed. For so the Eagle
of Ablek, the oldest animal in the world and the one who
could see the furthest, and had seen Sir Yvain, instructed
them.

Yvain wandered from the forest to the desert that lay all
around it. There in the desert stood a huge craggy mound, on
the side of which was a grey rock. He heard a loud roaring
from the grey rock. The roar rose to a yelp mixed with hissing,
and then to a sort of shrieking roar that made Yvain very
curious to find out what it was. When he came near, he saw a
cleft in the rock and a serpent coiled within the cleft. It had
bitten a lion by the tail, and every time the lion tried to leap
away the serpent opened its jaws and hissed, breathing fire at
it, burning its flank.

Yvain thought that if he was not killed by the serpent, he
would be killed by the lion, as he was weak and had only a
rusty sword with him. He tried to creep by. But the lion, which
was fierce and black, roared at him so piteously that he
thought he should help the lion as it was the more natural
beast of the two. So he raised his old sword and struck at the
serpent again and again, cutting it first in two and then into
tiny bits that slithered all around in their foul blood and filth.
Unfortunately as he was slashing at the serpent he had by
mistake cut the end of the lion's tail off, which the serpent's
venomous jaws were holding. So he supposed the lion would
snarl and roar and come at him, once it was free. But instead
the lion reared up nobly on its hind feet as if it was a great dog
begging, and then bowed its face down to earth with its
fore-paws joined together, doing homage to Sir Yvain, and
thanking him for having killed the serpent and rescued its life.
Sir Yvain was delighted at this fine behaviour. Then the lion
made him all the cheer that a beast might make a man,
fawning on him like a spaniel, playing about him like a

greyhound, and bringing him that evening a fine large roebuck for his supper.

Then Sir Yvain stroked the lion on the neck and the shoulders, and thanked God for the company of the beast, for he had been a long time all alone without any company. He took the roebuck, carved the skin along the rib, struck a spark from a flint, caught the spark in some dry brush-wood, and roasted the roebuck meat. While he was eating, the lion lay at his feet, not making a movement, but watching him steadily till he had eaten all he could. Then when Sir Yvain had finished, he gave the rest to the lion, who devoured it merrily, bones and all. That night the lion slept at his feet and sometimes Sir Yvain used its mane as a rest for his long legs; and ever after it followed him.

One day Sir Yvain and the lion came to a fine castle. Seven gatekeepers lowered the drawbridge but they were terrified at the sight of the lion and asked Sir Yvain to leave the lion at the gate.

'Certainly not,' said Sir Yvain, 'for this beast is as dear to me as I am myself. Either we shall both find shelter here, or else I shall stay outside with my dear companion.'

So they let them both, lion and knight, in. But the people of the castle were as sorrowful as though death were upon them. They went into the meal. The lord of the castle sat on one side of Yvain, and his daughter on the other. Sir Yvain had never seen any lady with a more graceful body or lovelier face than she, though it was stained with tears. Then the lion came and placed himself between Yvain's feet, and he fed him with every kind of food that he took himself. But he never saw anything to equal the sadness of that people.

At the end of the meal the lord of the castle had still not spoken a word of welcome.

'The knife was in the meat,' said Sir Yvain, 'and the drink was in the horn, but there was no revelry in this hall. Can we now be cheerful at last?'

'Heaven knows,' said the lord of the castle, 'it is not your coming that makes us sorrowful but the monster on the mountain. For he has captured my two sons, and tomorrow he will come down and kill them before my eyes — for this is a monster that devours men — unless I give him my dear daughter here.'

'This is cause for sadness enough,' said Yvain. 'But I was a knight errant of the Round Table, so give me armour and let me fight the monster.'

They all rejoiced then, thinking he must be a very good man, as they could see the lion by his side as trustful as a lamb would be. All the same the others dared not sleep in the same room as Yvain and the lion that night, but barred the door so tight they could not get out till next morning at dawn. That is how human beings treat even their friends when they are frightened.

Next morning, while Yvain was arming, he heard a great clamour. It was the monster coming. The monster's dwarf, puffed up like a toad, was beating the lord's two sons along in front of him with a four-knotted scourge.

When they lowered the drawbridge Sir Yvain rode out to do battle, armed and mounted as a knight should be. But the lion would not stay behind. It loped out alongside Sir Yvain's horse. At first it sat on its haunches and watched the battle, and roared with pleasure when Yvain slashed from the monster's cheek a slice fit to roast. But then the monster gave Sir Yvain such a blow that he sank in a heap on his horse's neck. At that the lion bristled up, and leapt at the monster, and tore away skin and nerves and flesh, fighting much more fiercely than Sir Yvain had done.

'You are no knight errant,' bellowed the monster in agony, 'to fight with that animal to help you.'

So Sir Yvain took the lion back to the castle, and scolded the beast, and had the drawbridge shut upon it. Then he returned to fight the monster alone.

But the lion leapt up from the hall to the battlements and

stood there on its hind-paws and watched the fight. He saw Sir Yvain's shield broken and dissolved like ice, and Sir Yvain himself being battered. Then the lion's heart was heavy and sad. Sir Yvain was knocked to the ground. At that the lion started quivering, bristled up again and thumped the stone tower with its tail. Sir Yvain looked up piteously, as the toad-like dwarf laughed. Then with a great spring the noble lion leapt from the top of the battlements of the castle right out over the moat to land on the hideous dwarf. And that was the last laugh the dwarf ever laughed. Then the lion turned on the monster and pulled him roaring and bellowing to earth like a tree-trunk, and with ten strokes of his claw tore his heart open, so that the monster lay stone-dead.

Thereafter Sir Yvain was known as the Knight of the Lion. Wherever he went, the lion went too, and they had many adventures together. But at last Sir Yvain went back to the Lady of the Fountain, and lived faithfully with her, guarding the magic Fountain, as long as she lived. When she died, the Giant Herdsman sent him on a quest to find Kerchevyn and Kerchevyn's followers: these were three hundred ravens, and at the quest's end they followed the Knight of the Lion instead and became his Raven Army. Sir Yvain took them back with him to his own land of Gore; and there was never an enemy that got the better of him thereafter.

HERE ENDS AN ADVENTURE OF SIR YVAIN

CHAPTER 11

The Adventure of
the Twrch Trwyth*

O N the first day of the year a young warrior of the
West rode up to the great gate of Camelot. Now in
the mountains of the West there were no knights in
those days, only chieftains, but their robes were rich,
their jewels splendid, and their speech silver ton-
gued. The youth rode a horse of dappled grey,
covered with cloth and purple on which was embroidered an apple of gold at each corner. Two
greyhounds followed him: each wore a collar of
rubies. In his hand he held two spurs of mottled iron,
sharp enough to cut the wind. His war-horse's
harness was of ivory, his bridle of linked gold.

'Open the gate, gatekeeper,' he said softly.

*Pronounced
Toorkh Trooith

169

'I will not open it,' said Asgard the Ancient, the gatekeeper.
'Why not?'

'The knife is in the meat, and the drink is in the horn, and there is revelry in Arthur's hall. None may enter but a king's son.'

'Open the gate now,' said the youth less softly.

'No,' said Asgard.

'If you do not open it, I will give three shouts that will echo from Camelot to the Mountains of the West.'

'Make as much noise as you like,' grumbled Asgard, 'but I will not let you in. You can have a guest chamber outside with peppered food and spiced wine and a damsel to smooth your sheets and lull you to sleep with songs.'

'If I gave the three shouts,' said the youth menacingly, 'all the ladies of King Arthur's court who are pregnant will lose their babies with fright.'

He opened his mouth wide.

'Wait,' said Asgard.

'If the ladies lose their babies, their knights will blame you, gatekeeper, and I think you will lose your life.'

The young man opened his mouth wider still and sucked in breath till Asgard found he had no air left around him to breathe.

So grumbling and muttering, the gatekeeper threw open the great gate. The youth rode straight into the Great Hall on his dappled grey horse, without dismounting.

'Greeting to you, High King of Logres and Lord of Camelot,' he cried. 'May this greeting be the same to the lowest as to the highest, to your knights and your chieftains, your ladies and your guests.'

'Greetings to you, young chieftain,' said King Arthur.

'It is not for meat or drink that I have come,' said the youth, 'nor even for a damsel to smooth my bed and lull me to sleep with her songs but for a boon. First though, Lord King, bless my hair.'

'Willingly,' said King Arthur. He knew it was the custom

for the Warriors of the West to have their hair cut and combed by kings.

So they brought him a golden comb and scissors, and he cut and combed out the youth's hair.

'Half of my life is past,' said King Arthur, 'but I have never set eyes on a more elegant youth than you, save only my nephew Sir Yvain. Tell me your name and your lineage, and the boon you ask.'

'I will tell you,' said the youth, 'I am Cealwin the Chieftain, son of Cynric the Chieftain, son of Cerdic the Chieftain, of the lineage of Woden. The boon I ask you I will ask for the love of your ladies, of the golden-haired daughters of Logres. I ask it for the love of Queen Guinevere, daughter of King Leodegrance of Camelard, for the sake of the Lady Morvyth, daughter of King Urien of Gore, for the sake of the red-haired damsel Gwendoline, for the sake of the dark-skinned damsel Inde. I ask you for their love and mine to obtain for me the dewy Olwen, daughter of the giant Yspaddaden.'

'Chieftain,' said Arthur smiling, 'I have never heard of this dewy damsel, but because you have asked me for the love of Guinevere my queen, I will send knights and men with you to seek her, even to the ends of the earth.'

Then Sir Kay said he would lead the quest, for the sake of the red-haired damsel Gwendoline, his paramour. Sir Conan said he would go too because he loved the beautiful Morvyth, sister of Sir Yvain. Sir Bedevere the one-armed said he would go too, for the dusky eyes of the Lady Inde.

King Arthur laughed aloud.

'Chieftain,' he said, 'you have cleverly chosen by praising their ladies three knights who will serve you well. For Sir Kay, the Seneschal, can go nine days and nine nights without sleep. Sir Bedevere, the One-Armed, never shrinks from any quest that Sir Kay goes on — besides he is a devil with giants — and Sir Conan is as good a guide in a land he has never seen as he is in his own. And I for my part will give you old Taliessin to go with you, because he speaks all languages.'

This Taliessin was a wizard who had come to the King after Merlin had left him.

The knights journeyed through far lands, and at the ends of the Earth they found Olwen. Her hair was more yellow than the flower of the broom, her skin was whiter than the foam of the wave, her cheek was redder than the reddest of roses.

'By the bones of God,' said the knights, 'she is fairer than our own lady loves.'

'Come away with me, Lady,' said Cealwin, 'for many a day have I loved you.'

'I promised my father I would not go without his permission,' said Olwen softly. 'Do you dare ask him for it?'

'We dare,' said the knights grimly.

They followed Olwen to the giant's castle. They slew the nine gatekeepers that were at the nine gates. Then they went into the Hall.

'The greetings of Heaven and Earth to you, giant Yspaddaden,' they said.

'What do you want,' he rumbled rudely.

'We want your daughter Olwen to marry Cealwin the Chieftain.'

'My life will end when Olwen marries,' said the giant sadly.

'All lives must end, giants' and men's alike,' said Taliessin.

'That sounds like a wretched wizard,' growled Yspaddaden grumpily, 'easy for them to say, they live for ever. Push up the wooden forks to open my eyelids that have fallen over my eyeballs. Then I may see my future son-in-law face to face.'

They pushed up his eyelids. The giant Yspaddaden did not much like what he saw. He saw armed knights with naked swords dripping with blood.

'Where are my porters and my servants?' he roared roughly.

The knights stood silent. Yspaddaden picked up one of the poisoned darts that lay beside him and hurled it at them in his ill-humour. Sir Bedevere caught it in his one arm, and flung it back so that it pierced the giant through the knee.

'A cursed ungentle son-in-law is this,' yelled Yspaddaden, 'I will always walk the worse now for his rudeness.'

He hurled another poisoned dart at them. Sir Kay caught it and flung it back. It went through the giant's belly and came out at his back.

'A cursed ungentle son-in-law I have,' yelled Yspaddaden. 'The cruel iron pricks me like the sting of a horse-fly. I will always be short of breath when I walk uphill after this, and my digestion will not be good now.'

He hurled a third poisoned dart at them. Sir Conan caught it and flung it back. It went through his eyeball and came out of the back of his head.

'A cursed ungentle son-in-law truly,' moaned Yspaddaden miserably. 'The stroke of this poisoned iron is as bad as the bite of a mad dog. My eyes will always water now when I walk into the wind. And I will have fits of giddiness every new moon because of his rudeness.'

The knights were amazed that they had not killed him, but they were Arthur's knights and no giants could dismay them.

'Fling no more darts at us, giant Yspaddaden,' they cried, 'unless you want even more pain than you are now suffering. Give us your daughter, and end this strife.'

'You do not understand,' groaned the grief-stricken giant, 'no one can kill me till the day my daughter marries. But everyone wants to kill giants in this Age. It is a bad time for giants, this Age of your King Arthur.' His groans died down. 'Who is the one of you who wants my daughter? Bring him here where I may see him.'

So they placed Cealwin in a chair face to face with Yspaddaden.

'He seems a fair young man, as men go,' said the giant

slyly, 'and in any case he threw no darts to hurt me. Well, well, daughters grow up and must marry. It will be done, it will be done.'

But he said this to trick the chieftain, for he hoped to make the marriage impossible.

'There is just one thing I need before the wedding day,' said Yspaddaden, 'and that is a comb and razor to comb my hair and beard. Will you take an oath to bring me the comb and razor I need? If you do, you shall have my daughter.'

'This is not difficult,' said Cealwin, 'and I take that oath willingly.'

'There is one little difficulty,' said Yspaddaden, 'my hair is so thick and matted that there is only one comb of ivory in the whole world that will comb it out, and that is the comb that lies between the two ears of the Twrch Trwyth.'

'I have taken my oath,' said Cealwin, 'and I will fetch you this comb, even though this Twrch Trwyth will not give it to you willingly.'

'There is one little difficulty more. You will have to hunt the Twrch Trwyth, and you will not be able to hunt him down without the whelp of the son of Eri. But the son of Eri lets no man take his whelp.'

'This is a small difficulty,' said Cealwin stoutly.

'There is one little difficulty more. Throughout the world there is only one huntsman who can hunt with this hound, and that is Mabon. He was taken from his mother when he was three years old, and no one knows where he is now, nor even if he is alive or dead.'

'This is not a great difficulty,' said Cealwin, 'and I will find him.'

'There is one little difficulty more. There is only one leash in the world with which Mabon the Huntsman can hold the whelp of the son of Eri, and that is a leash made from the live whiskers of Dillas Varvak, the greatest robber in the world. You will find it hard to steal even a whisker from him, for he knows all the crafts of thieving.'

'Is that all?' asked Cealwin proudly. 'You may think this is difficult, giant, but for me it will be easy.'

'No,' said the giant, 'there is one tiny difficulty more. It will not be possible to hunt the Twrch Trwyth to death without the help of the King of the Elves whom God has placed as guardian over the brood of devils in Annwen to stop them from destroying the race of humans. Elves call him Guiomar King, men call him Bran the Blessed and name Annwen Avalon. But, however you call him, he will never be spared from the Isle of Glass.'

Then Cealwin the Chieftain fell silent for a moment.

'Horses I will have, and chivalry; and my lord King Arthur will obtain for me all these things. I shall win your daughter, and you shall lose your life.'

Now when they came back to Camelot and told the King all that had happened, Arthur asked: 'Which of these marvels will it be best for us to seek first?'

'It will be best,' said Taliessen the wizard, 'to seek Mabon the Huntsman.'

Then King Arthur turned to his knights.

'Kay and Bedevere,' he said, 'I give you this quest.'

'Take my troll Gurr with you,' said Taliessen, 'for he can speak all languages, even those of the birds and the beasts.'

It was just as well they took Gurr with them, for without him they would not have even begun. Gurr guided them first to the ousels, then to the stags, then to the wise owls. None of them had ever heard of Mabon the Huntsman. But the most ancient of the owls, an owl so old that its wings were withered stumps, sent them to the Eagle of Ablek, the oldest animal in the world and the one that could see the furthest.

The Eagle of the Ablek scanned the Forest and the Sea and all the realms of the upper world, but not even his eagle eyes could pinpoint Mabon the Huntsman.

'Once,' he told Gurr, 'I went in search of food as far as

Loch Lure. There I struck my talons into a great salmon, thinking he would be my food for a long time. But he drew me down into the deep, and I was scarcely able to escape. So we made peace, his kindred and my kindred, the eagles and the salmons. The Great Salmon is the possessor of all the wisdom in the world. If he cannot help you, I cannot tell who will.'

So the Eagle of Ablek took them to the Great Salmon of Loch Lure. The Great Salmon listened to the tale of Gurr. Then he said:

'Fifty fish-spears this Mabon the Huntsman planted in my back, in the service of the Fisher King, so I do not love him. But fifty eagles pulled them out, so for love of the race of eagles I will help the men of Arthur. Let one of those knights stand on one of my shoulders and one on the other. What they will see they will see; and what they will hear they will hear.'

So Sir Kay stood upon one of the shoulders of the Great Salmon. But Gurr the Troll went upon the other shoulder, though he was no fighting man, because Sir Kay and the Great Salmon could not understand each other without him. They rode up the tide to the walls of a vast stone prison and heard a great wailing from inside.

'Who is it that cries so miserably in this house of stone?' called Sir Kay.

'It is I, Mabon the Huntsman,' a voice replied. 'No imprisonment was ever as grim as mine.' No wonder the Eagle of Ablek had not been able to see him: he was behind stone walls and under the water.

'Will they let you out for gold or silver?' shouted Sir Kay.

'No,' the voice shouted back, 'only by battle and fighting.'

So they returned to Arthur and told him where Mabon the Huntsman was imprisoned. Arthur brought his knights to attack the castle and, while they were attacking, Sir Kay and Sir Bedevere rode against the walls of the prison on the back of the great fish and broke them down. That was the way they found and rescued Mabon the Huntsman.

'Which of these marvels will it be best for us to seek now?' asked Arthur.

It would be long to tell how Arthur in his own ship trapped the son of Eri and obtained his whelp; how Sir Kay and Sir Bedevere made a leash to hold this hound from the whiskers of Dillas Varvak the greatest robber in the world by twitching them from his beard with wooden tweezers; or how Cealwin the Chieftain stole the wind-horse from the son of Aer. But at last Mabon the Huntsman was mounted on the wind-horse, and held the Eri hound on a leash made from the beard of Dillas Varvak. All was ready for the hunting of the Twrch Trwyth.

'Taliessen,' said Arthur, 'we have the huntsman, and we have the hound and the horse. But where is the Twrch Trwyth?'

'I am not sure,' said Taliessen.

'What do I have a wizard for,' cried the King impatiently, 'if he cannot answer a simple question? My Merlin would have known!'

'I said I was not sure,' said Taliessen icily. 'I did not say I could not find out. I will summon one of our Third Order, Mabinogion the Magician. He can fly in the form of a bird and see without being seen. This I will do for you, Arthur. I am sorry if I am not as good a wizard as Merlin. But he is of the First Order, and I am only of the Second. Besides, I prefer poetry to sorcery. So hunt the Twrch Trwyth as best as you can, for you will get no more help from me!'

Taliessen's eyes flashed like burning icicles. Arthur and all his knights stood abashed and afraid, for it was dangerous to anger wizards, even wizards of the Second Order. But then Taliessen swirled his great cloak around him and was gone, none knew where.

Sir Gawain bit his lip.

'Fair uncle,' he said, 'you know I do not like wizards, not even your Merlin. But it was wrong to treat this Taliessen with discourtesy. We will have much need of him in this adventure.'

But Sir Kay laughed Sir Gawain to scorn and declared that he and Sir Bedevere had followed the quest without a wizard so far, and would enchieve it easily.

'For what is the Twrch Trwyth after all? Bedevere and I have hunted and killed many monsters without a magician's help.'

Then Mabinogion the Magician took the form of a bird and flew to Ireland where he found the Twrch Trwyth. But when he flew back and changed his shape again, he was twitching and shaking, poisoned by the venom of one bristle of the Twrch Trwyth's back, and he was never the same again as long as he lived. At this Sir Kay stopped his bragging, and fell silent.

Then Arthur called to himself all the Warriors of the West, and set out for Ireland. In Ireland there was great fear and terror at his coming, for King Anguish had always dreaded the son of Uther Pendragon. So he sent all the saints of Ireland to beg Arthur for mercy. They met him when he landed. Arthur was filled with pity when he saw so many trembling saints, and granted Ireland his protection. So the saints all together shouted a great shout of Hallelujah! and joyfully gave the King their blessings one by one.

That was a good – though slow – beginning for the hunt. But what followed was not so good. The Irish led Arthur and the Warriors of the West to the bogs where the Twrch Trwyth lay with his seven sons. There they saw the monster for the first time. The Twrch Trwyth was a monstrous wild boar, as big as the Questing Beast, as black as a fighting bull, with small gleaming eyes, tusks as sharp and as long as pointed lances but ten times as strong; and his bristles were poisonous. As for his seven sons they were as big as buffaloes; the two fiercest and fastest were named Lug and Grotch.

Then the Irish let loose their dogs on the Twrch Trwyth from all sides. King Anguish's warriors fought with him till evening for seven days and seven nights without so much as killing one young hog. During that time the Twrch

Trwyth and his seven sons laid waste the fifth part of Ireland.

King Arthur in fear sent Gurr the Troll to the lair where the great boar lay with his seven young hogs. By the power of Mabinogion the Magician Gurr took the form of a bird and settled on a tree top above the lair. Then he called down to the Twrch Twyrth.

'Great Boar,' he said, 'Arthur the High King seeks a boon from you.'

But the Twrch Trwyth would not answer him. The only one who paid him any attention was the young hog Grotch, whose bristles glittered like silver wire.

'All we want this Arthur to do is to go away and leave us alone,' he said. 'We suffer enough from the Irish without you coming to hunt us as well.'

'Arthur will not hunt you if the Twrch Trwyth gives him a little thing. All he wants is the comb of ivory horn and the razor of ivory horn that lie between your sire's ears.'

'This king of yours will have to kill my sire first before he can take these precious things,' said Grotch.

'Then he will kill him, and all of you too.'

At this Grotch consulted with his sire the Great Boar.

'Tell Arthur the High King,' said Grotch, 'that the Twrch Trwyth defies him to do his worst; and for this insult we will cease ravaging Ireland and go into Arthur's country and there we will do all the damage we can.'

So the Twrch Trwyth and his seven sons swam across the Sea, and very swiftly they killed all the cattle and many of the men and beasts of the Mountains of the West before Arthur and the Warriors of the West had sailed back across the Sea in their ships.

When Arthur landed, he proclaimed the Hunt throughout the length and breadth of Logres. Sir Bedevere led out Cabal, the King's own hound. All the Warriors of the West ranged themselves around Glen Nyver. There the Great Boar made his first stand. He slew four of the Chieftains of the West. Then he made his second stand. He slew three more of the Chieftains of the West, but he himself was wounded.

Next morning some of Arthur's men came up with the Twrch Trwyth in his lair. But there he slew all the attendants of Asgard the Ancient, so that, heaven knows, the gatekeeper had only one attendant left to help him on the gate, a man called Erik the Churl, from whom nobody expected anything good. Then he and his seven sons came down from the mountains into the deep Forest, and there encountered Arthur's knights. At Castle Terrible he slew Sir Madoc and two other Knights of the Round Table. At Castle Perilous he made another stand, and slew Sir Guillaume of Gaule. Then he and his seven sons went as far as Glen Est, and there the men and dogs lost him.

Then all Arthur's household hunted the swine as far as the White Mountains of the land of Gore where Arthur himself first caught sight of him. So he set all his men and dogs on them. There at the Gates of Gore, in a great running fight that lasted three days and three nights, first two young hogs were killed, then with the help of the Raven Army three more. But the two fiercest and fastest of the Twrch Trwyth's sons closed on the King's huntsmen and killed them all with their dogs, so that only Sir Bedevere and Arthur's own hound Cabal escaped, and then only just.

Of the young hogs only Lug and Grotch went from that place of death alive. Lug parted from his sire and his brother, headed North, and slew Sir Peissac the King of Armorica and three knights who were uncles to King Arthur, being brothers of his mother, the beautiful Ygraine. There, by the waters of Loch Taw, Lug was killed himself in the end. But because of the deaths of so many noble knights there was terror throughout the whole realm of Logres. Men feared there would be many more deaths, for the Great Boar and his son Grotch were still rampaging side by side, slaying and pillaging and ravaging the realm.

Cealwin the Chieftain, whom men blamed for all this killing, remembered what the Giant Yspaddaden had told them.

'My lord King,' he said, 'we will never hunt the Twrch Trwyth to the death unless we have the help of the King of the Elves, the Ruler of Annwen, the Lord of the Glass Isle.'

Then King Arthur tore his beard in anguish because he knew he could never reach this realm that men called Avalon, not even in the best of his ships. There was only one person who could help him, now Merlin was gone; and that was his sister, Queen Morgan le Fay, for he knew she had visited Annwen, and men said Guiomar the Elf-King loved her, as Merlin had once done.

But King Arthur hated his sister because of the burning cloak she had sent as a treacherous wedding gift to Guinevere, and he had never seen her since he had tried to kill her in revenge.

All the same he sent a message to his sister, to beg her for help. They found her at her spell-defended fortress of Castle Chariot.

'So,' she said, smiling, 'does my little brother send me his pardon?'

'He does, Lady,' said the messenger, fearfully, for they knew Queen Morgan le Fay was a sorceress now, and sorceresses are most to be feared when they smile, as all the world knows.

'Tell Arthur,' said Morgan le Fay, 'that one day he shall sail with me to Avalon, and see all its wonders. Tell him too that I love him. But tell him that that day is not yet come. When it comes, the realm of Logres will be in greater danger than even the Twrch Trwyth could cause, for all the ravaging and the slaying.'

So the messengers went back to Camelot, and gave Arthur the message of Morgan le Fay. All the knights sat in silence, wondering at what she foretold, afraid of a great doom. It was Sir Kay who spoke up at last.

'My Lord,' he said, 'this quest for the ivory comb is a quest we shall never enchieve. It is not right for the sake of one damsel, even a damsel as beautiful as Olwen, to see the deaths of so many men, young and old alike, and the wasting of your realm. Let us halt the quest, and send Gurr the Troll to tell the Great Boar that he may leave our shores in peace and that we will hunt him and the one son left to him no more.'

'Kay, Kay,' said Sir Gawain, 'it was you who boasted that with Bedevere you could hunt and kill any monster living.'

'Kay was wrong,' said Sir Bedevere. 'I have only one arm left, and I nearly lost that when the Trwch Trwyth killed all Arthur's huntsmen except me. I would not want to be armless when that greatest danger comes to threaten Logres that the King's sister has foretold.'

'Yes,' said Sir Kay, 'I admit I am so proud and so hot-tempered that I am often wrong. Yet I was never afraid to ride into battle or challenge any knight or giant or monster, even though I have often been beaten and often nearly killed. But without Merlin's help we will never kill this Trwch Trwyth. Instead, he will empty every seat at the Round Table. Call off the Hunt, my lord Sir Arthur.'

'No,' said Sir Gawain, 'I never yet set out on an adventure that I did not enchieve. Nor did my fair uncle the King. Sire, you have forgotten one thing. Summon Mabon the Huntsman now, for with his help we may yet win the ivory comb and the razor.'

First the King summoned the whole assembly of the Knights of the Round Table, a hundred and fifty when all the seats were filled. But many seats were empty at this time because of the deaths the Trwch Trwyth had caused.

'The Great Boar and his son are heading for Cornwall,' he said. 'But if there is any valour left in the Round Table, for all their valour they shall not cross into Cornwall. I will stand against them, life for life, limb to limb. Do you as you will.'

Then Mabon led the Hunt, riding upon the wind-horse; and he unleashed the whelp of the son of Aer. They cornered the Trwch Trwyth and drove him into a great river, and there Arthur's own body-servant, Bloodaxe, seized hold of him by the feet and plunged him into the torrent so that it overwhelmed them both. On one side Mabon the Huntsman rode the wind-horse over the water and plucked the ivory comb. On the other side Arthur himself spurred his horse into the torrent, and there, struggling with the Trwch Trwyth, body to body, life for life, cut out the ivory razor from between his ears.

But the Great Boar shook King Arthur and his servant Bloodaxe off, and heaved himself out of the torrent. From the moment he reached the shore neither man nor hound nor horse could overtake him till he came to Cornwall. They could not stop him from ravaging all the land, but they hunted him out of Cornwall and drove him down into the deep Sea. From that day forward it was never known where he went; and his son the hog Grotch went with him.

Then King Arthur came back wearily to the Summer Country, to rest and heal his wounds with the ointment his sister so long ago had given him. But Cealwin the Chieftain, Sir Kay and Sir Bedevere, and all the other knights and warriors who now wished Yspaddaden ill, took the trophies with them to his castle. There Sir Kay shaved the giant grimly. First he shaved his beard off, then he shaved his skin off, then he shaved his flesh off, with the razor that King Arthur had cut from between the ears of the Trwch Trwyth.

'A cursed ungentle shaving is that,' groaned the giant, 'and I fear my beard will find it hard to grow again.'

'Are you shaved enough for your daughter's wedding?' asked Sir Kay.

'I am shaved,' said Yspaddaden sadly, for he knew that at his daughter's wedding he must lose his life.

'Then I will comb you as kindly,' mocked Sir Kay grimly.

He took the ivory comb that Mabon the Huntsman had

plucked, and pulled it through the giant's matted hair, so that Yspaddaden's neck was laid bare. Sir Bedevere who was standing by took his sword in his one hand, and with a great stroke cut off the giant's head.

'Are you combed enough for your daughter's wedding?' asked Sir Kay merrily. But at last Yspaddaden's tongue was silent.

And that is how Cealwin the Chieftain won Olwen the daughter of the giant Yspaddaden. He married her that very night.

HERE ENDS AN ADVENTURE OF KING ARTHUR;
AND ALSO OF SIR KAY AND SIR BEDEVERE
AND MANY OF HIS KNIGHTS; AND ALSO OF THE
GREAT BOAR, THE TWRCH TRWYTH, AND HIS SON
THE HOG GROTCH

CHAPTER 12

The Adventure of the Saint of Gaunes

WHENEVER he could, King Arthur rode out on quests for adventure, his arms and armour gleaming in the sun, and Excalibur flashing in his hand, a proud sight to see. But as he was the High King, his knights would not let him go alone. Two of them always went with him. And when he rode out into the rocky realm of Gaunes one winter the two who went with him were Sir Bedevere the One-Armed and Sir Lucan, his sword-companion.

Gaunes was a cold, bleak realm, especially in winter when the winds whistled over its plains and through the joints of the knights' armour. Arthur and his two companions rode in silence, too cold even to speak. Then Sir Lucan tapped the King's shoulder and pointed. Arthur looked up. Straight ahead of them rose a great mountain, like a pyramid in the desert. On its top was blazing an enormous fire.

'What is this mountain?' Sir Bedevere asked a man who was cowering in the fields.

'It is a holy mountain, Sir Knight,' said the man, 'and if you go up, you will go to Heaven and never come down again. Or else you will burn in that great fire and go to Hell. A great Saint guards the mountain top.

'Who is that Saint?' asked Sir Bedevere.

'Sant Michel,' said the man.

He meant Saint Michael.

'I never yet heard of a Saint that sent Christians to Hell as well as to Heaven,' said King Arthur merrily. 'I think I will go on a pilgrimage to Saint Sir Michael and see these marvels with my own eyes.'

So the three spurred their horses, and trotted together towards the foot of the mountain. When they came close to it, they found that they were trotting on sand, with the sea-water swirling round their horses' fetlocks. Seagulls cawed overhead, and night was falling.

At the foot of the mountain Arthur dismounted.

'Stay here,' he commanded, 'and guard the horses. For I will see this Saint and lord of this mountain alone.'

The King climbed up the crag. It was a hard haul in full armour. Near the top he found a woman wringing her hands, sitting by a new-made grave.

'Sir Knight,' she cried, 'what are you doing on this mountain? What use are your arms and your armour? Even if there were fifty of you, you would still be too feeble to match the Saint. He is the most fearsome Archangel alive. He will slit you from gizzard to navel like my dead man here.'

'This is the strangest Saint I ever heard of,' said King Arthur.

'Where do you come from, Sir Knight, that you have not heard of him?'

'I come from Arthur's Court.'

'Ah if you had brought Arthur's wife, the Lady Guinevere, the Saint would be happier than if you had given him half the kingdom of Heaven! He has been saving treasure for her, and he has more treasure than ever Arthur had, or any other king. One day, he says, he will descend from the mountain with flaming sword and drive Arthur and his knights down into Hell, as he once drove Sir Lucifer; and then he will take the beautiful Guinevere by force and live with her here on top of the mountain, with feasting and revelry, like God himself.'

'Indeed?' said Arthur grimly. 'This is a Saint I must meet.' And he went on his way.

'Have a care, Sir Knight,' cried the woman. 'The Saint is at his supper, with pepper and powder and many precious wines, and three fair damsels turning the spits, though they will be dead and in paradise within four hours. He does not like to be disturbed at his supper.'

Arthur paid no attention to her words. He climbed to the crest of the mountain and there saw the strangest sight that he had ever seen in his life. Three damsels were turning three spits over the flames of the fire. On the spits, being slowly roasted, were the bodies of twelve new-born babies. When he saw them, Arthur's heart was near breaking with sorrow. Standing by the fire warming his great breechless buttocks was the foulest being ever man saw. From head to foot he was twenty-five feet tall. He had teeth like wolves' teeth and he was gnawing the limb of a large man. There was never devil in Hell more horribly made.

'Hola! Archangel!' cried Arthur angrily. 'You are the foulest creature that was ever formed! You feed like a fiend! Why have you killed these Christian children? What will you do this night with these damsels, devil's son? Know that I am Arthur, Guinevere's husband, whom you so desire, spawn of Satan! For this and for your other sins you will die this day by the dint of my hands!'

The giant glowered and grunted. He dropped the limb he was gnawing, seized a club of clean iron, and swopped at the King with that mighty weapon. The blow crushed Arthur's coronet down to the cold earth. But the King had drawn Excalibur. It flamed and dazzled. He covered himself with his shield, and thrust the sword point up into the middle of the giant's forehead, right through to the brain. Then before the giant could raise his iron club and strike again, Arthur wounded him in the haunch and swopped his thighs asunder.

The giant brayed with pain and smote angrily at Arthur but he missed. His club cut a great swathe through the earth. Arthur slashed at him again, and cut his belly open so that blood and gore came pounding out and befouled the grass and the ground.

Then the giant gave a great bellow, threw his club away, leapt upon Arthur and caught him in his mighty arms. Never was the King in greater danger! His ribs were crushed, he dropped Excalibur. The three maidens called Christ to help — and perhaps even God himself heard their prayer. But the giant bore Arthur backwards, and so they tumbled all down the mountainside, locked in each other's arms, weltering and wallowing, rolling over crags and bushes, now one on top, now the other. But as they rolled, Arthur managed to draw his dagger Cern and he plunged it again and again up to the hilt in the giant's body, till at long last they tumbled to the foot of the mountain with a great fall and a great groaning from the giant, for that fall broke three of his ribs at once.

So Sir Lucan and Sir Bedevere galloped up and found them both lying there in each other's death clasp with the sea-water swirling round their broken bodies.

'Alas,' cried Sir Lucan in his grief, 'we are lost for ever! There is our Lord the King overthrown by a fiend!'

But then Arthur stirred, and slowly rose to his feet.

'Help me, Sir Lucan,' he said. 'I have brought this holy saint down from the mountain top.' He kicked at the giant's body but it did not move.

'It is a holy relic now, my lord,' joked Sir Lucan, dragging the body out of the sea-water.

'Saint Michael,' said Sir Bedevere to the body as he helped, 'it is a wonder God ever let you stay in Heaven! If all ye saints and archangels be like this, by the faith of my body I will forget to say my prayers. For I would rather go to Hell!'

'Sir Bedevere,' said King Arthur, 'leave the joking and leave the dragging. As to the joking, I was never so near death. As to the dragging, you have only one arm, and it is too much for you. So leave this giant's body to the waves, but draw your sword, and strike off his head. Then set it on a spear and ride with it to the King of this realm, King Bors of Gaunes, Sir Lancelot's uncle, and tell him that I have killed this fiend. As for you, Sir Lucan, climb to the mountain top and fetch me Excalibur and this giant's club of iron. Set free the three maidens, and if you find treasure bring it with you. For the Saint meant it for Guinevere, and by the Saint's bones Guinevere shall have it.'

'No wonder men call you Sir Lucan the Lucky,' grumbled Sir Bedevere, as he fixed the giant's head to the top of his lance. 'I carry great ugly fiends' heads round the country, while you have the treasure and the damsels.'

'What shall we do for the wretched people of the country, Sire?' asked Sir Lucan.

'We will tell them the false Saint Michael was a devil's spawn and is rightly gone back to Hell,' decided King Arthur, 'and we will build for them a great church on the top of the mountain in honour of the true Saint Michael, the Archangel, and there we will bury with great honour the bodies of the twelve poor babies that this fiend was going to devour and pray for them to God's Twelve Apostles.'

So it was done. Ever after the people of Gaunes called that place in their language the mountain of Sant Michel.

HERE ENDS AN ADVENTURE OF KING ARTHUR;
AND ALSO OF SIR LUCAN AND SIR BEDEVERE

BOOK THREE

The Book of Doom

Prologue

Doom comes to all mortal men. It came in the end to King Arthur and Queen Guinevere and to the whole fellowship of the Round Table.

But, first, doom struck a warning blow. Evil enchantments befell the whole realm of Logres and the Seven Kingdoms. The land was laid waste; knights and men killed each other treacherously, even the Knights of the Round Table.

Sir Balin and Sir Balan were the first to die. Though they were twin brothers they killed each other by mischance. Men became half-mad. Sir Lancelot himself lost his wits and lived like a wild beast in the woods. Sir Yvain the gold-green knight quarrelled with his uncle King Arthur and set his

Raven Army at the Knights of the Round Table, to their great despite. Worse still, Queen Morgawse of the Orkeneys, King Arthur's eldest sister, was killed by her own son Sir Gaheris in the sea-girt fortress of Rethenam. King Pellinore was killed too – sadly he never caught the Questing Beast. Then his two sons were killed: Sir Tor and the noble knight Sir Lamorak de Galys. They were killed, like their father, by Sir Gawain and his brethren. They were all killed treacherously.

But Merlin came back to Camelot; and he saved the realm from doom. At his urging the Knights of the Round Table set out on the greatest of all their quests, the Quest of the Grail. Many lost their lives on that Quest; but they lost their lives nobly. They were united in the Quest; there was an end to feuds and killings; and King Arthur's heart was glad again.

When the Quest of the Grail was at last enchieved, the knights – or at least those that had survived, like Sir Gawain and his kin and Sir Lancelot and those of his blood – rode wearily back to Camelot.

'The evil enchantments are over,' said Merlin. 'The land is healed.'

He was standing on the topmost tower of Camelot, side by side with Arthur, gazing at the knights as they came straggling in. The scent of many flowers lay thick and heavy in the still air. But for all that Merlin did not look happy.

'Why so melancholy, old friend?' asked Arthur merrily.

'Old?' said Merlin impatiently. 'I was old already in the days of Middle Earth! What do you know, King of this little time, of the spreading menace of those dark days?' Then he fell musing. 'Yet even at that time there were humans, as proud, as brave and as foolish as you and your knights. They called themselves the Riders.'

'If these Riders had you to guide them, old friend,' said Arthur affectionately, 'then men of those ancient times must have blessed the name of Merlin.'

'I was not known as Merlin in those days,' said the wizard,

'but by another name.' He laughed harshly. 'Then, as now, the wheel of destiny turns. Wizards can see the turning, yet they cannot halt the wheel. So it has been, so it will always be.'

Merlin fell silent. Then he put his hand on Arthur's shoulder, as he had not done since Arthur was a boy in the Fenland. 'Your own Day of Destiny approaches,' he said.

Arthur felt cold at heart. For now he knew why the wizard had been talking of the wheel of destiny which carries mortal men up to the highest point and then dashes them down to ruin. But he did not show his fear, even to Merlin.

'I am a King,' he said proudly, 'and kings, unlike wizards, must all die some day. I accept my destiny.'

'Yet it grieves me,' muttered Merlin, paying no attention, 'that the shadow of Mordor looms once more over earth, even in these, the Later Ages. Much can it yet destroy.'

'Mordor?' asked Arthur sharply.

'Mordor the Dread,' mumbled the wizard. For a moment he seemed to shrink and shrivel. But then he stood upright and grew tall and menacing again.

'King,' he said, 'it may yet be given me to save you and this most noble Fellowship of the realm of Logres for the Last Age of earth. I must leave you at once. There is much that I must contrive, in many places, and many webs must I weave.'

'When shall I see you again?' asked Arthur anxiously. He could tell – he had seen it so often – that Merlin was about to swirl his great cloak around him and disappear.

'In the elfin kingdom,' said Merlin, 'if all goes well. There Nudd the Dwarf forged your sword Excalibur in the deep pits. There Nimiane the elf-queen once knew peace, and may yet know it again. There your own sister Morgan le Fay has been for the love of Guiomar the Elf-King. There, Arthur, if Wyrd decrees, I will see you again, you who have been like a son to me. For wizards can have no sons of their own, which is great pity.'

'I too have no sons,' said Arthur, 'which is also great pity for me. But the sons of my fair sister Queen Morgawse have been like sons to me, and especially ruddy-bearded Gawain who shall inherit this realm when I am gone.'

'Alas,' said Merlin.

Arthur looked at him pleadingly. 'Or if Gawain should not,' he went on, 'then one of her other sons. There are so many. Sir Gaheris or Sir Agravaine or Sir Gareth or Sir Mordred. They are all my dear nephews, even Sir Gaheris who slew my own sister in his madness.'

'Arthur,' said Merlin even more sadly, 'do you know what your greatest good fortune is? It is that you are only a mortal man and cannot foresee what will come to pass. Were you a wizard, your heart would be full of foreboding!'

These were the last words Arthur ever heard from Merlin in Camelot. The wizard swirled his great cloak around him and disappeared, leaving the King to face the dark future alone.

CHAPTER I

The Great Tournament

IT was the lusty month of May when men and women rejoice and are glad at the coming of summer, and every heart buds and flourishes with lusty deeds.

'Now that my knights are back from the Quest of the Grail, those that are left alive, I will proclaim a Great Tournament. For in all these past seven years I never have seen such a noble fellowship together.'

So King Arthur proclaimed a Great Tournament. From all over the Seven Kingdoms, knights came riding into Camelot, eager to win glory and to fill the empty seats at the Round Table. Sir Lancelot was staying at a castle that belonged to an old knight, the Castle of Astolat, but this old knight did not know who his guest was. 'Fair sir,' said Sir

Lancelot to his host, 'I would go to this Great Tournament. But I pray you to lend me a shield that is not known, for my own shield is too well known.'

'Sir,' said his host, 'you shall have whatever you want, for you are one of the finest knights that I ever saw, and I will do all I can to show you my friendship.'

Now the old knight had a young daughter who grew hot with love for Sir Lancelot.

'Almighty God preserve you wherever you ride,' she said to him, 'for you are the most courteous knight I have ever met, and the kindest to ladies and damsels. But one thing, Sir Knight, is wrong: you seem to be a knight wifeless.'

'Fair damsel,' said Sir Lancelot, 'I am a knight errant, and I do not ever want to be a wedded man. For, if I marry a fair damsel, then I would have to couch with her and give up arms and tournaments, battles and adventures. And that I will never do.'

Now the girl turned pale, for she was so very beautiful and hot with love that she had hoped Sir Lancelot would make her his wife. But now she saw that he would always prefer battles and adventures. She begged Sir Lancelot at least to wear in the joust a token for her sake.

'Fair maiden,' said Sir Lancelot, 'I never wore any token in any tournament for the love of any lady.'

But then he remembered that he was going to the Great Tournament disguised, with a shield that was not his own; and he thought that if he wore a lady's token, he who had never worn a lady's token before, nobody would ever believe that the unknown knight could be Sir Lancelot.

'For you,' he said gravely, 'I will wear a token on my helm.'

So she thanked him with great joy, and brought him her token. It was a red scarf, of scarlet cloth, embroidered with great pearls. Sir Lancelot fastened it to his helm, left his shield in her keeping, took leave of her father, and rode out to the Great Tournament.

There had been many famous tournaments before in King Arthur's time, but there was never a tournament to equal the Great Tournament at Camelot. King Anguish of Ireland brought with him a hundred good knights to joust, and King Royance brought as many. Sir Galehalt the Haute Prince brought fifty good knights, so did Duke Chalaunce of Claraunce. When the trumpets blew into the field, King Arthur himself rode into the field with two hundred knights, of whom most were Knights of the Round Table.

Then a great melée began. Sir Palomides, who was of Arthur's party, encountered Sir Galehalt, and each smote the other down, but their companions helped them up into the saddle again. King Royance smote down King Anguish of Ireland. At this King Arthur's blood boiled: he ran at the King Royance and smote him down, horse and man, and after this with the same spear he smote down three other knights till his spear broke. Then Sir Gawain and Sir Gaheris, Sir Agravaine and Sir Mordred rode in; each of them smote down a knight, and Sir Gawain smote down four knights. Then a great turmoil began, for the knights of Sir Lancelot's blood rode into the field, and Sir Gareth with them. They began to hold so hard against the three kings and the mighty duke that all their knights fell back.

Then Sir Lancelot rode in at the thickest of the press, and there he smote down Sir Sagremor the Desirous, Sir Grifflet le Fiz Dieu, Sir Kay, and Sir Bedevere, all with one spear. Then he took another great spear and smote down Sir Agravaine and Sir Gaheris, and also Sir Mordred. Then he encountered Sir Palomides, and there Sir Palomides had a fall. And so Sir Lancelot, without a pause, smote down thirty knights; most of them were Knights of the Round Table.

'Jesu mercy!' cried King Arthur as he saw all his best knights smote down. 'What knight is this that does such marvellous deeds in the field?'

'Sire,' said Sir Gawain, 'I would say it was Sir Lancelot by his riding and by the buffets I see him give. Yet it cannot be Sir

Lancelot, for he wears a red scarf on his helm, and I never yet knew Sir Lancelot at any joust or tournament wear the token of any lady.'

Then Sir Bors, Sir Ector de Marys, and Sir Lionel called together all the knights of Sir Lancelot's blood, like Sir Blamour de Ganys and Sir Bleoberis and four more, all noble knights, and thrust in grimly, hurling together and smiting down many knights. When Sir Lancelot saw his kin do this, he took a great spear in his hands; at this Sir Bors and Sir Lionel and Sir Ector all rode down on him at once, and smote him so mightily that they threw Sir Lancelot's horse backwards onto the earth. By mischance Sir Bors smote Sir Lancelot through the shield into the side. The spear broke, but its point stayed in Sir Lancelot's side.

Sir Gareth had encountered Sir Palomides, and gave him such a buffet that both he and his horse were dashed to earth. When Sir Gareth saw the Knight of the Red Scarf lying there, he was full of pity. He brought Sir Lancelot's horse back and helped him to mount again. Then Sir Lancelot took a spear in his hands, and smote Sir Bors, horse and man, to the earth, and he smote Sir Lionel, horse and man, to the earth, and his own brother Sir Ector de Marys too. They all three horsed themselves again, and came in; all three smote with their swords upon Sir Lancelot's helmet. Then Sir Lancelot drew his own sword, for he felt himself so badly wounded that he feared he would meet his death, and gave Sir Bors such a buffet that he made him bow his head low; and then he raced off his helm and could have killed him. But when he saw his face, his heart would not let him do it. So he left him there, and in the same manner he treated Sir Lionel and Sir Ector.

Then he hurtled into the thickest press of all, and there did the most marvellous deeds of arms that ever men saw.

'Jesu mercy!' cried King Arthur again. 'Who is this Knight of the Red Scarf?'

'I will assay him,' said Sir Gawain grimly.

Then Sir Gawain took a great spear in his hands, and rode

into the thick of the press and first he encountered his own brother Sir Gareth and smote him down, horse and man, to the earth. Then he encountered Sir Lancelot. But Sir Lancelot gave Sir Gawain such a buffet that the saddle-bow of his saddle broke, and Sir Gawain went hurtling down to the earth and lay there for a long while, stunned, so that King Arthur feared that his neck was broken. Then Sir Lancelot hurtled here and there, smiting with spear and racing off helms, and there was none who could stand against him.

It was near evening, so they blew to lodgings. King Arthur sent to the two kings, and the mighty duke, and the Haute Prince and prayed them that they should not allow the Knight of the Red Scarf to leave, for he thought he might be of their fellowship. But when they had all unarmed and washed and came to dinner, each said that they did not know who the Knight of the Red Scarf was.

King Arthur turned to his nephew Sir Gareth.

'Well, fair nephew,' he said, 'I saw you help this knight to mount again, and I think that you are the only knight he did not encounter or throw to earth, so you will tell us who he is. For you have both done marvellous deeds of arms this day. You, fair nephew, have unhorsed thirty-five knights, but he has unhorsed more than fifty knights, and so he must have the prize.'

But Sir Gareth said that he did not know who the Knight of the Red Scarf was. He had only helped him to remount out of pity and courtesy.

'For this,' said King Arthur, 'all the days of my life I shall love you the better and trust you more, Gareth. A worshipful knight should always help another worshipful knight when he sees him in danger, as you did this day. As for this knight, I have no doubt he will come tomorrow to the second day of the Great Tournament, and then we will speak with him and give him the prize he has so richly won.'

But Sir Lancelot did not come back the next day. He was so badly wounded that when he left the Great Tournament he rode, groaning, to a hermitage in the deep Forest. When the hermit drew the head of Sir Bors' spear out of his side, the blood came bursting out, nearly a pint all at once, so that even Sir Lancelot shrieked and swooned.

The Great Tournament was over. Sir Gawain rode out and came by chance to the Castle of Astolat. The old knight and his daughter asked him who had done best at the Tournament.

'God help me,' said Sir Gawain, 'a knight with a plain white shield, who wore a red scarf upon his helmet. He was certainly the best knight I ever saw joust in a tournament. For I dare say that one knight smote down fifty Knights of the Round Table, myself included. He left me all stunned on the ground.'

'Now blessed be God!' cried the girl.

'That is a discourteous prayer, fair maiden,' said Sir Gawain, smiling, 'that you should bless God because I was left stunned upon the ground.'

The young girl blushed.

'It was not for your mischance, Sir Gawain,' she said, 'for all ladies know you are a mighty knight of prowess, and I am sure you had a fall only by mischance.'

'You have a fair tongue, fair maiden,' said Sir Gawain, smiling even more, 'and you are so very beautiful and look so hot with love that I hope you may be my paramour.'

The girl blushed even more.

'There is one man in the world I loved first,' she said, 'and truly he will be the last that I will ever love.'

Sir Gawain laughed gaily.

'Those are the sweetest words any damsel has ever said to me!'

'Oh, but it is not you, Sir Gawain,' she cried hastily, 'it is the knight who threw you down. The knight who, you told me, did best in the Great Tournament. That was why I blessed God.'

At first Sir Gawain scowled. But when he saw the girl looked a little frightened, he smiled again.

'Well, well,' he said, 'then that knight must be the luckiest knight in the world to have so beautiful a damsel as you so hot with love for him.' Then he thought for a moment.

'If you love him so much, beautiful maiden, you must know his name. For he rode away from the Tournament without claiming his prize and no one knew his name.'

'Truly, Sir Gawain, I do not know his name nor where he came from. But he will come back here, for he has left me his shield.'

'Why did he do that?' asked Sir Gawain.

'Because his shield is so well known among many noble knights.'

Then Sir Gawain persuaded her to show him the shield the knight had left behind, and he knew at once it was Sir Lancelot's.

At that Sir Gawain was regretful for what he had said to the girl.

'For God's sake,' he said, 'please do not be angry with me for what I said. It is true that of all the damsels in the world you are the one I wish most of all would love me deeply. But I would never have asked for your love if I had known it was this knight you have the heart to love. He is a better knight than I am, nobler, more handsome and more charming. There is no maiden anywhere, however truly she might love, who would not be right in leaving me for him.'

'As for love,' said the girl, 'I promise God and you I love him. And I think he loves me too, because for love of me he wore my token of the red scarf.'

'That amazes me,' said Sir Gawain. 'I have known that noble knight for four and twenty years, and never till that day did I or any other knight see or hear that he had ever worn a token for any lady or damsel at any joust or tournament, not even for the Queen.'

Then the maiden of Astolat trembled.

'Tell me,' she cried, 'tell me, Sir Gawain, who this knight is.'

'I will tell you,' said Sir Gawain. 'It is the most noble knight Sir Lancelot du Lac.'

At that she burst into tears.

'Why are you weeping,' asked Sir Gawain, amazed, 'when I tell you that the knight you love is the finest knight in the world?'

'Because,' sobbed the damsel, 'it is said that Queen Guinevere loves him and she has enchanted him so that he may never love any other damsel or lady, only her.'

'Well,' said Sir Gawain, 'that is as it may be. But I will tell you this. He is not now at Camelot at the Queen's side, and no man knows where he is — if he is still alive. For at the Great Tournament he had a fearful wound in the side from Sir Bors' spear.'

Then the maiden of Astolat wept all the more, for fear that Sir Lancelot might be dead.

Sir Gawain rode back to Camelot, and told King Arthur who the Knight of the Red Scarf was.

'By my head, uncle,' said Sir Gawain, 'the maiden of Astolat loves him so marvellously well that she even rejected me. What it means I cannot say.'

When Queen Guinevere heard that it was Sir Lancelot who had worn the token of another beauty, she nearly went out of her mind with jealousy. And when Sir Lancelot had been healed of his wound and rode back, still feeble, to Camelot, she spoke to him as she had never before.

'Sir Lancelot,' she said bitterly, 'now I can see that you are a false recreant knight and a common lecher. You love and uphold other ladies, but for me you have only disdain and scorn. Know this well, that now I know your falsehood, I will never love you any more. I forbid you to be with me! You shall never see me again!'

Then she sobbed and wept with fury, and would not listen to what Sir Lancelot had to say but thrust him out of her chamber.

Sir Lancelot departed in great sorrow. He called his cousins, Sir Bors and Sir Lionel, and his brother Sir Ector de Marys, and told them that the Queen had sent him away and that now he would go to his own country.

'You were the Knight of the Red Scarf then?' asked Sir Ector, who was rather slow-witted and needed time to think things out. Sir Lancelot admitted it. 'Then in God's name, brother,' said Sir Ector indignantly, 'you made me feel the hard ground when I had no need of it!'

Sir Lancelot only laughed. But Sir Bors sternly told Sir Ector to be quiet, because a fall in a tournament was not important. What was important was the Queen's anger; and her command to Sir Lancelot to go away.

'Fair cousin,' said Sir Bors, 'do not leave this country. Women in their hastiness often say things they are sorry for afterwards. I suggest that you go to the Castle of Astolat, for you are not yet cured of the great wound I gave you by mischance, and the maiden there is very beautiful. She will look after you lovingly till we can send you better news.'

Sir Lancelot took Sir Bors' advice. He rode away to Astolat where the young girl was overjoyed to see him, and gave him great cheer.

'I wish to God,' said Sir Bors to Sir Lionel and Sir Ector, 'that Sir Lancelot could love her, though as to that we neither may nor dare advise him.'

Only the three of them and no other creature knew what had become of Sir Lancelot.

CHAPTER 2

The King at Castle Chariot

WHEN King Arthur learnt that Queen Guinevere had sent Sir Lancelot away, he reproached her bitterly.

'My Lady,' he said, 'you have always been a good wife to me and never acted foolishly up till now. I have never regretted marrying you, though Merlin did tell me that he could find me many other princesses to marry, as beautiful or even more beautiful than you, and warned me that you were not wholesome for me. I did not know what he meant then, but now I think I know and I am very angry.'

Guinevere trembled then, for she was not used to Arthur being angry with her. She had never been very brave.

'But now,' said King Arthur sternly, 'you have sent away, disgracefully, the most worshipful of all my knights, and the one who had always promised service and proved love to you. I mean Sir Lancelot du Lac. Heaven knows where he is now: men say he has gone to his father's lands in Benwick.'

'Ah my Lord,' said Guinevere, 'I thought you might be angry with me because I love Sir Lancelot so much. But I swear to you I have always loved you more. You ought to be glad that I have sent Sir Lancelot away. That shows how much more I love you.'

King Arthur thought this was a very foolish thing to say, and he remembered that his sister Morgan le Fay had once called Guinevere a foolish, empty-headed girl. But he knew it was no use arguing with Guinevere, and he was too courteous to show her how angry he really was. Besides, he loved her very much. He simply asked her whether she would like to see Sir Lancelot back at Camelot.

'No,' said Guinevere angrily. 'Some damsel has snared him with a magic potion or spell. I never want anything to do with him again.'

King Arthur thought this was an even more foolish thing to say. But all he did was explain courteously to Guinevere that, whatever she wanted, he wanted Sir Lancelot back because Sir Lancelot was the flower of knighthood, the greatest honour to the Round Table, and the finest knight in the world. 'I will set out on a quest myself,' said Arthur, 'and bring Sir Lancelot back, even if it means riding as far as Benwick.'

So King Arthur set out through the Forest, and rode for many days and nights, till one day he and his companions completely lost their way. It was growing dark.

'What shall we do?' said Arthur.

'My Lord,' said his companions, 'as far as we know there are no castles in this part of the Forest. We had better set up our tents here for the night.'

So they did; but as they were putting up the tents, a horn sounded nearby: it was blown twice.

'There must be people near here,' said the King. 'Go and see who they are.'

So Sir Sagremor the Desirous, who bore the King's standard, mounted and rode towards the sound of the horn. When he came back an hour later, he told the King that he had found a fine strong castle, enclosed with a high wall, that belonged to a lady; and that when the lady had learnt King Arthur was nearby, she had invited him to spend the night there. So they took down their tents, mounted, and followed Sir Sagremor. They found that the castle was beautiful, delightful, rich and splendidly kept. There was no wall that was not covered in silk hangings, and so many candles that they gave out a more intense light than Arthur or his companions had ever seen in their lives before.

As soon as the King had washed his hands, the tables were set and all his companions were asked to sit down – or at least those that were knights. The handmaidens began to bring food, as if they had known long beforehand that the King was coming. The tables were so plentifully adorned with rich dishes of gold and silver that the King could not have been more richly served in his own castle of Camelot. When they had eaten their fill, fair music filled the room. It was as if all the different musical instruments they had ever heard in their life were playing. They all sounded together so sweetly that Arthur had never heard music that was so gentle and pleasant to his ear. When the music faded away, two beautiful damsels came in carrying two large burning candles in golden candlesticks.

'My Lord,' they said, 'if it pleases you, it is now time for you to rest. It is very late at night, and you have ridden so far we think you must be very tired.'

'I would like to be in bed already,' replied Arthur, 'because I am so very sleepy.'

'My Lord,' said the damsels, 'we have come to accompany

you to your bed because the Lady of the Castle so commands it.'

'Certainly,' replied the King.

He followed the damsels to a large and beautiful chamber. As soon as he lay down, he fell asleep.

Next morning the sun rose splendid and bright, and its light penetrated all the King's chamber. Arthur woke up, rubbed his eyes, washed and dressed. Then he looked around the chamber. It was very beautiful, and richly painted. At first he did not look very closely at the paintings; but then he saw that all the walls were painted, and that they told the story of the adventures of a knight.

'Jesu mercy!' said Arthur to himself, 'this knight is Sir Lancelot, and there are all his adventures painted here! Here he is jousting with Sir Caradoc of the Dolorous Tower. Here Sir Tarquin is riding with Gawain slung over his saddle-bow. Here he slays Sir Tarquin. Here he rescues Sir Kay and all the other prisoners from Dolorous Garde. Here I am coming to Joyous Garde, where at first his men stopped me at the river and would not let me go in.' Then he laughed. 'Here he is in his shirt-tails at the top of an elm-tree, going after a hawk. Yet he was always a bad climber.'

'But there is one adventure he never painted here,' said a lady's voice behind Arthur, 'and that is the adventure of the apple tree.'

King Arthur turned around swiftly. There was a lady standing there, in beautiful rich clothes, with golden hair and green glittering eyes. Arthur realized she must be the Lady of the Castle.

'Yes,' she said, 'Sir Lancelot du Lac painted all these paintings with his own hand.'

'Fair Lady,' said King Arthur uncertainly, 'he never told us of this. When was he here, that he had the time to paint all these adventures?'

'Many years ago,' said the Lady of the Castle, 'I kept him prisoner here for a summer and a winter, and during those months he had much time for painting because he could not go out. He never told you, my Lord King, nor any of his companions or kin because he was ashamed of having been made captive by a woman. I trapped him while he was asleep, under an apple tree.'

'This is a strange tale, Lady,' said King Arthur very puzzled. 'But is Sir Lancelot by any chance here now? For I am on a quest to find him.'

The Lady of the Castle shook her head.

'No, Arthur,' she said. The King was amazed that she dared call him by his Christian name alone without any title of honour. 'You will not find Sir Lancelot here. But you will find the woman who loves you more than any other woman in the world.'

'Is my queen, Guinevere, here then?'

The eyes of the Lady of the Castle glittered.

'I can tell you, Arthur,' she said, 'there is no woman that loves you more than I do, and so I should unless human love does not exist.'

King Arthur was more and more puzzled.

'My Lady,' he said, 'who are you that love me as much as you say?'

'My Lord,' she said mockingly, 'you ought to know me better than you do. I am the person closest to you in blood in the whole world.'

'Morgan!' cried Arthur, and his hand leapt to his sword Excalibur. He recognized his sister then, though so many years had passed since he had last seen her; and at that time he had been trying to hurt her to the death.

Queen Morgan le Fay stood her ground without flinching.

'Put Excalibur back in its sheath, little brother,' she said. 'Next time you draw it, it will be for a greater need and in a greater quarrel; and that will be on your Day of Destiny. Then, I can assure you, you will be glad that I love you still.'

'I thought that you had left this world and were dead,' said Arthur uncertainly.

Brother and sister stood looking at each other in silence for a long time. The years rolled away, and they remembered how they had lain side by side joyfully in the green glades of Gore, and how they had feasted and laughed together at that time. Those had been joyful times, before Arthur had married Guinevere. Then both sadly remembered their eldest sister Morgawse, the dark Queen of the Orkeneys, who had been slain by her own son Sir Gaheris. Morgan le Fay did not tell King Arthur how nearly she had once come to being slain by her own son too, the noble Sir Yvain. But Arthur talked much of Sir Yvain, the gold-green nephew he had so loved.

'He stays beyond the Gates of Gore and comes no more to Camelot,' he said sadly. 'He loves his Ravens more than the Round Table.'

'Yet if Merlin's plans go right, brother,' said Morgan le Fay, 'Yvain and the Raven Army will be of greater service to the realm of Logres on the Day of Destiny than the Round Table itself.'

'What do you know of all this, sister?' asked Arthur uncertainly. 'What do you know of this Day of Destiny and Merlin's plans? Has Merlin been here?'

But all Morgan le Fay would tell him was that Merlin had passed by, and that there were many secret schemes afoot to match the menace of the Dark Shadow; but what they were she would not or could not tell him. Then she took Arthur by the hand, and he forgot all his past anger as they took pleasure in talking together, just the two of them. They asked each other many questions about their past lives. Morgan le Fay told Arthur a part, and kept a part secret from him.

'I shall take you back to Camelot when I leave here,' said the King joyously.

'Brother,' said Morgan le Fay, 'I swear to you that I shall never go to Camelot. When I leave here I shall most certainly go to Avalon, which is the homing-place of all the magic in the world.'

'I was forgetting,' said King Arthur, 'for when I leave here in any case I cannot go directly back to Camelot. First I must find Sir Lancelot, wherever he is, and bring him back with me, for without Sir Lancelot my Round Table is bereft.'

'Brother,' said Morgan le Fay, 'before you go on with your quest for that knight, there is something else I must show you. For while Sir Lancelot stayed here as my prisoner he painted this chamber with the paintings of all his knightly deeds. But there is another smaller chamber that he slept in, and he painted the walls of that chamber also. Would you like to see those paintings too?'

The King joyfully said that he would. Then Morgan le Fay led him by the hand to the chamber where Sir Lancelot had slept. There the walls of the chamber were covered with golden apples painted very large; and inside each apple was a scene of love between Lancelot and Guinevere.

The King's brow grew dark as he examined all the paintings set inside the apples, one by one; and there were twenty-four apples.

'In God's name, sister,' he said, 'tell me if these paintings show the truth.'

'I will tell you what I know without lying about anything,' said Queen Morgan le Fay. 'It is true that Lancelot loved Queen Guinevere since the first day that he received the order of knighthood, and she with her own hands girded him with the Sword of Brightness. He has loved the Queen as much as any mortal man can ever love a lady, but at first he never revealed the fact to himself or through anyone else. His love spurned him on to perform all the deeds of chivalry he painted in the great chamber.'

But then, Morgan le Fay explained, because Sir Lancelot was wasting away for love and he would not eat or drink, Sir Galehalt the Haute Prince kept pressing him; until in the end he admitted that he loved the Queen and was dying of love for her. Then the Haute Prince had gone to Guinevere and implored her until she gave in and, with a kiss, had granted Sir Lancelot her love.

'You could have known this at the Castle of Joyous Garde,' said Morgan le Fay, 'when you first went there and could not enter because you were stopped by Sir Lancelot's men at the River. Then Guinevere escaped without you knowing. But now you do know and if you do not punish them, God and the whole world will hold you in shame. No true king or true man can tolerate being dishonoured in this way.'

The King and his sister spoke a great deal more about this matter. The King made Morgan le Fay promise to let no one enter the chamber where Sir Lancelot had slept, because he feared the story would spread and would dishonour him too much. He did not promise he would punish Lancelot or Guinevere. But his love for them both was half-destroyed, and never again did he fully trust them. He gave up his quest for Sir Lancelot and stayed with his sister instead, in her great fortress of Castle Chariot. The place was so beautiful and pleasant, and the woods were full of game which he spent all his energy hunting. Arthur was very happy there; which was just as well, for after he left there he was never happy again in this life.

CHAPTER 3

The Poisoned Apple

G UINEVERE was sad at heart. First Sir Lancelot had gone, then King Arthur had gone, and no one knew when either of them would return to Camelot. She hoped with all her heart that Arthur would bring Lancelot back from Benwick despite the harsh words she had uttered; for she wanted to see Lancelot again very badly. She also wanted to see Arthur back for he was her king and her lord. She loved them both. She had no idea that Sir Lancelot was staying at the Castle of Astolat with the old knight's daughter, or that Arthur was staying at Castle Chariot with Morgan le Fay. If she had known she would have been furious with both of them; for she was jealous of the great beauty of the maiden of Astolat and fearful of the great powers of Morgan le Fay. But she did not know, and so she was only sad.

Yet a queen must never let the knights of her court see that she is sad. So outwardly she seemed merry and cheerful, hiding her inner feelings. To show that she did not miss Sir Lancelot, and loved the other knights just as much, she held a splendid dinner for twenty-four Knights of the Round Table. She invited Sir Gawain and his brothers, that is to say, Sir Agravaine and Sir Gaheris, Sir Gareth, and Sir Mordred; also Sir Bors, Sir Lionel, Sir Ector de Marys, Sir Blamour and Sir Bleoberis de Ganys, Sir Hud, Sir Eliodyn, Sir Palomides the Saracen and his brother Sir Saphir, Sir Kay the Seneschal, Sir Bedevere the One-Armed, Sir Persaunt, Sir Ironside, Sir Brundelis, Sir Mador de la Porte and his kinsman Sir Patrice of Ireland, Sir Alyduke, Sir Ascamor, and Sir Pinel le Sauvage — who was a cousin of Sir Lamorak de Galys, King Pellinore's son, the good knight whom Sir Gawain and his brothers had slain treacherously.

Anyone who gave a great feast at Camelot and invited Sir Gawain always made sure there was plenty of fine fruit at the feast. For Sir Gawain loved all manner of fruit, especially pears and apples. So Queen Guinevere, to please Sir Gawain, made sure there were plenty of delicious apples with red skins, which he loved best of all.

It was a marvellous feast. All the knights enjoyed themselves and praised Guinevere for her kindness and for her beauty. This pleased her very much, especially as she was the only lady there. Sir Patrice, the knight of Ireland, had had too much wine, for the knights of Ireland often drank too much wine by mischance.

'I will take an apple,' he joked, 'before Gawain eats them all!'

Sir Pinel le Sauvage tried to stop him, for it was not yet time to eat the fruit.

'Leave go my arm, Sir Pinel,' shouted Sir Patrice, 'for an apple I will have!'

He picked out the reddest of them all, waved it under Sir Gawain's nose to tease him, and then munched it. All the other knights laughed at Sir Patrice's joke and Sir Gawain's discomfort, and Queen Guinevere laughed as merrily as the knights. But then suddenly she stopped laughing; for she saw Sir Patrice was choking and his face was swelling up.

'Ah God,' she cried, 'Sir Patrice, what is the matter?'

Sir Patrice staggered to his feet; his face was all bloated and purple. Then he cried out, clutched at his throat, and fell forward onto the table, scattering the dishes. Sir Kay pulled his head back.

'He is dead,' said Sir Kay, slowly, looking up.

Then all the knights rose to their feet and stood there in silence, angry and frightened, not knowing what to think or what to say.

At last Sir Gawain spoke.

'My Lady the Queen!' he said. 'Every person here who knows me knows that I love fruit well. Therefore if these apples are poisoned, as they seem to be, it was with the intent of killing me, and indeed I came very near to death.'

Queen Guinevere stood very still. She did not know what to say. She knew that she had chosen the apples herself especially for Sir Gawain and she knew also that she had not poisoned them. But how could she prove it?

'There is some treason here,' she murmured. 'Why should I wish to kill you, good Gawain?'

'As to that, madam,' said Sir Gawain grimly, 'I am afraid that you may have lost your honour.'

Then Sir Mador de la Porte broke in, who was the dead knight's cousin.

'That may be as that may be,' he said sternly, 'but Sir Gawain is alive. It is Sir Patrice who is dead. Here I have lost a noble knight of my blood, and therefore for this shame and outrage I will be avenged to the uttermost!'

Guinevere's heart beat then with fear.

'In the presence of you all,' said Sir Mador slowly, 'I call the Queen to account for treachery, for the poisoning of the good knight Sir Patrice of Ireland.'

All stood still and silent, and no knight challenged Sir Mador. Guinevere knew that they were all full of suspicion against her because she had arranged the dinner. She was so fearful and ashamed that she could do nothing but weep so bitterly that she fell into a swoon. So her servants carried her into her chamber and there she stayed, weeping and swooning, till at last King Arthur came back to Camelot.

King Arthur was heartbroken when Sir Mador de la Porte stood before him and repeated the accusation. Yet he did not now trust Guinevere as well as he had done before, though he did not tell her he had been at Castle Chariot or what his sister Morgan le Fay had shown him there.

'In this matter,' said King Arthur, 'I must be a rightful judge. But, Sir Mador, be not too hasty!'

'My gracious lord,' said Sir Mador, 'you must hold me excused. For though you are our king, in this matter you are only a knight as we are, and you are sworn to the laws of knighthood just as all Knights of the Round Table are. Therefore I ask you to judge sternly, for there is not one of all these twenty-four knights that were invited to the dinner that has not grave suspicions of the Queen.'

'What say you all, fair sirs?' asked the King.

Then they answered, one by one. Each said the Queen must be guilty of the poisoning and that it could be no one else, for she had arranged the dinner.

Guinevere alone knew she was innocent.

'I swear to you all, my lords,' she cried, 'I made this feast for joy and good fellowship, not for evil purpose. God be my witness!'

She could not understand why even King Arthur did not seem to believe her.

'My Lord the King,' said Sir Mador fiercely, 'I require you, as you are a righteous king, name me the day that I may have justice.'

'Well,' said King Arthur, 'my Queen shall be judged fifteen days from now. If she is not proved innocent before, then she shall suffer the rightful punishment for so foul a treachery as poisoning.'

'What is that, my lord?' asked the Queen, trembling.

'Guinevere,' said Arthur gently, 'if you are not innocent, there is no help for it. You must be burnt at the stake.'

'I am answered,' said Sir Mador, content.

They carried the Queen to her chamber. If she had wept and swooned before, she sat still, shivering with fright, now. When Arthur came to see her, he had pity on her, and his heart melted.

'But if you did not poison the apple,' he said, 'who did? Guinevere, you must tell me who did.'

'Sire,' cried Guinevere, 'as God is my witness, I do not know. Why should I poison the apple? Why should I want to murder Sir Patrice or any other of the twenty-four knights? Arthur, why should I?'

King Arthur did not answer her. But he was still not sure. He thought that perhaps she had wanted to poison Sir Gawain because Sir Gawain would inherit the realm when he himself was dead. So all he did was to ask her gloomily where Sir Lancelot was.

'Why is it that you cannot keep Sir Lancelot at your side?' he complained. 'If he was here he would put heart into you, he loves you so well.'

At these words Guinevere felt ever more miserable. She thought King Arthur meant that he did not love her any more himself.

'Arthur!' she moaned with misery.

'Well,' said the King more kindly. 'I mean that if Sir Lancelot were here, I am sure he would uncover the treachery. Whoever has Sir Lancelot's love has the man of most worship in this world upon their side.'

He left her then. He thought that perhaps the Queen knew where Sir Lancelot was and would send for him in her great peril. She did not know but she thought of someone who might do. She sent for Sir Bors.

'Ah, madam,' said Sir Bors, 'now you miss Sir Lancelot. He has never failed you whether you were right or whether you were wrong. But now to your dishonour and to ours you have driven him out of this realm.'

'Gentle knight,' said the Queen, 'I put myself wholly at your mercy.'

Sir Bors was moved by Guinevere's sorrow; but he still thought she must be a poisoner.

'Madam,' he said, 'what can I do? I myself can do nothing to help you for fear of the knights who were at the dinner. They think you are a poisoner. Indeed many say you have long been a destroyer of good knights.'

Then Guinevere went down on both her knees to Sir Bors, and begged him to help her: 'Else I shall die a shameful death, though I swear by God that I have done nothing evil.'

Sir Bors thought then that if the Queen humbled herself on her knees it meant that not even the King would help her. Yet if she swore by God, then she was probably innocent.

'Madam,' he said, at last, 'you ask me the greatest thing that has ever been asked of me. Many of the fellowship of the Round Table, and especially Sir Gawain and those of his blood, will hold it against me if I help you. Yet I will do what I can.'

With that he raised the Queen to her feet, and left her. But Guinevere was much happier because she knew that Sir Bors was one of the noblest knights and most perfect of men then living.

Sir Bors rode out to the Castle of Astolat where Sir Lancelot had been living in secret and told him the whole story.

'Ah God,' said Sir Lancelot in great confusion, 'it was an

evil day that ever I took such offence and let the Queen send me away.' He sent for his arms and his armour at once, and ordered his war-horse to be made ready. For he had sworn always to be the Queen's good knight in right or in wrong, from the day when Arthur first gave him the order of knighthood and Guinevere girded him round the waist with his knight's sword.

But the young maiden of Astolat, when she heard that Sir Lancelot was about to leave, came rushing to him.

'My lord Sir Lancelot,' she said, 'fair and courteous knight, have mercy on me. Else I will die for love of you.'

'What do you want from me?' said Sir Lancelot.

'Marry me!' she cried.

'Ah, fairest of maidens,' joked Sir Lancelot, 'I could often have married if I had wanted to. But I never wanted to. And, to tell the truth, I do not want to now – though I thank you from the bottom of my heart. It is not often so beautiful a girl as you asks me!'

'Then, fair knight, if you will not marry me, will you be my paramour?'

Sir Lancelot stopped smiling and looked very shocked.

'God forbid!'

'Then I swear I will die for your love.'

'This much I will promise you, fair maiden,' said Sir Lancelot desperately, 'that all my life long I will be your true knight and wear your scarf in tournaments. But you are too young to talk of marriage and far too young to talk of dying for love.'

Then the young maiden of Astolat lost her temper.

'Fool,' she said, 'scarfs and tokens and such like toys mean nothing to me. You may be the mighty Sir Lancelot du Lac; but for all that you are a man of flesh and blood. And I? Am I not a woman of flesh and blood, as much as any queen? I take God to witness, I never have loved and I never will love anyone on this earth except you. Ah, sweet Sir Lancelot,' she cried,

'unless you marry me or at least become my paramour, my days are done.'

'Fair maiden,' replied Sir Lancelot, 'you must forgive me. Neither the one nor the other.'

He turned his horse's head towards Camelot, and rode away side by side with Sir Bors.

'My Lord,' she cried after him, 'as soon as I saw you, I loved you more than it is possible for a woman's heart to love a man's. And since then I have not been able to eat or drink, rest or sleep. My thoughts have been tormented all the time, and I have suffered every pain and every grief by night and day.'

Sir Lancelot did not look round. But he was very upset and angry, and did not say a word to Sir Bors all that journey. As for Sir Bors, he wondered whether he had been right to come for Sir Lancelot; for perhaps the young maiden of Astolat loved his cousin more deeply than Queen Guinevere had ever done. But what could he do? He had given the Queen his word that he would help her in the best way possible.

Night was falling when they came within sight of the towers and battlements of Camelot. Sir Lancelot broke the silence at last.

'I will go to the Queen at once,' he said.

'Fair cousin,' said Sir Bors, 'not tonight. My advice is that you do not go tonight.'

'Why?' asked Sir Lancelot angrily.

'King Arthur is not at Camelot tonight, and I think you should not go to the Queen when the King is not with her.'

'Guinevere has sent for me,' said Sir Lancelot abruptly, 'not Arthur.'

Then Sir Bors had a feeling that the great friendship between the three of them was near to being broken.

'I have never had so strong a feeling as I have now that you should not go,' he said.

'Then why did you bring me here from Astolat and break that beautiful maiden's heart if it was not to see and help the Queen?' shouted Sir Lancelot. 'Why?'

'I dread some treason,' said Sir Bors quietly.

Then Sir Lancelot quieted down too.

'Have no dread, fair cousin,' he said, 'I will go to the Queen but I shall not stay long.'

'I am much afraid your going this night will bring death to us all.'

'Bors,' replied Sir Lancelot, 'the Queen has sent for me. I will see her. Else I am a coward.'

Sir Bors saw there was no help for it.

'Then God speed you well,' he said, 'and keep you safe and sound.'

Sir Lancelot dismounted, disarmed, took his sword only with him under his cloak, and crept silently by a secret way he knew towards the Queen's chamber.

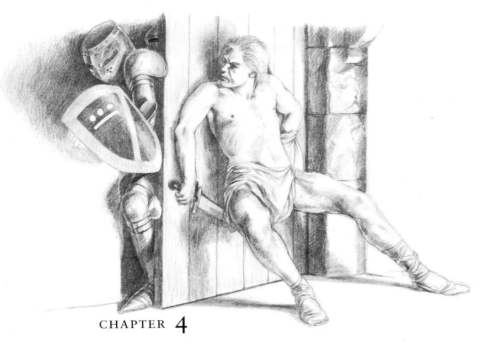

CHAPTER 4

The Fight in
the Queen's Chamber

SIR Agravaine had always hated Queen Guinevere. He was sure that Sir Lancelot was still in the realm, for his brother Sir Mordred had told him so and Mordred had secret powers. So he had set a watch on the Queen's chamber, day and night. 'For I do not doubt,' he told his brothers, 'that she will send for Sir Lancelot, and if he comes secretly then we will catch them together and destroy them.'

'God help me,' said Sir Gaheris, 'you have always been a knight causing unhappiness, brother, and I will have nothing to do with this plan.'

He and Sir Agravaine were twin brothers; but Sir Agravaine had all his life long been jealous of Sir Gaheris, because men loved Sir Gaheris but did not love him. The two twin brothers glared at each other. Sir Gareth who was the youngest of them all, stood unhappily in silence.

Sir Agravaine turned to Sir Gawain.

'Gawain,' he said, 'you are the eldest of our mother's sons. I know that even your golden tongue could never persuade Gareth to do anything against the man who made him a knight. But talk to Gaheris – since he loves you better than he does his own twin brother and always will do what you say. Tell him you will help me in this plan, and so must he.'

'I wish you would not meddle with all this,' said Sir Gawain uneasily, 'for I warn you that great unhappiness will come of it.'

Sir Agravaine thrust his angry face close to Sir Gawain's.

'Gawain,' he said, 'have you forgotten that this traitorous Queen tried to poison you? Have you forgotten that our uncle the King has rightly decreed that she must suffer death for this foul crime?'

'That is true,' admitted Sir Gawain.

'So if Sir Lancelot comes to her,' added Sir Agravaine, 'it will be to your dishonour, Gawain. For he will rescue this poisoner and save her from the punishment she deserves. You must stop him, Gawain. We must all stop him, for the sake of justice and the love of our uncle the King.'

'Ah, but brother Sir Agravaine,' said Sir Gawain, 'you must remember how often Sir Lancelot has done great service to our uncle King Arthur, yes, and to all the Knights of the Round Table too. For even the best of us would have been many times cold at the heart-roots if Sir Lancelot had not come to our rescue. And for my own part,' said Sir Gawain, 'I will never be against Sir Lancelot, because of that one day when he rescued me from Sir Caradoc of the Dolorous Tower and slew him and saved my life.'

'Nor will I,' said Sir Gaheris, 'for he rescued me from Sir Tarquin of Dolorous Garde, and I swore I would always do him service and love him.'   So neither Sir Gareth nor Sir

Gaheris nor even Sir Gawain would help Sir Agravaine because of their great love for Sir Lancelot, though they still all thought that the Queen had tried to poison Sir Gawain and deserved to die.

'Do as you like then,' said Sir Agravaine bitterly, 'but, come what may, I will act.'

So he kept the watch set about Guinevere's chamber. On the night when Sir Lancelot came secretly in, a scullion hurried out to Sir Agravaine.'

'My Lord,' said the scullion, 'Sir Lancelot is here!'

Sir Agravaine sent him to fetch Sir Mordred, and twelve other knights of their kin. He himself hurried to a window in a tall tower, just in time to see Sir Lancelot in his cloak creeping along the secret path that led to the Queen's chamber.

'Now we have him!' he said when Sir Mordred and the other knights arrived. 'Arm, kinsmen, for neither the Queen nor Sir Lancelot shall escape us now. He is caught in a closed trap!'

'We will surprise him,' they said gleefully, 'naked and unarmed.'

When Guinevere saw Sir Lancelot come into her chamber, she was overjoyed. She knew then that he still loved her – the best knight in the world. She told him she had never really meant to send him away. She told him with tears in her eyes that she had never poisoned the apple and had never wanted to murder Sir Gawain – and Sir Lancelot at least believed her. He promised he would find out who had poisoned the apple and vowed that he would never allow Arthur to burn her at the stake. So Guinevere made Lancelot great cheer, and they took their joy of one another in the cool comfort of the night.

Then, at that moment, to their horror they heard a great clattering of armed knights on the stone staircase and a great hammering outside, at the door of the Queen's chamber.

'Traitor Sir Lancelot,' came the clamour of many voices. 'Now you are taken!'

Luckily Sir Lancelot had barred the door. He leapt up, seized his sword, and looked wildly around.

'Armour,' he cried. 'Guinevere, is there no armour here?'

'There is nothing,' said the Queen wildly. 'My lord, there is neither helmet nor shield nor spear nor armour.'

'By the bones of God,' cursed Sir Lancelot, 'in all my life I was never so likely to be shamefully slain as now, and all because I have no armour!'

But Sir Agravaine and Sir Mordred were battering still more violently on the door.

'Traitor knight, come out of the Queen's chamber!' they shouted exultantly. 'There is no escape for you this time.'

'Ah Jesus mercy!' cried Sir Lancelot. 'Death itself were better than this shameful noise . . .'

'My Lord,' sobbed Guinevere, 'by the sound there are many noble knights out there, fully armed. There is no escape for us this time. You will be slain, and I will be burnt.'

Then Sir Lancelot put down his sword, took the Queen in his arms, dried her tears, and kissed her softly.

'Most noble queen,' he said, 'you have always been my special good lady, and I at all times your own knight, true to you as far as I could be. I have never failed you, right or wrong, since the first day Arthur made me a knight. My own lady, I have always loved you well, as a noble knight should. But now it seems the day is come when our love must end. Therefore, I beg you, pray for my soul if I am slain.'

At that Queen Guinevere wept many bitter tears.

'Ah God,' said Sir Lancelot tenderly, 'I am a thousand times more sorrowful for you than for myself. As for me, I will sell my life as dearly as I may. But as for you, as for the fire, do not worry. I am sure Sir Bors and the others of my blood will rescue you, whatever becomes of Lancelot du Lac.'

Then Sir Lancelot wrapped his cloak around his arm to protect it, and took up his sword again.

226

'Now, fair lords,' he called softly, 'stop your battering and your clamouring. I shall throw open this door, and then do with me what you will. But ah God,' he muttered below his breath, 'I would rather have armour upon me now than be lord of all Christendom. Then men would speak of my deeds before I die!'

Sir Lancelot unbarred the door. But he did not throw it wide open, no. With his left hand he opened it just a little, so that only one man could come in at a time. The first to come striding through was the stern knight Sir Mador de la Porte. Guinevere trembled when she saw him: she knew Sir Mador hated her most because it was his cousin Sir Patrice who had dropped dead of the poisoned apple.

Guinevere trembled all the more when Sir Mador smote mightily at Sir Lancelot. But Sir Lancelot avoided the stroke, and raising his own sword in anger, struck Sir Mador so violently with all his great force that neither his helmet nor his steel cap could save Sir Mador from being split from teeth to shoulders. Sir Lancelot wrenched out his sword, and Sir Mador fell dead across the doorway. Then there was a great uproar and crying, and tumult.

'Agravaine,' yelled Sir Lancelot, much less calmly now the battle-fury was upon him. 'You shall not have me tonight for all your noise!'

He dragged the dead knight inside the chamber and called to Guinevere. She stopped her sobbing then, and started disarming the body of the dead knight. Meanwhile Sir Lancelot stood in the doorway, smiling a grim smile.

'Who will be the next hero to taste my sword's bite?' he jeered, as Guinevere passed him Sir Mador's shield.

It was Sir Meliot. Then when Lancelot had killed Sir Meliot, came his brother Sir Melion. By the time Sir Melion had had his death blow, the Queen had armed Sir Lancelot with iron cap and helmet; and the bodies lay so thick across the door that the next knights could not push their way in.

'We defy you, traitor,' called Sir Agravaine and Sir Mordred furiously. 'For we will have you for all your prowess, and take your life. The King our uncle has told us to take you alive if you yield. But if not, then dead.'

This was not true. But how could Sir Lancelot know it?

'Ah, sirs,' he cried furiously, 'is there no other grace in you? Then keep yourselves!'

With that he threw the chamber door wide open, and came striding out, in full armour now, terrible to behold. He smote on the right and he smote on the left, and at every blow a knight fell dead.

'Now, Agravaine,' he said, 'let us see which of us two is the mightier.'

Then it was Sir Agravaine's turn to tremble. But for all that, he was no coward, Agravaine of the Hard Hand.

'Traitor Sir Lancelot,' he cried, 'if you kill me, Arthur's sister's son, the King will have your life!'

He whirled up his sword and rushed upon Sir Lancelot. But Sir Lancelot whirled up his sword too and smote Sir Agravaine such a mighty blow between neck and shoulders that Sir Agravaine's head flew from his body, and that vengeful knight fell down dead. Of all the knights who had assailed the chamber, only Sir Mordred was now alive. The bodies of all the others lay in their armour and blood on the cold stone. Never had there been such a killing before in Camelot.

'Sir Mordred,' said Sir Lancelot, 'you are too young to be fighting me. Go. You can still save your life.'

'Ah, traitor,' said Sir Mordred, 'do you think I am afraid of you?'

And he rushed upon Sir Lancelot as Sir Agravaine had done.

But Sir Lancelot, to his amazement, found he could not wound or kill Sir Mordred.

'Sir traitor,' laughed Sir Mordred through his teeth. 'No sword forged by mortal men can harm me!'

Sir Lancelot remembered then that many thought that Sir Mordred's father was a fiend.

'Ah, warlock,' he cried, 'let us see which of the two of us is the mightier, for all that!'

Dropping his sword, he plunged at Sir Mordred and seized him round the waist. They struggled like two great bears. Then with a mighty twist of his shoulders Sir Lancelot lifted Sir Mordred off his feet, armour and all, and hurled him down a flight of stone stairs. Mordred's body went banging and clattering to the bottom, and lay there still.

Sir Lancelot staggered back to the Queen's chamber and sat down wearily on her bed.

'Guinevere,' he said, 'now King Arthur will always be my enemy, for these killings. Come with me now, and I will save you and myself both. Else his vengeance will be terrible.'

But Guinevere stood there, pale with horror, looking at the savage face of Sir Lancelot and his armour and weapons, all dripping with the life-blood of so many noble knights.

'Come,' said Sir Lancelot urgently.

But the Queen only shook her head.

'Sir,' she said at last, 'not so. You have done so much harm it were best you did no more. Leave me now.'

'Alas,' said Sir Lancelot heavily. 'Now I see that our true love is at an end, and I dread that the fellowship of the Round Table that was the noblest fellowship in the whole world is here undone.'

He turned with his bloody sword in his hand, and strode wearily from the Queen's chamber by the way he had come.

CHAPTER 5

The Judgment of the King

SIR Mordred had not been killed. For a long time he lay stunned at the foot of the stairs where Sir Lancelot had thrown him. When he came to his senses, the cold dawn was breaking and a hush lay over Camelot. Then there was jangling of harness, and the clatter of horses' hoofs. King Arthur was riding back from the hunt, with Sir Gawain beside him. For Sir Gawain, Sir Gaheris, and Sir Gareth had ridden out to fetch their uncle, since they feared some misfortune by cause of their brother Agravaine.

Sir Mordred lay there still, not moving, dreaming and half listening to voices that suddenly died away into silence as they saw the massacre by the Queen's chamber. Once he heard the Queen scream as men spoke sternly to her, then all was silent again.

At last he heard voices directly over his head.

'Here is Mordred,' said Gawain's voice, 'our half-brother. Another to be buried.'

'At least Agravaine did not run away like Mordred,' said Gaheris' voice. 'Agravaine died sword in hand. I did not love my twin brother, but, Gawain, he was no coward like this one.'

'Wait,' said Gareth's voice, 'I see no blood or wound. I think Mordred is alive, unless his neck is broken.'

Then Sir Mordred stopped dreaming and stirred, and his brothers knew he was alive. They unlaced his armour, took him up gently, and brought him to the King. There Mordred told Arthur the whole story.

'Jesu mercy!' said King Arthur. 'Sir Lancelot is a marvellous knight of prowess. Alone, he killed thirteen knights. Nephew, you were lucky indeed that he spared you.'

'It was God who spared me, fair uncle,' said Sir Mordred, 'not that traitor knight. Think of vengeance, not prowess. Think of my brother Sir Agravaine, your own sister's son, whom he killed.'

'In truth,' said King Arthur heavily, 'there must now be mortal war against Sir Lancelot for the slaying of my nephew. But alas, that even Sir Lancelot should be against me, for now I am sure the noble fellowship of the Round Table is broken for ever.'

Then all the knights who heard King Arthur stood silent in mortal sorrow, for they could not imagine that the fellowship of the Round Table, the most noble fellowship in all the world, should be ended. Only Sir Mordred smiled secretly, for he had long planned for this breaking.

'If you lay hands on Sir Lancelot now, fair uncle,' said Sir Mordred, 'he should have as shameful a death as our Queen must suffer.'

'God forbid,' said Sir Gawain, much shocked, 'that I should ever hear such a thing.'

King Arthur looked from Sir Mordred to Sir Gawain.

'Gawain,' he said, 'why should you be tender to Sir Lancelot? Last night he slew your own brother Sir Agravaine and twelve knights more of your kin, and would have killed the young Mordred here if God had not saved him.'

Sir Gawain looked scornfully at Sir Mordred, as if he did not believe that it was God who had saved him, but rather the Devil.

'My Lord,' he said, 'I know all this, and for their deaths I am full of sorrow. Yet I warned them. I told my brother Agravaine beforehand how it would end. He would not take any advice, so I will not meddle with it or avenge their deaths. For Agravaine and my other kinsmen caused their own deaths, not Sir Lancelot.'

King Arthur looked both miserable and angry.

'And what of my poisonous Queen?' he said. 'Will you pardon her too, Gawain, though it was you she tried to poison?'

Without waiting for Gawain's reply he went furiously up the stairs to Guinevere's bedchamber, and closed and barred the door. What passed between the two of them then, between Guinevere and Arthur, no man may say. But when the King came out at last he was silent, and his face was so grim that no one, knight or page, dared say a word to him. He did not eat or drink that whole evening.

Next morning the King announced that according to true justice his Queen must suffer a shameful death: first, because the fifteen days were ended and she had not been proved innocent of the poisoning of Sir Patrice; secondly, because Sir Lancelot had come secretly to her chamber and there killed so many noble knights of the Round Table for her sake.

King Arthur commanded a great fire to be prepared in the meadows outside the walls of Camelot, on which Guinevere would be burnt. For a queen who was guilty of treachery could die no other way, because she was sacred.

Then a great noise of shouting arose through the whole

city of Camelot; for the people had not believed that Arthur would ever really allow Guinevere to be burnt. There was mourning and weeping, and all the people were as grief-stricken as if the Queen had been their own mother.

The noise of the wailing rose to the Queen's bedchamber. But Guinevere wept no more, though she knew that she faced a fearful death. Perhaps Arthur had told her of the paintings he had seen in Sir Lancelot's secret chamber at Castle Chariot, and she was ashamed. Or perhaps she thought that she might have gone with Sir Lancelot and escaped if she had wanted. But since she had not done so, how could she now complain? At any rate when the noise of the shouting and wailing reached Guinevere's ears, she knew very well what it meant.

About midday Sir Kay came to her chamber.

'Madam,' he said, 'your lord and mine has given his judgment.'

Guinevere looked him calmly in the eyes.

'Sir Seneschal,' she said, 'the King is a just ruler; I have always loved my husband Arthur's judgments as much as his person. So do not hesitate to tell me what he has adjudged for me.'

'Lady,' said Sir Kay, 'it is a bold judgment. You are to be burnt at the stake.'

'Sir Kay,' said Guinevere bravely, 'you have often spoken unkindly, but never as unkindly as you speak now.' Sir Kay looked down, abashed. 'When and at what time?'

'Madam, tomorrow, at this time,' said Sir Kay. He bowed and went out.

The Guinevere called her handmaidens, and prepared herself to die as a queen should.

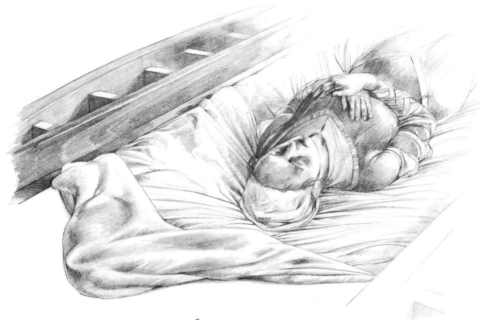

CHAPTER 6

A Message from Astolat

THE shouting and the wailing from Camelot reached Sir Lancelot's ears too. He had not gone far away. He had hidden in a place in the deep Forest, by the side of a secret lake, that only he and Sir Bors knew.

Sir Lancelot did not know what the shouting and the wailing meant till late that afternoon when Sir Bors and twenty-two knights of his blood came to him, all armed.

'What does this mean?' asked Sir Lancelot, amazed.

'Fair cousin,' said Sir Bors, 'the King has said this: that if he lays hands on you, you will suffer the same shameful death as his Queen. So we of your blood think there is great strife at hand; and we have made ourselves ready to ride with you to Joyous Garde or to your father King Ban's lands of Benwick or wherever else you should wish, and to guard you from all treason.'

'What does the noise and wailing mean?'

Sir Bors hesitated. It was Sir Ector who spoke.

'Brother,' he said, 'it is for the Queen. She is to be burnt at the stake tomorrow at midday.'

Then Sir Lancelot was silent for a long time, and they all too, not knowing what to say.

'My fair lords,' said Sir Lancelot at last, 'my kin and my friends, advise me what shall I do. For if we attempt to rescue the Queen there are few of us, and there will be many of them. Yet if we do not attempt to rescue the Queen, I will be dishonoured, and all of my blood with me, for my sake.'

Then many said that it would be foolish to try and rescue the Queen, for she would surely be closely guarded by Sir Gawain and all his kin.

'And if there is any more killing,' said Sir Bors, 'there will never be peace again in Logres but always mortal war. But once Guinevere is dead, I think the King will pardon you the death of his nephew Agravaine. For Agravaine was always an unhappy knight.'

But Sir Bors really thought that King Arthur would never be jealous of Sir Lancelot ever again, for with the death of the Queen the reason for jealousy would be gone.

Then others said that in any case the Queen deserved death, for she had surely intended to murder Sir Gawain. At this Lancelot was angry because the Queen had sworn to him she was innocent. Yet even he was unsure now, because Guinevere had refused to escape with him when she could. So perhaps, he thought, Guinevere is guilty. Perhaps she knows she deserves punishment.

'Fair lords,' he said in the end, 'leave me. For I would be alone to think on all these things. Keep your armour, and meet me here tomorrow two hours before midday; and then we will ride where destiny decides.'

So Sir Lancelot sat down on a little mound by the side of the lake to think about all these difficult things, and what he should best do. As the sun set, the lake grew very still. Its surface was like glass. A voice, soft and silvery, seemed to whisper, 'Lancelot!' Sir Lancelot looked round. He could see nothing and no one. Then on the surface of the lake a shimmering shape slowly took form, that of a beautiful nymph, far more beautiful, Lancelot saw, even than Queen Guinevere, even than the maiden of Astolat. Her eyes were all the colours of the rainbow; they sparkled now like ice diamonds, now like rich rubies.

'Lancelot,' said the silvery voice, 'do you not know who I am?'

Then Sir Lancelot's thoughts went back to his boyhood that he had spent in the shimmering glass castle under water.

'We have not seen each other,' he said unsteadily, 'since the day that Merlin came for me, to take me to the upper world. Because of you he called me Sir Lancelot du Lac, I think.'

'Indeed he did,' smiled the Lady, 'to try and win his way to my heart. But now I have left the Lake where I brought you up, for great things are afoot and I must go to Annwen, to the side of my brother Guiomar the Elf-King. The Dark Shadow is falling again over earth. All the forces that can oppose the menace of Mordor are gathering in the Half World. There is much to be done if the evil that once fell on Middle Earth is to be repulsed in this Later Age.'

'Lady,' said Sir Lancelot humbly, 'you speak of matters that are too high for me.'

'One matter I will speak of then that is not too high even for simple minds like yours,' finished the Lady. 'Guinevere the Queen did not poison the apple.'

'Who did then?' asked Sir Lancelot, amazed.

'Ah, you knights who always accept the obvious and never seek beneath the surface! I will be glad to be free of you all, yes, even of you, Lancelot. But I do you this last favour because I

trained you to be unmatched of any earthly knight, and brought you up to be my own son. Of course it was not the gentle Guinevere. Why should she seek to kill Sir Gawain?'

Then the Lady told him the name of the knight who had poisoned the apple and explained why he had done it, and gave Sir Lancelot instructions what to do.

'If all goes well,' she said, 'this will save Guinevere from an unjust death, and preserve the fellowship of the Round Table. Yet if the Dark Shadow is too far advanced, even this will fail, and you mortal men and women must act as you think best, without our help. For we are all summoned to Annwen; even Morgan le Fay the sorceress. Merlin, your friend, will be there too, whom I once taught a bitter lesson because he dared to love an elf-queen.' She laughed. 'So there will be none of the Wise left to advise you.'

For a moment the Elf-Queen looked sadly at Lancelot. Then her eyes sparkled and her shape shimmered. 'Little human, farewell,' she called, as she disappeared beneath the waters from which she had come.

That night a boy came secretly to Sir Gawain in his chamber at Camelot, bearing a letter written to him by Sir Lancelot. This is what the letter said.

To Sir Gawain, most noble of knights, King Lot's son of Orkeney and sister's son to the most noble Lord and High King Arthur. Greetings from King Ban's son of Benwick, Sir Lancelot du Lac.

Know that my Lady Queen Guinevere is unjustly accused of plotting your death. It was Sir Pinel le Sauvage who empoisoned the apple. He had always hated you because he was a cousin of Sir Lamorak de Galys, King Pellinore's son of the Outer Isles, whom you slew. By your knighthood, Sir Gawain, most noble of knights, have the noble Lord King Arthur put Sir Pinel to the ordeal if he denies this. And I

beseech you for the love I have always had for you and all your
blood, except only for Sir Agravaine and Sir Mordred, save the
life of the noble Lady Queen Guinevere.

Sir Gawain did not stop to ask how Sir Lancelot had
known this. Swiftly he woke Sir Gaheris, who always slept by
his side, and told him to bring Sir Pinel le Sauvage before the
King. Then he hurried to Arthur's bedchamber and woke the
King.

'Sire, fair uncle,' he said, 'a message has come from that
most noble knight Sir Lancelot.' And he showed King Arthur
the letter.

Meanwhile Sir Gaheris with naked sword in his hand
woke Sir Pinel in his nightshirt and drove him in front of him
like a sheep to the King's chamber. And there Sir Gawain
accused him of treason.

'Sire,' he said. 'Now I remember how this Sir Pinel laid his
arm on Sir Patrice and tried to stop him from eating that apple.
Why should he have done this if it was not to save the apple for
my lips, since he knew that I love apples best of all fruit?
Rightly is this Sir Pinel called le Sauvage, for he is a savage
recreant knight.'

'And you,' burst out Sir Pinel, 'you brothers Gawain and
Gaheris, are you not savage too, and recreant? For you
treacherously slew that good knight Sir Lamorak, though
there were three of you against one.'

'Gaheris was not there,' burst out Sir Gawain. 'It was
Mordred and Agravaine.' Then he bit his lip, for they had all
always denied the killing of Sir Lamorak, and now he had
revealed the secret.

King Arthur looked sternly at his nephew.

'It was in the time of the evil enchantments, fair uncle,' said
Gaheris defensively. 'We were all half-mad.'

That was a foolish thing for Gaheris to say. It reminded the
King that it was Gaheris who had killed his own mother
Queen Morgawse.

'For all that,' burst out Sir Pinel, 'my good cousin Sir Lamorak is dead, and his father King Pellinore too, and the good knight Sir Tor, all slain by you grim brood of the Orkeneys treacherously, because King Pellinore killed your own father King Lot in fair battle, for our Lord King Arthur's sake.'

Then they all fell silent, thinking of those old feuds and of so much blood shed on so many sides.

'There must now be an end to these blood feuds,' said King Arthur at last. 'Sir Patrice of Ireland is dead, but now Sir Mador de la Porte his cousin is dead too, by mischance, who demanded judgment for that poisoning. Gaheris, put up your sword; you are an unworthy, recreant knight, and like your twin Agravaine, you have always loved killing and murder.' King Arthur said this for the bitter sorrow he still felt for the death of his eldest sister Queen Morgawse. 'Sir Pinel, for your cousin the good knight Sir Lamorak's sake, I pardon you even this treachery of poisoning. But you must go from Camelot, and swear to end this feud.'

So Sir Pinel swore. He rode away from Camelot that night. Never was man so glad to escape with his life.

'What of the Queen, my Lord?' said Sir Gawain.

'Let her sleep,' said King Arthur shortly, 'and us too.'

But Sir Gawain was content, because he was sure the King would now pardon her; and then Sir Lancelot would return in peace and the joyful fellowship of the Round Table would be restored.

But Sir Gaheris could not sleep that night. He took his horse and rode down to the river that flowed by the walls of Camelot. His mighty young brother, Sir Gareth, worried about him, and at dawn went in search of him. When he found him, he thought that he had never seen Sir Gaheris look so miserable ever before, not even after the slaying in the Orkeneys.

Sir Gaheris told Sir Gareth how the real poisoner had been discovered at last: it was not the Queen, but Sir Pinel le Sauvage.

'But then why are you so gloomy, Gaheris?' asked Gareth. 'Is it because you want to ride after Sir Pinel and kill him for trying to poison our eldest brother Sir Gawain?'

This made Sir Gaheris gloomier still.

'Gareth,' he said, 'I have not Gawain's golden tongue or your sweet courtesy. I may be too violent. But do not imagine that all I ever want is killing and feuds. That is what our uncle King Arthur accused me of, to my dishonour. But for all that I would never disobey him, and he commanded that Sir Pinel should ride free.'

Gareth was glad that there was to be no more killings but he was sorrier than ever for Sir Gaheris. He had looked after Sir Gaheris in the great troubles that followed the killing of Queen Morgawse, when Sir Agravaine and even Sir Gawain had wanted to slay Sir Gaheris in revenge for the killing of their mother. In his remorse Gaheris, who had before been quick-witted, grew morose and sullen. But for all that, Gareth loved him still and tried to protect him from his fits of gloom. For Gareth was always happy, always thinking of his wife the Lady Lynette or of Sir Lancelot, the knight he loved more even than his own brothers.

So Sir Gareth made Sir Gaheris good cheer. But Sir Gaheris sat silently in his saddle, looking even more gloomily down into the river. At last he told Sir Gareth why he was sadder than ever before. It was because he feared his own death was upon him. For he remembered that the twelve sorceress-damsels of La Roche aux Pucelles had foretold that he would die within days of his twin brother Sir Agravaine.

'Ah, dear brother Sir Gaheris,' said Sir Gareth, 'probably you frightened those beautiful damsels, and in their fright they turned their tongues on you, as the Damsel Sauvage did on me when I rode to Castle Perilous. But women are often like that. They often say things they do not mean.'

But Sir Gaheris remembered how they had foretold the death of Sir Marholt; and he had died. Also how they had foretold that he himself would die at the hands of the knight he loved best in the world, without defending himself. He suddenly felt a feeling of worry for his brave young brother Gareth too, who had always been so kind to him in his distress.

'Fair brother,' he said urgently, 'I pray you with all my heart to leave Camelot now, at once, and ride home to your sweet wife, the Lady Lynette.'

'Why?' laughed Gareth. 'Now that the Queen is sure to be freed, there will be no danger here, only joy. Am I to leave all the jousting and feasting to you? No, Gaheris, I will bid my sweet wife ride here, for all the happiness – and together we will make you forget your gloom!'

But then all of a sudden the argument ceased; for their horses shied backwards in alarm, and a strange and pitiful sight caught their eyes.

A barge decked in black cloth was floating down the river towards them. On the barge lay a rich bed, covered in black velvet; and it seemed to them that under the coverlet lay a body.

Sir Gaheris trembled. He feared it was Death itself come for him. But Sir Gareth went onto the barge, lifted the coverlet of black velvet and saw underneath it a girl who was not long dead. To judge from how she still looked, she must have been very beautiful.

'Ah, Gaheris,' said Sir Gareth for pity, 'do you not think Death was wicked to enter the body of such a beautiful girl as she was not long ago?'

But Sir Gaheris was already riding back to Camelot, to tell the King of this sad marvel.

Arthur rode down with his knights to the riverside and looked long and sadly at the beautiful maiden that lay dead.

'My Lord,' said Sir Gawain, 'do you remember the beautiful girl of whom I spoke to you the other day, the one I said loved Lancelot? This is the girl we were speaking of – the maiden of Astolat.'

'How did she die?' said Arthur.

Then he saw that there was a very rich purse hanging from her belt, and it did not seem to be empty. Sir Gawain opened it for him; inside was a letter, which Sir Gawain passed to the King. And this is what the letter said:

To all the Knights of the Round Table, greetings from the maiden of Astolat. If you ask for whom I suffered the pains of death, I shall reply that I died for the noblest knight in the world, and also the wickedest: Sir Lancelot du Lac. He is the wickedest, as far as I can tell, because however much I begged him with tears and weeping he refused to have mercy on me, for the wicked love he bore to Queen Guinevere, King Arthur's wife. I took it so much to heart that I died from loving faithfully.

King Arthur read this letter slowly and in silence.

'Indeed, young woman,' he said almost to himself, 'you can truly say that the man you died for is most valiant in the world and the wickedest.'

Then he commanded her body to be taken from the barge and buried at Camelot. Over her grave he commanded a very rich and beautiful tomb to be raised with this inscription, in letters of gold and azure:

HERE LIES THE MAIDEN FROM ASTOLAT
WHO DIED FOR LOVE OF LANCELOT.

Guinevere, looking down from her window, saw the black barge at the riverside, heard all the knights and ladies weeping for pity, and watched the body of the girl being carried up to Camelot for burial. When her handmaidens told her the sad story, she wept too, for pity's sake. Yet in her heart she rejoiced: for she knew now that Sir Lancelot had never truly loved the maiden of Astolat, however beautiful, but had always loved her.

That was what King Arthur thought too. He knew now that Lancelot had always loved Guinevere and she had loved him in return. Sir Mordred stood always at his side as they watched the maiden of Astolat being buried, whispering to the King about Guinevere's wickedness, and Lancelot's too.

When the burial was over, King Arthur turned to Sir Gawain. 'Make yourself ready in your best armour,' he said, 'you and your brothers, Sir Gaheris and Sir Gareth.'

'My Lord, why?' they all asked.

'To bring my Queen to the fire,' said Arthur sternly.

Sir Gawain was astonished.

'But, fair uncle,' he said, 'she is not the empoisoner of the apple. Are you not going to set Guinevere free?'

'She is guilty of the deaths of thirteen good knights,' said King Arthur grimly, 'she and that wicked knight Sir Lancelot. She shall have a shameful death, as I have judged, and so shall he, if he falls into my hands.'

'Mordred,' said Sir Gawain threateningly, 'is this your evil doing?'

But King Arthur pushed Sir Mordred aside and turned angrily on Sir Gawain.

'Arm yourselves,' he thundered, 'as I have commanded you.'

'Nay, my most noble king,' said Sir Gawain, 'that I will never do. I will never be in that place where so noble a queen as the Lady Guinevere shall meet such a shameful end. My heart will not let me see so great a treachery.'

Sir Gawain went straight to his lodgings, lamenting. But the King did not say a word in reply to Gawain's insolence. He ordered Sir Gaheris and Sir Gareth to arm and fetch the Queen.

'Well,' said Sir Gaheris heavily, 'I have never yet disobeyed you, fair uncle, and I may not do it now; though it is much against my will.'

Sir Gareth went with him, to keep him company. So they armed, and led out the Queen towards the meadows outside the walls of Camelot where the great fire that had been prepared had just been set alight. Guinevere was crying bitterly when they led her out through the streets, wearing a dress of crimson, a scarf of cloth of gold, and a cloak of black velvet.

'Ah, my Lady,' shouted the people of Camelot, 'where will we ever find pity now? Ah, King Arthur, you have treacherously sought her death, you can still repent.'

Indeed when the King saw her, he felt such great pity for her beauty that he was unable to look at her. But for all that, he ordered that the judgment proceed; and he ordered Sir Gaheris and Sir Gareth to take eighty armed knights with them, and escort her to the fire; and there to set her on the flames, and burn her.

Then there was weeping and wailing and wringing of hands.

'Listen, Gaheris, fair brother,' said Gareth, 'do you think I have come to fight with Sir Lancelot if he tries to rescue the Queen? I tell you I shall not fight with him.'

'Nor shall I, Gareth,' said Sir Gaheris as they rode out. 'For if he does this, he acts as a noble knight should, and as I would do too if I were in his place.'

CHAPTER 7

The Burning of Guinevere

S IR Bors and the knights of the blood of King Ban and
King Bors had ridden out to Sir Lancelot. All was
joy, for they had the best tidings to tell him: that Sir
Pinel le Sauvage was the poisoner and that the
Queen was sure to be released. So they took off their
armour and bathed, splashing, in the secret lake,
themselves and their war-horses alike, and made
great cheer. The Forest rang with their joy.

But then came the sound of weeping and wailing,
moaning and groaning, faintly through the trees
from Camelot, yet louder than before. A boy came
running.

'What news, boy?' said Sir Bors.

'Bad news, my Lord,' he said. 'They are leading

the Queen out to die. They have already lit the fire to burn her on.'

Then Sir Lancelot did not hesitate.

'Arm and mount, fair lords,' he said. 'There are some who expect to put Guinevere to death but who will die themselves. May God grant, if ever he listens to the prayer of a sinner, that I find Mordred. For I know this must be his doing.'

Then they counted themselves to see how many knights they were, and they found there were thirty-two in all. Each one armed and mounted his war-horse. Then there was spurring and plucking of horse, and galloping such as has never been seen before.

When the people from the City saw them spurring out of the Forest they all shouted together:

'There is Lancelot! Flee, flee!'

But of the eighty knights who had come out with Sir Gareth and Sir Gaheris only three turned to flee.

Sir Lancelot, who was riding ahead of all the others, saw Sir Mordred close to the Queen, close to the great fire.

'Traitor, recreant,' he cried, 'you have come to your end!'

He struck him so hard that no armour could have saved him; but the great lance broke in Lancelot's hand; and Mordred laughed his sneering laugh again, knowing that Lancelot for all his might could never kill him.

Then there was rushing and hurling and thranging and lashing, as all the knights clashed and the press became thick. Sir Bors, riding as fast as he could urge his horse to gallop, shouted to Sir Gareth to defend himself. But Sir Gareth would not feutre his lance or draw his sword against any of Sir Lancelot's kin. Sir Bors could not stop but struck him so violently that no armour could turn the point of his lance. It did not break. It drove deep into Sir Gareth's chest, and with a great cry Gareth toppled to the ground.

Sir Gaheris then saw that his dear brother Gareth was dying. He could not support the grief of it. Though he had sworn not to fight with sword or spear, he hurled his spear against Sir Meliadas the Black, one of Sir Lancelot's kin, and struck him so hard that he knocked him shrieking, into the middle of the great fire — and there he burnt to death. Then Sir Gaheris put his hand to his sword, and struck Sir Belleus to the ground, dead at Sir Lancelot's feet. But Sir Lancelot would not strike him.

'If Sir Gaheris lives much longer,' said Sir Ector de Marys to himself, 'he will do us much harm, he is such a valiant knight.' For there was now killing and slaying on all sides, and many knights lay dead on the ground. Then Sir Ector spurred his horse, rode up behind Sir Gaheris, brandishing his sword, and struck him so violently that his helmet flew off his head.

When Gaheris felt his head unprotected, then he knew his death hour had come, and the prophecy would be fulfilled. But he did not care, he was so wild with sorrow for the death of Sir Gareth. He dashed into the thickest of the press, brandishing his sword.

Sir Lancelot was ranging to and fro, smiting and killing all who withstood him, putting the rest to flight. He did not see it was Sir Gaheris. He struck him so hard on the bare head that the sword drove through the brain to the teeth.

When King Arthur's knights saw Gaheris fall, and both he and Sir Gareth dying upon the field, their courage failed and they fled, those of them that were left alive. There many a noble knight was slain; and by Sir Lancelot alone Sir Girflet was slain, and Sir Aglovale, a son of King Pellinore, and the Green Knight of the Green Lands, whom Sir Gareth had once conquered.

With all his enemies dead or dying or in flight, Sir Lancelot rode straight up to the Queen, snatched her from the fire, mounted her behind him, and rode deep into the thickest part of the Forest. There he and those of his blood counted their losses. Seven of their knights had been killed.

'I saw three of them die at the hands of Sir Gaheris,' said Sir Ector.

'What?' said Sir Lancelot. 'Was Gaheris there, then?'

'My Lord,' said Sir Ector, 'you killed him. You killed him as surely as Bors killed Sir Gareth.'

Sir Lancelot looked from one to the other of them, with horror.

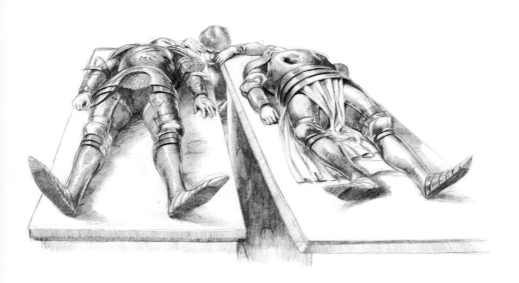

CHAPTER 8

The Wrath of Gawain

Sir Mordred and two companions staggered into the Great Hall of Camelot, covered in blood, and threw themselves on their knees in front of the King.

'My Lord,' said Sir Mordred, 'I have bad news to tell you and all those present. My Lord, I have to tell you that of all the knights that were leading the Queen to the fire only the three of us have escaped. The others are all dead or badly wounded or in flight.'

'Lancelot?' asked the King. 'Was it Lancelot?'

'Yes, my Lord,' Mordred replied, 'and that is not all he has done. He has rescued the Queen from death and disappeared with her into the deep Forest.'

'They will not go free if I can help it,' said the King grimly.

He commanded all the knights who were with him to arm. They mounted as soon as they could and rode out of Camelot, covered in steel, into the deep Forest. King Arthur rode out with them, to the place where the fighting had been fiercest. He looked to the right and he looked to the left, and then tears came to his eyes, for on all sides his noblest knights were lying dead. Then he saw the body of his nephew Sir Gareth. At that, no man had ever seen the King in greater distress. He struck his hands together, which were still armed, as he was wearing all his armour except his helmet. He was so heartbroken he could not hold himself upright in the saddle but fell to the ground with a cry. He took off Gareth's helmet, and looked at him: then he kissed his eyes and mouth, which by now were cold, and had Gareth placed on his shield so that he could be carried back to Camelot.

'Ah, Gareth,' he groaned, 'now you will never see again your fair wife, Lynette.' Then to the left, in the thickest of the press, he saw the body of Sir Gaheris whom Lancelot had killed. Arthur ran up to him as fast as he could, and kissed his eyes and his mouth, bloody as they were, for Sir Gaheris was his favourite nephew apart from Sir Gawain, and, whatever he might have said to him, he loved him as much as any man might love another.

'Ah, God,' cried Arthur, 'now is all my joy gone! Ah, Gaheris! Must I live to see all my dear nephews that I have brought up die in such a wretched way? Cursed be the knight who struck you down. He is destroying me and all my race.'

Then they told him that it was Sir Lancelot who had struck Sir Gaheris down, and Sir Bors Sir Gareth.

'Jesu mercy!' cried Arthur. 'These deaths will cause the greatest mortal war that ever was. For when Sir Gawain hears that both his brothers are slain, I am sure that he will nearly go out of his mind with anger and grief.'

Then he had the body of Sir Gaheris laid on his shield too, and carried back to Camelot.

At all this noise and shouting Sir Gawain came out of his lodgings, thinking that the Queen was dead and the lamentations were for her. As he walked through the streets of the city, he looked to the right and to the left, and saw everyone weeping together, young and old. As he went past they all said to him: 'Sir Gawain, now you will know the greatest pain you have ever known.'

Sir Gawain did not say a word in reply but was more dismayed than ever, though he did not let it be seen. Outside the Great Hall everyone was weeping as if they had seen the deaths of all the princes in the world.

Seeing Gawain come in, Arthur turned to him: 'Gawain, Gawain,' he said, 'know your great grief and mine too. For here is your brother Gareth, the most courteous of our race.'

He showed his body to Sir Gawain, still all bloody in his arms and to all the other knights too.

'Beaumains,' said Sir Kay, 'how much I regret now that I ever mocked you. For you were a knight of great prowess and courtesy. And they say that Sir Bors slew you, though you would not raise a sword or lance against him, in despite of your gentle courtesy.'

'But why did Sir Lancelot let my brother be killed?' cried Sir Gawain in anguish. 'For I dare say, as for Sir Gareth, he loved Sir Lancelot most of all men on earth.'

They did not dare tell him then that Sir Gaheris was dead too, killed by Sir Lancelot. But Sir Gawain saw the body of Sir Gaheris lying dead in front of the King on his shield. Never had Sir Gawain imagined his heart would be so near breaking.

'Ah, God,' he sobbed, 'I have lived too long when I see my flesh and blood killed so grievously.' He kissed Sir Gaheris' mouth as best he could, but because he had been struck so hard it was not easy. He sat near him, looking down at his body. 'Ah, Gaheris,' he wept, 'cursed be the arm that struck you in that way! Dear brother, the man who struck you in that way must have hated you! Now I have seen you dead, dear brother, I no longer have any wish to live myself.' He gazed wildly around. 'Who killed him?'

'Sir Lancelot,' they said.

'That I will never believe,' shouted Sir Gawain, 'for I dare say Sir Gaheris loved Sir Lancelot, next to me, better than all his kinsfolk and the King himself.'

But they assured him that it was so. Then he ran, crying and moaning and threw himself, grovelling at the feet of the King.

'Arthur, my lord, my uncle,' he panted, 'now I will make you a promise that I will hold by my knighthood: that from this day forth I will seek out Sir Lancelot until one of us two is dead. I promise to God,' said Sir Gawain, 'that for the death of my good brother Sir Gaheris, I shall seek out Sir Lancelot through the Seven Kingdoms. I will be revenged upon Sir Lancelot, I swear and promise it!'

King Arthur looked down at Sir Gawain.

'Now we shall never have peace,' he said mournfully, 'till Sir Lancelot and all his kin have been destroyed.'

CHAPTER **9**

The Siege of Joyous Garde

THAT night there was such great sorrow in the city of
Camelot that there was nobody who was not in
tears. The dead knights were disarmed and en-
shrouded. Coffins and tombs were made for them
all.

For Sir Gaheris and Sir Gareth two coffins were
made which were as beautiful and rich as was
suitable for a king's sons. At the moment when their
bodies were let down into the earth, all the poor
people wailed with grief and all the knights paid
them the greatest honour they could, because they
had been such good men and such fine knights.
These were the inscriptions on their tombs:

HERE LIES GARETH, KNOWN AS BEAUMAINS,
WHO WAS KILLED WITHOUT PITY BY SIR BORS
DE GANYS.
HERE LIES GAHERIS, KING ARTHUR'S NEPHEW,
WHO WAS KILLED WITHOUT MERCY BY SIR
LANCELOT DU LAC.

But Sir Gawain was not at the burial of his brothers. He lay in his lodgings, half out of his mind with grief. He would speak no word, good or bad, to any man.

The knights whom King Arthur had sent out into the deep Forest had come back; they had not been able to find a trace of Sir Lancelot or his companions.

'I know where Lancelot will have gone,' said Sir Kay. 'He will have gone to his castle of Joyous Garde.'

'Kay,' said King Arthur, 'tell me if you think he has taken Guinevere with him.'

'My Lord,' said Sir Kay, 'you can be sure the Queen is there. But I do not recommend you to go. I know the castle very well. I was once imprisoned there and feared I should die, until Lancelot sent Gaheris to release me and my companions. It is so strong that it is in no danger of a siege from any side. And those inside are so noble that they would have little fear of your attacks.'

When Arthur heard this, he was not pleased.

'Kay, you are right about the strength of Joyous Garde and the courage of those inside,' he said. 'But since I first became king, I have never waged a war that I did not bring to an end with victory. Now know that nothing will hold me back from fighting the men who have caused me such a loss among my own blood and lineage. Dishonour has befallen us not through God's justice but through Lancelot's pride – that man whom I have treated for so long as one of my own flesh and blood!'

Then all present knew that King Arthur was determined to wage mortal war on Sir Lancelot and had forgotten all the love he had once felt for him. Messengers were sent far and wide throughout the whole realm to summon knights and men to Camelot.

The news reached Joyous Garde.

'Have things then come to this?' asked Sir Bors.

'Yes, my Lord, before long you will see King Arthur here and all his forces.'

'In God's name,' said Sir Ector, 'it is a pity they are coming. But the pity will be for them, not for us, for they will much repent it.'

Not many mornings later, before sunrise, many thousands of armed men left Camelot. They rode day after day through the Forest till at last they came within half a league of the great fortress of Joyous Garde.

When Sir Lancelot saw how his castle was besieged by King Arthur, the man he had loved most in the world and whom he now knew to be his mortal enemy, he was so saddened that he did not know what to do; not because he feared for himself, but because he loved the King. He would not go out of Joyous Garde or even show himself on the battlements for fear of having to fight either King Arthur or Sir Gawain, whom he also loved. For he knew Sir Gawain to be one of the most noble knights in the whole world.

But Sir Lancelot's kinsmen did not agree with Sir Lancelot.

'If we stay shut in here much longer,' they said, 'our enemies will think we are cowards.'

That evening Sir Bors and Sir Ector, and forty knights, slipped out into the Forest. There they lay all night in hiding, waiting for the signal that they should attack.

Next day those in the castle armed and made ready to break out. From the highest tower of Joyous Garde a purple flag fluttered.

'Now we must be ready to move,' said Sir Bors as soon as he saw the flag. 'This means that Sir Lionel has mounted, and he will be coming out straight away with all his company.'

Then the besiegers saw the great gates of Joyous Garde thrown open, and six companies of armed knights ride out to the attack. King Arthur armed himself hurriedly, and so did Sir Gawain and all their knights. But as they rose out to meet the knights of Joyous Garde, there was a great hue and cry behind them and the thundering of hoofs as Sir Bors and Sir Ector galloped out from their hiding place in the Forest. The noise in the camp became so loud that one would not even have heard God thundering. The King saw his own tent fall to the ground, with the Dragon Standard above it; for the knights from the Forest were smiting and striking at all the tents, hoping to capture the King.

When Sir Gawain saw the astonishing things they were doing, he spurred his horse against Sir Ector. Sir Gawain hated Ector mortally, because men had told him that Ector had first smote off the helm of Sir Gaheris, treacherously, from behind, before Sir Lancelot killed him. So Gawain smote Sir Ector such a blow on the helmet that he dazed him, and he would surely have killed Sir Ector with his next stroke if Sir Bors had not come riding to his rescue. Sir Bors rode up to Sir Gawain, brandishing his sword, and struck him so hard that his sword went two finger breadths into his helmet. At this Gawain was so stunned that he rode away, shaking his head with the pain; and so Sir Ector, who would have fallen to the ground if he had not clung to his horse's neck, was saved.

The fight raged fiercest in front of the King's fallen tent. Bors and all his men would have been killed there if his brother Sir Lionel and the knights from Joyous Garde had not spurred to his rescue. Men were dying in great pain; they hated each other mortally, though they had been each other's dear companions shortly before.

Sir Gawain did marvels when he had recovered his wits, and slew nearly thirty knights. At last he came up with Sir Bors again and he was far from sorry because Sir Bors was the man he hated most in the world.

'Ah, Bors,' he cried, 'false and recreant knight. What cause had you to kill my good brother Sir Gareth, defenceless and in his despite?'

Sir Bors had not time to answer before Sir Gawain was upon him. They clashed so violently and with such hatred that their lances passed through each other's bodies. They fell to the ground, and did not move.

At the fall of these two great knights the battle ended. Each side feared their own champion was killed, and made haste to bear the bodies back to safety. But Sir Gawain was only slightly wounded. Sir Bors was in a very different way. He seemed likely to die, and never was there seen man or woman in such grief as the Queen when they carried him injured and bleeding back into Joyous Garde. With her own hands Guinevere drew out the fragment of Sir Gawain's lance from the deep wound in his side.

'Ah, Bors,' she cried sadly, 'you alone were ready to help me when all men believed I had poisoned Gawain. And now Sir Gawain has slain you.' Then the tears came into her eyes. 'This is all because of my evil doing,' she wept, 'and because I have left my true lord King Arthur.'

But Bors did not die, though he took many weeks to heal. As the siege of Joyous Garde continued and more and more noble knights were killed, King Arthur grew very sad, and regretted both the war and his dear wife. At last it was agreed that the Queen would be returned to King Arthur, but that Lancelot would leave the realm of Logres and go, with all his kin, to Benwick.

That night when the news was proclaimed throughout the camps there was great joy among the besiegers, because the war was over. But there was great sadness in Joyous Garde.

'My Lady,' said Sir Lancelot, 'tomorrow I leave Logres and I do not know if I will ever see you again. Here is a ring that I beg you always to wear for love of me as long as I live.'

'Nay, Sir Lancelot,' said Guinevere sadly, 'that shall I never do. Sir Lancelot, for all the love that was ever between us, go to your realm, and there, I beseech you, take a wife and live with her in joy and bliss.'

'My sweet lady,' said Sir Lancelot, 'do you think I will wed a damsel in my own country and be false to you? Nay, madam, that I will never do; and you never knew me false of any promise yet. For I call God to witness now, that if you had wished, I would have taken you to my own realm. But for the love of my lord King Arthur this may not be.'

On the next day Sir Lancelot dressed richly, mounted and rode out to the King's camp, clothed in cloth of gold. The Queen rode at his side, dressed in green velvet. A hundred knights followed them, their horses covered in silk; and in his hand each knight held an olive branch, the sign of Christian peace. The horses pranced, and the knights jousted joyfully as they rode out. When the moment came that Sir Lancelot saw Arthur approaching him, he dismounted and took the Queen by the reins of her horse.

'My Lord,' he said, 'here is the Queen whom I give back to you. She would have died some time ago if I had not risked my life to save her. I did not do it because of any kindness I have ever had from her, but only because I know her to be the finest lady in the world. She comes to you of her own will, and begs you to receive her lovingly.'

At these words Arthur was very miserable and pensive. 'Sir Lancelot,' he said, 'you are truly the flower of knighthood and the most noble knight in all the world.'

And he stretched out his hand to Guinevere. But then Sir Gawain interrupted.

'As for my lady the Queen,' said Sir Gawain, 'I will never blame her. But you,' he said turning to Sir Lancelot, 'you, false and recreant knight, what cause had you to let Bors kill my brother Gareth that loved you more than me and all his kin? It was you that made him a knight with your own hands; and he would not defend himself against any of your kind. And what cause had you to kill my good brother Sir Gaheris so cruelly and so traitorously?'

'I was ranging in the thick of the battle,' said Sir Lancelot, 'and unhappily I smote Sir Gaheris without realizing who he was. But by the faith I owe the high order of knighthood I swear that I would as soon have slain my own cousin Sir Bors.'

'It could have been better if you had,' said Sir Gawain grimly, 'for you are both recreant knights. Many a long day you have envied all of us, and many a time destroyed the good knights of my blood.'

'Ah, Sir Gawain,' said Sir Lancelot, 'your grief has made you mad. You are cruelly causing bitterness between my blood and the King; yet you should not feel any hatred for me. Remember, rather, how I rescued you from Sir Caradoc of the Dolorous Tower, and Sir Gaheris from Sir Tarquin of Dolorous Garde.'

'Lancelot,' said Sir Gawain bitterly, 'there is nothing you have done for us that recently you have not made us pay for very dearly.'

Then Sir Lancelot saw that he would never be forgiven by Sir Gawain. He turned to the King.

'My Lord Arthur,' he said, 'I will now leave this noble realm of Logres and for all the services that I have rendered you since I first became a knight, I shall take away nothing in return. But when I am in my own country, shall I be safe from you? What can I expect from you, peace or war?'

It was Sir Gawain who answered him.

'Sir,' said Sir Gawain, 'the King my uncle may do as he will. But you and I will never be at peace. You will have war, mortal war, more violent than you have had up till now, and it will last till my brother Sir Gaheris, whom you killed wickedly, is avenged by your own death. I would not take the whole world in exchange for the chance to slice off your head.'

'I can believe well enough,' said Sir Lancelot grimly 'that if you lay hands on me I will get little mercy from you.'

Then Sir Lancelot sighed, and the tears fell on his cheeks.

'Most noble Christian realm,' he said, 'which I have loved above all other realms! For in this realm I won glory, and by me and my kin the glory of all the Round Table has been increased. I fear that in this realm there will be peace no longer but always war and strife, now that the fellowship of the Round Table is broken. And here, my Lord King Arthur, I make my boast. By the noble fellowship of the Round Table were you upheld and all your realm, and in great part this was by my own prowess.'

Then he turned to Queen Guinevere.

'Madam,' he said, 'I must now depart from you and Logres and all this most noble fellowship.'

Then he, and all his company, took their sad leave.

CHAPTER 10

War with Sir Lancelot

ALL that winter King Arthur remained in the realm of Logres. But Sir Gawain gave his uncle no rest. In the spring after Easter, when the cold weather had passed, the King summoned all his knights and warriors. Sir Gawain swore that together they would destroy the fortresses of Benwick and Gaunes until not one stone was left standing on another.

So the great army marched out, thousands upon thousands of them. King Arthur left Sir Mordred to rule the realm while he should be away. He gave him the keys of all his treasures in case he should be in need of gold or silver and made the people swear on the saints that they would do exactly as Sir Mordred wished.

'Peace is better than always war,' said the Lady Luned, as the great army marched past Castle Perilous. She turned to her sister the Lady Lynette. 'Even if they kill Sir Lancelot and Sir Bors, it will not bring poor Beaumains, your dead husband, back to life.'

'My lord Sir Gareth loved Sir Lancelot best of all knights,' said the Lady Lynette sadly. 'What would he say now if he knew that there was mortal war between King Arthur and Sir Lancelot?'

'He would say that it must stop,' said the Lady Luned, 'and so do I.'

She mounted her palfrey, and rode down to try and see the King.

'Alas,' said Sir Lucan, 'my lord Arthur would make peace with Sir Lancelot, but Sir Gawain will not let him. I pray to God, Lady, that you may persuade them better.'

'If I am as lucky as you, Sir Lucan,' said the Lady Luned, 'I will.'

He took her into the King's presence.

'Sir King,' said the Lady Luned, 'turn back. This is great madness, and you are ill advised. No honour will come to you from this war.'

Sir Gawain saw that the King was hesitating, and that all the other knights were for turning back.

'My lord, my uncle,' he said, 'will you turn back? All the world will speak of your cowardice and shame.'

'You know well, Gawain,' said King Arthur miserably, 'that I will do as you advise me.'

'Ah, Gawain,' said the Lady Luned angrily, 'you have persuaded the king to begin this war. But are you sure you are not pursuing your own destruction? You are more of a madman these days than a courteous knight.'

'Damsel Sauvage you called yourself,' retorted Sir Gawain furiously, 'but Sorceress Sauvage I call you for your ill will, and ugly face, and evil tongue. The best thing you can do now is ride to Sir Lancelot and tell him that I, Sir Gawain, send him word that I so promise him by the faith I owe to God and to my knighthood that I shall never let him alone till he has slain me, or I him.'

The Lady Luned did not ride to Sir Lancelot to deliver Sir Gawain's proud message. For she saw that there was no stopping the war with Sir Lancelot. Instead, she rode to see the knight whose life she had once saved, Sir Yvain. The Raven Army would have turned her back, as they turn back all intruders who have ever tried to pass the Gates of Gore; they would have turned her back too if she had not had with her the Ring of Power that, by twisting, rendered her invisible. So she passed into Gore, out of the power of the Shadow that was now spreading over Logres, and there she contrived many things.

King Arthur's knights and warriors swept down into the realm of Gaunes and the land of Benwick, destroying and burning and wreaking havoc and vengeance. But Sir Lancelot would not come out to fight against King Arthur or Sir Gawain, because of the great love he had always had for them. There was much slaughter on both sides, and so it went on for half a year. King Arthur's heart grew heavy.

'Now alas,' said the King, 'that ever this unhappy war began!'

Sir Gawain had no wish to see his uncle miserable and spent that night deep in thought. Next morning he called one of his squires and said:

'Go to the city of Benwick and tell Lancelot du Lac that I defy him to single combat. If he can conquer me, then King Arthur and all his army will return to the realm of Logres. If I overcome him, I shall ask no more, and the war will end straightaway.'

When Sir Gawain's squire heard this, he began to sob tenderly.

'My Lord,' he said, 'may it please God, I will not carry that message! Sir Lancelot is the most hardened knight in the world, and in that message I see your death too clearly. And I would be disloyal if such a noble man as you went to his death through anything I did or said.'

'I well know that he is the finest knight I have ever met,' said Sir Gawain. 'But what you are saying is nonsense. For everyone knows that wrong and treachery make the world's finest knight a coward. That is the reason I fear Lancelot less, since I know I am on the side of justice and he is guilty of having slain my brother Gaheris. So take the message – or else this war will never end.'

So the squire rode out to Benwick and defied Sir Lancelot on Sir Gawain's behalf.

'My fair lords,' said Sir Lancelot to his kin, 'Sir Gawain is the man, out of all those in the world that have ever meant anything to me, that I have most loved and still do, excepting only the King. I should never wish in all my life to fight against Sir Gawain for anything in the world because of his nobility and the companionship he has given me since I was first made a knight.'

'It is remarkable,' said Sir Bors, 'that you love him so deeply when he hates you so mortally.'

'Find it strange if you like,' said Sir Lancelot, 'but he will never be able to hate me so much that I stop loving him.'

When the squire rode back and told Sir Gawain that Sir Lancelot had refused single combat, Sir Gawain said very little. He rode out next day himself, alone, right up to the wall of Benwick and there he accused Sir Lancelot of cowardice and recreancy and treason.

Sir Lancelot and his kin stood on the high walls of Benwick, listening to Sir Gawain's shouts.

'He is grieving so much for his dead brothers,' said Sir Lionel, 'that he would rather take his revenge on Sir Lancelot than on anyone else, and that is why, fair cousin, he accuses you so wickedly.'

'It is all the same to him whether he lives or dies,' said Sir Bors.

'Brother,' said Sir Ector with a grim smile, 'if he challenges you to single combat, he would certainly rather die than live.'

Then they all told Sir Lancelot he had rested over long.

'I will lose all my honour if I do not defend myself,' admitted Sir Lancelot at last, 'because he now accuses me of treason. Therefore send to him and say that he will find me armed and on the battlefield at any time he wishes.'

Then all the kin of Sir Lancelot rejoiced because they were sure Sir Gawain would be going to his death. King Arthur was miserable for the same reason.

'Fair uncle,' said Sir Gawain, 'if God were so courteous as to permit me to put Lancelot to death and avenge my brothers, I would never be saddened by anything that might happen to me. But if he managed to kill me, at least that would be the end of my grief that afflicts me day and night. In one way or another, either alive or dead, I will be at peace after this battle.'

'Gawain,' said King Arthur, 'may God help you, for you have never undertaken anything that dismays me as much as this!'

Sir Gawain smiled.

'God will help me surely, fair uncle,' he said, 'but you may too by giving me your sword Excalibur to fight this battle.'

King Arthur did so willingly. But all the same he was not hopeful.

'I am so worried for you,' he said, 'that I would rather lose the best city I possess than this, for Lancelot is a battle-hardened knight.'

But Sir Gawain was much less worried. He did not rely only on God's help and Excalibur. When he had fixed the day of the combat and the time, he rode out alone without a squire or any companion for many leagues till he came to a great circle of stones, that marked the crossing of the earth-lines that flow beneath the Earth's surface. There at noon, through a sorcery that he had learnt in the Orkeneys, he absorbed the strength of the earth-lines that flow beneath the surface of the Earth.

'Now, Wing Mane,' he said, patting his great war-horse on the neck, 'let us see, old friend, how Lancelot will face your might and mine.' For Wing Mane's might had also increased, by the sorcery. Then they rode back, horse and man, towards Benwick.

Sir Lancelot kept vigil all night before the day of the battle dawned. The sun rose, fine and bright; he asked for his arms and they were brought to him, strong, tenacious, and light. In the courtyard he mounted his strongest horse, covered in steel down to its hoofs. Sir Bors took him by the right hand and led him on to the field, outside the walls.

'My Lord, go forward,' he said, 'and may God grant you victory in this battle.'

Sir Lancelot saw Sir Gawain waiting there, sitting on his great war-horse, grim and unfriendly.

'Sir Gawain,' he cried, 'needs must I defend myself, since you have accused me of treason. I am heavy for your sake, for it is greatly against my will that I should ever fight against any of your blood. But now I am driven to it, as a beast at bay.'

'Cease your babbling,' was all that Sir Gawain replied, 'and let us ease our hearts.'

The sun reflected on their arms. Noble and proud, the two knights spurred their horses on against each other. They came together like thunder. Sir Lancelot's spear broke into a hundred pieces, so violent was the shock, but Sir Gawain and his great war-horse struck Sir Lancelot so fiercely, horse and man together, that Sir Lancelot's horse reared up and toppled over backwards, throwing its rider down onto the cold earth. Sir Lancelot was quite stunned by his fall and lay there dazed. If Sir Gawain had attacked him in unknightly fashion, he could have killed him then and there. Instead, he dismounted and put his hand to Excalibur, King Arthur's good sword. By this time Lancelot was up on his feet, though still dazed and not knowing what to do. Gawain ran at him and gave him such a great blow on his helmet that he dented and twisted it. That cleared Sir Lancelot's head, and he rained blows back at Sir Gawain.

With that a great battle began between the two of them, the most violent combat that was ever seen between two knights. They struck each other so often that their coats of mail split on their arms and their legs. Their shields were so torn at top and bottom that you could have put your fist through the middle of them. Their helmets were so damaged by blows from their swords that they were almost useless. Both of them had many wounds, the least of which would have killed a lesser man. By the time they had fought for an hour, they were so exhausted and weary that their swords often turned in their hands when they went to strike each other. They had to rest then, because they could endure no longer. First Sir Gawain drew back and leant on his shield to regain his breath; then Lancelot did the same.

When Sir Bors saw this, he said to Sir Ector: 'This is the first time ever Sir Lancelot has had to rest before being able to overcome a knight.'

'In truth,' said Sir Ector uneasily, 'he seems to be regaining his breath a little. But do not be dismayed, Bors. You can be sure he does not really need to.'

Sir Ector was wrong. When the battle restarted Sir Lancelot was still tired and suffering from loss of blood, but Sir Gawain seemed as fresh as if he had not struck a single blow. His might increased, his strength doubled, and he struck and smote Sir Lancelot so vigorously that Sir Lancelot was quite dazed and sore adread.

'Ah, God,' cried Sir Bors, 'what do I see? Lancelot, can you do nothing except only suffer?'

Indeed all Sir Lancelot could do was dodge and parry, and cover himself with his shield as Sir Gawain rained down blows upon him. But on King Arthur's side hopes rose higher than they ever had before.

'By God's grace,' cried Sir Gawain's squire, 'my lord is right, and treachery has made Sir Lancelot a coward.'

It is Excalibur, thought King Arthur, as Sir Lancelot stumbled backwards. It is Excalibur that will save Gawain. I could not bear it if he was killed by Lancelot like my other dear nephew Gaheris.

The sun was directly overhead, and Sir Gawain's strength seemed to double again. Excalibur flashed in the sunlight, as with a mighty stroke he beat Sir Lancelot to his knees. A great groan echoed round the high walls of the city of Benwick, so loud that it drowned out, almost, the ringing of the bells which sounded the hour of noon. But Sir Gawain, though he did not hear the bells, felt his strength suddenly fail, and a great weariness came over him. Sir Lancelot was on his feet again, and gave Sir Gawain such a great blow sideways that he sent him staggering.

'Now I feel you have done your mighty deeds, my lord Sir Gawain,' cried Sir Lancelot joyfully, 'and so it is my turn.'

Then Sir Lancelot strode at Sir Gawain, doubling his strokes and driving him backwards.

So the battle raged on, and the ground over which they fought was strewn with links from their coats of mail and pieces of their shields. Sir Lancelot's blood was flowing from his body in more than thirteen places where Sir Gawain had wounded him, and he was nearly dead from exhaustion. But as for Sir Gawain, he defended himself with such difficulty that with all his great efforts the blood burst out of his nose and mouth, as well as from his other wounds. All those watching on both sides had fallen silent with the pity of it, and now there was neither cheers nor groans but only the sound of the panting of the two men, and the swish of swords that rang on armour or bit deep and silently into flesh.

'Ah, God,' muttered Sir Bors, 'those are the two finest knights in the world.'

The sun was sinking. Evening was approaching. Sir Gawain was so exhausted that he could hardly hold his sword.

He felt the greatest fear that he had ever known, but he held out and parried the blows Sir Lancelot rained on him, striving on for fear of death. All who watched could see that there was very little fight left in him. Then Sir Lancelot smote him such a stroke upon the helm that the blow glanced off the helmet and cut into the head, and Sir Gawain sank slowly down upon his side. At that Sir Lancelot put up his sword and turned wearily away.

But even though Sir Gawain was lying on his side, he still waved Excalibur and thrust feebly at Sir Lancelot as he lay. 'Traitor knight,' he gabbled, 'you have not slain me yet. Come back, come closer, if you dare, false recreant, finish this battle to the utmost.'

'I will do not more than I have done,' said Sir Lancelot, looking down in pity upon him.

'As soon as I am cured,' groaned Sir Gawain, 'I will do battle with you again, so slay me if you can.'

'I will do battle with you when I see you stand upon your feet,' said Sir Lancelot, 'but to smite a wounded man that cannot stand – may God defend me from such a shame.'

Sir Lancelot turned then, and limped wearily back to Benwick. Sir Ector came out to meet him.

'My Lord,' he said, 'what have you done? Will you let your mortal enemy escape? Go back, my Lord, and swop off his head – then the war will be over.'

'May God help me,' said Sir Lancelot, 'I would rather be struck through the body with a lance than kill such a noble man.'

'He would have killed you if he could,' said Sir Ector; and even Sir Bors said that he feared Sir Lancelot would repent it.

But, as for King Arthur, he felt sick with his sorrow for Sir Gawain, who was so badly wounded, and all because of the war with Sir Lancelot. They brought Sir Gawain to him, on his shield.

'Alas, Sir Gawain, my sister's son,' lamented King Arthur, 'here now you lie, the man in the world that I loved most. Now all my joy is gone! For now, my nephew, Sir Gawain, I must tell you that in you and in Sir Lancelot I had my greatest delight and trust. Now I have lost my joy of you both, wherefore all my earthly joy is gone from me.'

Then everyone there, high and low, rich and poor, wept because they all loved Sir Gawain so dearly. But Sir Gawain had not the strength to reply. He did not open his eyes or say anything or do any more than if he were dead, except that after a time he groaned bitterly. They thought he might die in their hands at any time.

'My fair lords,' said Sir Lancelot to his kin, 'I can tell you that ever since I first bore arms I have never been afraid of any single knight except today. When we rested, I knew Gawain was near defeat and surrender, but in a very short time he was swifter and more valiant than he had been at the beginning.'

'Indeed,' said Sir Bors, 'if he had continued that prowess for long, you would not have escaped with your life.'

That was how they talked, on both sides, of that battle. But Sir Gawain did not die. Slowly he recovered, except for the deep wound in his head; and he swore that when he was whole again he would challenge Sir Lancelot once more and this time defeat him. For his hatred had not grown softer nor his grief less violent.

Yet it was not to be.

The Day of Destiny

STRANGE things had been happening in Logres while King Arthur and Sir Gawain were away.

It was lucky for the Lady Luned that, when she rode back from Gore to Castle Perilous, she went by secret paths that only a damsel errant would know. It was night when she neared Castle Perilous. She had a feeling that all was not well. The night sky was too bright, flickering and glowing over the tree-tops of the deep Forest. She spurred her palfrey on till she came to a little rise, and from its top at last caught a glimpse of her sister's great castle. To her horror it was all ablaze, from the drawbridge to the topmost towers. She was about to gallop on when a tall figure stepped out of the shadows in her path.

271

'Go no further, Lady,' said a voice that Luned recognized at once. 'It is too late.'

'Who are those with you, Merlin?' she asked, unsteadily.

'My night-riders,' said Merlin, 'my own fellowship.' He laughed grimly. 'For even I, even I Merlin, do not dare go abroad by day now or by night without protection. The Shadow of Mordor has fallen over Logres, and the whole realm is in mortal danger.'

Luned looked at the blazing castle.

'My sister?' she asked.

'The Lady Lynette is dead,' said Merlin, 'burnt alive with all her knights. They resisted bravely but they could do nothing. The Orcs were too strong.'

'What are these Orcs?' asked Luned fiercely.

Merlin gave a tired smile.

'I forget,' he said, 'I keep forgetting that there is so much you and the humans of this Age do not know. I myself had thought Orcs were extinct but they are not. They have swarmed out of the Land of Stones. They are like enormous trolls, only ten times as dangerous. Not so dangerous, though,' he muttered looking anxiously up at the sky, 'as the Nazguls who even now are hunting me and my fellowship.'

The Lady Luned paid no attention to that. She cared more for her dead sister than for any wizard.

'But who summoned these creatures, these Orcs?' she said. 'At whose service are they?'

Merlin seemed amazed that she did not know.

'Why, at the service of Mordred of course,' he said. 'Do you not know that Sir Mordred has proclaimed himself High King of Logres, and that great forces are rallying to him?'

'But how can that be?' cried the Lady Luned. 'What of Arthur? And what of Sir Lancelot and Sir Gawain?'

'That gives him no difficulty,' said Merlin sombrely. 'He has told the people that they have all killed each other, that they are all dead.' Luned looked very shaken. 'It is not true, of course,' Merlin added hurriedly. 'But they are fighting each other in Benwick while the realm perishes, and indeed they may well end up by killing each other. There is no hope in them. No, the only hope for Logres now is Sir Yvain.'

Then it was the Lady Luned's turn to look very sombre. She told Merlin how she had ridden to Gore and by the use of the Ring of Power had passed the Raven Sentinels, and come at last into the presence of Sir Yvain.

'But he is very different now,' she said, 'from that young knight who was so beautiful and so valiant, who overthrew the Lord of the Fountain and married the Lady, my cousin. He sits by himself in silence, with only a mangy toothless lion for company. He speaks only to the birds and the beasts, not to man. He called me a sorceress, like his own mother Morgan le Fay, and told me he would never again come to Camelot, not even if his uncle King Arthur and his cousin Sir Gawain begged him on bended knee. I think he would have thrown me to his Ravens if I had not twisted the Ring and made myself invisible even more.'

'So the Shadow has fallen over Gore too,' said Merlin. 'Now is all hope lost, for I was counting on the Raven Army in my plans.'

'Ah,' sighed the Lady Luned, 'when I remember how courteous and elegant Sir Yvain was! Mind you, I told him what I thought of his bad manners nowadays just before I made myself invisible.'

'There is no time for this foolishness,' snapped Merlin. Far away the howling of the Orcs rose to a crescendo as the towers of Castle Perilous toppled down at last in the flames. 'In a little while, if I and my night-riders escape the Enemy, I will go to Gore myself. For the Raven Army is the only force left that can stop Mordred, of that I am almost sure.' He pointed a long menacing finger at Luned. 'As for you, Lady, ride to Guinevere and take her to a hidden place of safety. Use the Ring of Power if you must. For if Mordred lays hands on a sacred queen, his might will be the more increased.'

'Who is this Mordred?' asked the Lady Luned fearfully.

But all Merlin said, as he swirled his great cloak around him and looked up, just as fearfully, at the lightening sky was: 'Who indeed is this Mordred? Who knows?'

In one way Merlin's question was very foolish, and the Lady Luned's too. Everybody in Logres knew who Sir Mordred was. He was the youngest son of Queen Morgawse of Orkeney, King Arthur's sister. But the mystery was that nobody was sure who Sir Mordred's father was. King Lot of Orkeney, the father of Gawain, Gaheris, Agravaine, and Gareth, had been killed long before Mordred was born. In any case Mordred did not look at all like his half-brothers. He resembled his mother: he was dark, and rather silent. When he was angry, his voice became mocking and his eyes grew red and savage. People were afraid of him. It was rumoured that his father was a fiend and he himself a warlock, because he never seemed to be badly wounded in battle, not even when he fought with knights of ten times his strength. But nobody really knew; and as Queen Morgawse was dead too, nobody could ask her. Sir Mordred himself told no one.

When he announced that he had had news of the deaths of King Arthur and Sir Gawain and Sir Lancelot in wars in Benwick, nobody was surprised when he proclaimed himself High King. The people had sworn on the saints to obey him in King Arthur's absence, and he rewarded the knights richly with the gold and silver that King Arthur had left behind. If any refused to accept him as High King and demanded proof of King Arthur's death, as the Lady Lynette and the knights of Castle Perilous had done, it was the worse for them. Logres shivered with terror, and Mordred smiled.

But when the news finally reached King Arthur in his camp at Benwick, then his anger was terrible to behold.

'Ah, Mordred,' he said, 'you are the serpent I once saw issuing from my stomach which burnt my lands and attacked me. Ah, God, if I now had in my company the knights that I once used to have, I should not fear the whole world if it was against me!'

But even though he had so few noble knights left since the noble fellowship of the Round Table had been destroyed, King Arthur acted as a great king should. He ordered his whole army to be ready to leave the next morning, to abandon the siege of Benwick and to march back to Logres.

'I will go by ship, secretly, seize Camelot, and slay this traitor,' said Sir Kay.

King Arthur thanked his foster brother, and Sir Kay rode away with a company of knights.

When Arthur and his army reached Logres, there was bad news waiting. A messenger came to them.

'King Arthur,' he proclaimed, 'I shall not greet you because my lord is a mortal enemy of yours, Mordred the High King of Logres. You have unwisely entered his realm. But if you leave at once, he will do you no harm.'

'Tell my half-brother Mordred,' growled Sir Gawain, 'that I will kill him, traitor that he is, with my own two hands.'

The messenger threw a basket down at King Arthur's feet.

'That is what Sir Kay your Seneschal threatened,' he said, 'Mordred the High King sends you this gift, as a sign of how he will deal with such threats.'

Sir Gawain opened the basket. Inside it was Sir Kay's head. King Arthur gazed in horror at the glazed eyes of his foster brother who had been brought up with him in the Fenland.

'He did not die a knightly death,' said the messenger. 'His head was smashed by an oar wielded by an Orc. Mordred has eyes everywhere.'

'Well, Kay,' said Sir Gawain, 'you were always too bold for your own strength, and now your mocking tongue is stilled for ever. I for one am glad that you did not slay Mordred. Tell that perjurer he will die by my hands alone.'

The messenger looked at the King.

'Go and tell your lord,' said Arthur, 'that this is my land

and my realm, and that I defy him as a false traitor and always will until my death day.'

'That will soon come,' said the messenger, 'for my lord King Mordred says that you will have your fill of battle tomorrow since you so desire it.'

For all his bold words Sir Gawain was not so confident as he sounded. He and King Arthur rode out onto the Great Plain that afternoon. The clouds scudded across the gloomy sky and a cold drizzle chilled them to the bone as they rode up and down, gazing at the ranks of Mordred's men. Further away, raucous cries rose from the dark edge of the Forest.

'What are those?' asked King Arthur.

'Those are the Orcs, fair Sire,' said Sir Bedevere. 'They are fearsome trolls from out of the Land of Stones, and it is said Sir Mordred has thousands upon thousands of them.'

King Arthur turned to Sir Lucan.

'We will need all your luck tomorrow,' he said, trying to be cheerful.

'The fewer we are, the greater the glory,' said Sir Gawain boldly.

For indeed King Arthur's great army that had set out so valiantly for the war against Sir Lancelot was much shrunken. Many of the ordinary soldiers had gone to their homes. 'With King Arthur,' they said, 'there is always war, but with Sir Mordred there may be peace.' Many of the knights had been killed or, like Sir Gawain, badly wounded in the battles in Benwick and were not so confident as they had been before. But for all that it was a great, battle-hardened army, and they comforted themselves that Orcs were only trolls grown larger and no match for armoured knights – though, to tell the truth, the cries of the Orcs even from a distance struck terror into their hearts.

Sir Gawain turned Wing Mane's head and rode off by himself into the middle of the Plain. He came across a high and solid rock. On it were the written runes. He could see they were wizard's runes, but as he could not read runes very well, he called over his uncle King Arthur. King Arthur read the inscription out aloud:

On this plain will take place the mortal battle which will orphan the Realm of Logres.

When the King had read this out, he fell silent. His knights looked at one another in great fear. They all rode back, saying nothing, to King Arthur's camp.

'What did this inscription mean, my Lord?' said Sir Gawain, when he went to King Arthur's tent that evening.

'It means, fair nephew,' replied King Arthur calmly, 'that my Day of Destiny has come, as Merlin foretold.

'Wizard's runes, wizard's trickery,' said Gawain. 'I have never trusted them. It could mean I will be killed, as I am the heir to Logres.' He cheered up. 'It could even mean that Mordred will be killed as he calls himself ruler of Logres now.'

All the same Sir Gawain slept badly. He had a nightmare: he dreamt he fell into a hideous black water in which all manners of horrible snakes were swimming. A serpent seized him by the leg, and was pulling him down, when he woke sweating and crying, 'Help! Help!' His squire came to him and washed him and dressed him, and Sir Gawain went to the King. He remembered now that the sorceresses had foretold he would die in the greatest battle of all; but that, if he lived, he would save the whole realm.

'Fair uncle,' he said, shaking him awake, 'we must not do battle with Mordred tomorrow. God has sent me a dream: if we do battle, I will be pulled down into the Pit, and our whole army may be defeated. Make him fair promises, but do not do battle with him.'

'Now we miss Sir Lancelot,' said King Arthur sadly.

Then Sir Gawain, who was the noblest knight in the world, knew what he must do.

'Through me and my pride, my Lord,' he said, 'is all this evil come. For if that noble knight Sir Lancelot were here with you, as he should be, this unhappy battle would be as good as won: for always through his noble knighthood and his noble blood he has held all your enemies in subjection. Therefore, fair uncle, I pray you that I may have paper, pen, and ink, that I may write to Sir Lancelot a letter written with my own hand.'

They brought him paper, pen and ink, and very slowly in the old spelling Sir Gawain formed the words and wrote out this letter:

Unto thee, Sir Launcelot, floure of all noble kynghtes that ever I hurde of or saw bye my days, I, Sir Gawayne, kynge Lottis sonne of Orkeney, and systirs son unto the noble Kynge Arthur sende thee gretynge. I woll that all the worlde wyte that I, Sir Gawayne, knyght of the Table Rounde soughte my owne dethe of thyn hande and thorow myne owne sekynge; for of a more nobelar man myght I not be slayne. Wherefore I beseche thee, Sir Launcelot, for all the love that ever was betwyxte us, make no taryyng but com in all the goodly haste that ye may, wyth youre noble knyghtes, and rescow that noble kynge that made thee knyght, for he ys full straytely bestad wyth an false traytoure whych ys my halff-brothir, Sir Mordred.

So in the morning when the battle lines were drawn up, King Arthur sent Sir Lucan and Sir Bedevere across the Great Plain, which was called Camlann, to treat with Sir Mordred. They came to Sir Mordred; behind him, rank after rank, men and Orcs alike, was a grim host of a hundred thousand warriors drawn up.

Sir Mordred agreed then that he would meet King Arthur between the hosts under the Truce of God, and that each of them should bring fourteen knights only with them. But when Sir Lucan and Sir Bedevere had ridden away gladly, Sir Mordred warned his knights that if they should see any sword drawn on King Arthur's side, they should draw their own swords and come on fiercely and slay the King. 'I in no way trust my uncle,' said Sir Mordred darkly, 'and I know well my half-brother Sir Gawain will be avenged on me.'

Both hosts watched as the thirty knights, fifteen from each side, rode out slowly and met in the midst of the Great Plain; and the men on both sides rejoiced because it seemed that they were making peace and that therefore many men, who would otherwise be doomed to die, would save their lives. Indeed wine was brought, and they drunk together like dear companions, though Sir Gawain always watched Sir Mordred as closely as a hawk, for he suspected treachery. Yet Sir Mordred was very pleasant and spoke fair words.

The hosts watching loosened their armour and leaned on their shields. Then suddenly they saw a single sword flash out on King Arthur's side and heard Sir Mordred call out, in a high thin voice as if he were surprised, 'Treachery!' Then the hosts saw in a single second fifteen swords flash out in the hands of Sir Mordred and his knights as they fell on King Arthur and his startled companions.

It would have gone hard with Arthur then if Sir Gawain had not been on his guard. But Sir Gawain had seen Sir Mordred give a secret signal to a young knight on King Arthur's side, who was ready for treason. That was the young knight who had drawn the sword, pretending that he had seen a snake, an adder that was striking at him. But in fact Sir Mordred had won him over before the battle: and it was all a trap to ensnare King Arthur falsely.

So Sir Gawain drew his sword, and hurled himself in front of Arthur the King. When Mordred's knights saw Gawain there, savage and smiling, like a hawk of battle, they hesitated; so the King was saved. But with a scream of fury Mordred hurled himself on Gawain. He struck him a great blow on the helm and then turned and galloped back to his own hosts, with all his knights. Wing Mane the war-horse started in pursuit of him without any urging, but then he felt his rider's weight grow heavier and his rider's hands fall lifeless, as they had never done before. Sir Gawain slowly toppled from his horse's saddle to the ground; his armour clanged about him, and as his helmet fell away, his companions could see that Sir Mordred's single stroke had by mischance reopened the deep wound in his head that Sir Lancelot had given him. 'Jesu mercy,' was all Sir Gawain said as the crimson blood gushed from his head, 'do not judge me by my sins.' Then he groaned and died.

'Ah, God,' cried King Arthur bitterly, 'why did you allow me to see the worst traitor in the world kill one of the noblest men ever to live?'

'Cursed be Death,' cried his companions, 'who has robbed us so shamefully of his company.'

But Sir Sagremor the Desirous, who was bearing King Arthur's Dragon Standard, raised his eyes from Gawain's body and saw on the edge of the Great Plain the hosts of Mordred's army rolling slowly forward, knights in armour and light-armed warriors on foot, trolls with stone slings, and bowmen with long bows, and in the midst rank after rank of fearsome Orcs with their great double-edged axes, their flails and their maces.

'My Lord King,' he said. 'Fortune is making you pay very dearly for the great prosperity and honour you used to have. God grant that things do not become worse!'

Then they all raised their eyes and saw what Sir Sagremor was seeing. Swiftly they laid Sir Gawain's body across his war-horse, and led them back as fast as they could to their own battle line.

When King Arthur's army saw that Sir Gawain was dead, they were more frightened than they had ever been. Asgard the Ancient, the Gatekeeper, had to keep his one assistant Erik the Churl from running away by patting him gently on the head with the flat of his axe.

'But the Orcs, Asgard,' cried Erik, 'look at some of these Orcs. How they frighten me.'

'You should be more frightened of me than of any oversize trolls,' said Asgard grimly. 'The bigger they are, the better the target.'

'I know I am no use to anyone,' said Erik, 'but I am young, Asgard, and you are old. I do not want to die.'

'Even when a man is as old as I am,' joked Asgard, 'he does not much want to die. Come, Erik, remember we are gatekeepers, you and I. Grip your club and make ready, for before we die, we will open Hell's gates for as many of those demon's spawn as we can.'

Then King Arthur rode up and down the ranks, encouraging his host. He divided his army into ten great companies, each led by a famous knight or king, but the last and finest company, of a hundred household knights and a thousand household warriors, he commanded himself. He drew Excalibur, flashing and flaming like a serpent's tongue, and ordered Sir Sagremor to advance the Dragon Standard across the Great Plain. Then the warhorns sounded and the banners fluttered, and even cowards such as Erik felt their hearts filled with courage. But for all that a hundred great companies of Mordred's hosts were advancing to the boom of deep drums, ten against one, and as they rumbled forward, like a black swarm over the green grass of the Great Plain, a great dark shadow seemed always to stretch out, overhanging them, in the sky, a sign of what no mortal man could tell.

The hosts clashed. The noise of battle rose. Far far away in Annwen Merlin felt the power of Mordor waver; and his wizard's heart went wild with joy. For he knew then he had been wrong when he had foretold that there was no hope left in Arthur. The Day of Destiny had come.

CHAPTER 12

Morte Arthur

NEVER was there a more doleful battle in any land, before or since, than the last great battle King Arthur fought at Camlann. The noise of the first clash of the hosts was so great that you could not have heard God thundering. Then there was rushing and riding, thrusting and smiting, many a grim threat spoken and many a deadly stroke given.

Of the Kings who had come to the aid of Arthur, King Royance and King Anguish did the noblest deeds before they were killed, though they were old men by this time. King Royance had more steel in him than any other man before he fell; his companions carried him to a tree because they loved him very dearly, so that he could die there in greater comfort.

King Anguish had brought a company of saints from Ireland. Shouting their war cries, they charged into the black mass of the Orcs, and were swallowed up there like angels by devils. Not one came out alive. King Yon, a younger man, challenged Sir Mordred himself; he struck the bearer of the Standard of the Shadow so hard that he clove him to the teeth and Mordred's standard fell to earth. But then more than five hundred of Sir Mordred's knights rode over him at a gallop, so that for all his armour he was crushed to pulp.

The battle continued all day long. Many a noble knight and many a warrior lay stretched on the cold earth; and even Orcs were wearying for all their great might. At last, of all King Arthur's companies only one remained, and that was his own company, the Company of the Household; but the rest lay dead on the Great Plain. King Arthur sent his own body servant Bloodaxe to climb a hill to see how many men remained on Mordred's side.

'Arthur,' said Bloodaxe returning, 'they have only one host left in arms. But the host is Mordred's own, and with him are the mightiest of the Orcs as well as the best of his own knights.'

'How many of them are there?'

'There must be a thousand in all,' said Bloodaxe.

'This battle is the most fearful we have ever seen,' said Sir Lucan gloomily. 'Soon we will all be dead and buried.'

Then King Arthur looked round. He saw that he had only thirty-two Knights of the Round Table left alive, and about seventy other warriors with them.

'If only I had Lancelot and Gawain armed and standing next to me,' he thought, 'then even now we would be victorious. Why did they leave me alone?' The Shadow passed over King Arthur's spirit and for a moment his heart failed him. Then he remembered who he was: he was Arthur, son of Uther Pendragon, the High King, the Lord of Logres. What need was there of Gawain or Lancelot while he could still wield Excalibur? He turned to his knights and warriors.

'We will not wait here like cowards for them to attack us,' he cried. 'Keep together, all of you. Sagremor, advance the Dragon Standard!'

Then the sun came out and the hearts of Arthur's knights and warriors lifted with joy, for they saw that even if they must die, they would die nobly and their deaths would always be remembered. They charged with such great violence that the whole earth seemed about to collapse for the great noise of the striking down of Mordred's knights. They killed on the right and they killed on the left, and Bloodaxe broke ranks, dashed through the thick of the press, seized Mordred by the leg, and hurled him off his horse. But then twenty knights, all in steel, rode to his rescue, every single one prepared to risk his life for love of Mordred. With twenty swords they hacked Arthur's poor servant to death, and set their own lord on his horse again. But of all Mordred's four hundred knights in his own company these were the last twenty that were left alive. There was such mortal hatred between them and the Knights of the Round Table that blows were given on both sides such as have never been given before or since.

The greatest blow was struck by Asgard the Ancient; with a single swipe of his battle-axe he clove the head of Arcan the Orc Lord, from skull to teeth, and sent him toppling down to Hell. Sir Mordred slew Asgard for that, and the trembling Erik too, but nevertheless the Orcs that remained alive fled. Yet of the Knights of the Round Table that remained almost all had been killed too: Sir Palomides the Saracen, and his brother Sir Safir, Sir Grifflet le Fiz Dieu, and the Chieftain Cealwin – they all took their death wounds on that field. Only four remained alive: King Arthur himself, Sir Lucan, Sir Bedevere, and Sir Sagremor the Desirous. But Sir Sagremor had received such a grisly body wound that he could hardly hold himself upright in the saddle; and Sir Lucan and Sir Bedevere were both bleeding and weary.

'Jesu mercy!' cried Arthur. 'Where are all my noble knights gone? Alas, that ever I should see this doleful day.'

Then King Arthur looked about and saw Sir Mordred not far away, sitting still and silent on his war-horse, leaning on his spear, alone amidst a great heap of dead men.

'Now bring me my spear,' said King Arthur to Sir Lucan, 'for there is the traitor that has wrought all this woe.'

'Sire, let him be,' said Sir Lucan, 'for he is unhappy. Blessed be God, there are four of us alive, and no one alive with Sir Mordred. For God's sake, my Lord, leave off this slaying, for we have won the field. If we leave off now, this wicked Day of Destiny is past.'

But then Sir Mordred raised his dark eyes and met the eyes of the King. Then for all his weariness he urged his horse on against Sir Sagremor, raised his double-handed sword and struck him so violently that his head flew off in the air and landed in front of the King.

'Now tide me death, tide me life,' swore King Arthur. 'I vow to God that either Mordred or I must die on this field.'

Sir Lucan and Sir Bedevere looked fearfully at each other.

'God speed you well, my lord King,' said Sir Bedevere.

Then Arthur took his lance in both hands and ran on foot towards Sir Mordred, crying: 'Traitor, now is your death day come!'

He struck Mordred so violently that the links of his coat of mail broke, the lance passed through his body, and when Arthur wrenched it out, a ray of sunlight passed through the wound so clearly that Sir Bedevere saw it. But Mordred only laughed. Slowly he got off his horse, like a man hardly wounded, and strode towards Arthur, brandishing the great double-handed sword.

'Did Merlin never tell you, fair uncle,' he sneered, 'that no weapon forged by mortal men can kill such beings as I am?'

Holding his sword in both hands, he lifted it high and smote King Arthur so violently through helmet and through head that the King lost a piece of his skull, and a great pain pierced his brain. The dark closed over him.

Yet, as he tottered, Arthur remembered who had forged Excalibur. He drew that flaming sword with his last strength and thrust it to the hilt through the body of his enemy, so that his black heart broke and his black blood came pouring out. Mordred gave one unearthly shriek. Then he fell down to the cold earth, stark dead.

The King leant on Excalibur. Sir Bedevere heard him murmur, 'This is the last battle of Arthur's time.' Then he saw him topple and fall.

At that Bedevere and Lucan who had been sitting bleeding among the piles of dead staggered to their feet. They took King Arthur up, one by one side and one by the other, and with great difficulty left the battlefield and led him towards the Sea until they came to a chapel called the Black Chapel. All the time the King was fainting for loss of blood and could not speak; and nor could they, they were so weary. A strange thing happened just before they entered the Black Chapel. Sir Lucan looked back at the darkening sky over the battlefield and saw a swarm of ravens flying in low and hovering there, over the dead.

'See, Bedevere,' he said. 'Carrions come to feast on the bodies of noble knights!'

At that Arthur opened his eyes.

'No, Lucan,' he said weakly, 'it is the Raven Army of Gore at last. But for me they come too late!'

They carried the King into the chapel, but he would not let them lay him down. He knelt on his knees and the other two knelt beside him and so they passed the whole night, all three on their knees, sobbing and praying for the great suffering of the battle, for the orphans and widows, and for all their friends that were dead. When the cold light of morning came Sir Lucan saw that the King was rigid and silent. He feared he was dead. He tried to lift him up but Arthur swooned and clutched at him so tightly that he burst Lucan's heart inside him. For Arthur was still in all his armour but Sir Lucan had disarmed. And Lucan's guts burst out of his belly.

'Sir,' said Sir Bedevere, 'leave him be. His luck is gone at last. Lucan is dead.' And he wept for pity, for he had loved Sir Lucan well.

But King Arthur did not seem to realize what he had done. He looked at Sir Lucan's body with unseeing eyes. He did not even seem to remember Sir Bedevere's name.

'Leave your mourning and weeping, gentle knight,' he said, 'for my time is passing on fast. Take me down to the sea shore.'

So Sir Bedevere bent his back and carried the King down from the Black Chapel to the sea shore. There Arthur ungirded the sword he was wearing and drew it from its scabbard.

He looked at it for some time, then he said: 'Ah, Excalibur, you fine rich sword, the best in the world! Where will you find a man who will put you to such great use as I have done, unless you come into Lancelot's hands, or perhaps Yvain's, if he is here?'

Then the King was deep in thought. After a while he called Bedevere and said: 'Take Excalibur, my noble sword, go up that hill, and there you will find a lake. Throw my sword into that lake, then come back, one-armed knight, and tell me what you have seen.'

Sir Bedevere climbed the hill, came to the lake, drew Excalibur from its scabbard, and gazed at the sword. Its pommel and hilt were all of precious stones. 'If I throw this fine rich sword into the lake,' said Sir Bedevere to himself, 'no good will come of it but only harm.' So he thought that instead he would throw his own sword. He laid Excalibur down in its scabbard, on the grass, ungirded his own sword, and threw it in. Then he went back to the King. 'My Lord,' he said, 'I have done as you said and thrown your sword into the lake.'

'What did you see?' asked the King.

'Sire,' said Sir Bedevere, 'I saw nothing but the wind and the waves.'

'Go back and throw it in,' said Arthur wearily, as if to a child, 'because you have not done so yet.'

Sir Bedevere went back to the lake, ashamed, and drew Excalibur from its scabbard.

'You splendid and beautiful sword,' he said, 'what a pity it is that you should not fall into the hands of some noble knight, as the King himself has said.'

Then he thought he would throw the scabbard in but hide the sword for Sir Lancelot or perhaps Sir Yvain.

'My Lord,' he said when he was back at the sea shore, 'now I have done as you said.'

'And what did you see?'

'Sire,' said Sir Bedevere, 'I saw the waters lap and the waves darken.'

King Arthur had been sitting on a rock, looking out to sea. He turned sadly towards Sir Bedevere.

'Who would have thought,' he said, 'that you, who have been so noble a knight and so dear to me, would betray me for the riches of this sword? Go again quickly, now, and this time do as I have commanded you. The longer you delay, poor traitor, the less time I have before my life blood ebbs. Already I fell the cold chill of death upon me.'

Then Sir Bedevere was never so ashamed in all his life, as for this, for endangering his Lord King Arthur by his delaying and his lies. He went straight back to the lake's side, picked up Excalibur without gazing on the sword's beauty, and with all the strength of his one arm hurled it as far out into the water as he could. As Excalibur fell, he saw a marvellous sight: an arm that might have been his other arm, if he had been born with both, rose above the surface of the water. The hand caught Excalibur by the hilt, shook and brandished it three times, and then vanished with the sword below the surface of the water.

Sir Bedevere came back to Arthur and told him what he had seen, marvelling.

'By the way the sword came, by the same way it is gone,' said the King. 'For this alone did Destiny spare you. For if you had betrayed me a third time, gentle knight, the realm of Logres would be doomed for ever.'

Then the King sighed deeply.

'Help me to the water's edge,' he said, 'for I dread I have tarried over long.'

Sir Bedevere put his arm round Arthur's waist then, and brought him to the waves' edge. Arthur stood then unsteadily, looking out to the Sea. There were tears in his eyes. Then he turned to Sir Bedevere.

'You must go from here and leave me, last of my knights,' he said.

'My Lord,' said Sir Bedevere, 'I shall do what you command, as sadly as can be. But please tell me if you think I shall ever see you again?'

'No,' said the King, 'but comfort yourself and do as you best may, for in me there is now no more trust to trust in.'

'Where do you expect to go, my dear Lord.'

'I may not tell you,' said the King. 'If you hear never more of me, pray for my soul.'

Sir Bedevere left the King and climbed up the hill again, as Arthur had commanded. As soon as he had left, heavy rain began to fall. When he had reached the hill, he waited under a tree for the rain to stop. He looked back to where he had left the King. A great ship with billowing sails had come sailing in to the sea shore. A queen stepped down from it into the waves' edge; and she was wearing a black hood: She took Arthur's head on her lap. Then Sir Bedevere heard her voice whispering clear over the water's edge and the land's shore.

'Ah, my dear brother,' she said, 'why have you tarried overlong from me? Alas, I dread that this grievous head wound of yours has caught over much cold for all the healing powers of Avalon.'

Then two more queens rowed out from the great ship in a little boat, and they too were wearing black hoods. Moaning and weeping, they laid Arthur gently in the boat; his head rested in his sister's lap. They rowed back then and raised him from the boat to the great ship. Another squall of rain came down again and hid the shore from Sir Bedevere's view. When it had passed and he looked up, the great ship was already far out at sea.

Then Sir Bedevere wept for misery.

'My Lord King Arthur,' he called, 'how can you go away from us and leave us here alone amidst our enemies?'

The sails of the great ship billowed and it disappeared out of sight, over the far horizon, leaving Logres behind.

HERE ENDETH THE BOOK OF DOOM;
AND HERE IS THE END OF THE WHOLE BOOK OF
KING ARTHUR AND OF HIS NOBLE KNIGHTS OF
THE ROUND TABLE.

Epilogue

WHEN Sir Lancelot received Sir Gawain's last letter, begging him to come and rescue King Arthur, he made no tarrying. He and Sir Bors gathered all their kin from the land of Benwick and the realm of Gaunes and rode day and night till they came to the Sea. They found their ships ready and, with a good wind, reached Logres the same day.

They found a very different realm from the one they had left. There were bandits everywhere. The land was in disorder, the people frightened, the Forest threatening, and no one could tell them what had happened. Only there were rumours of a great battle and many deaths. No man knew what had become of King Arthur or Queen Guinevere, but Sir Mordred and Sir Gawain were dead, that was certain.

At last Sir Lancelot's company reached the Great Plain; they rode sorrowfully over it, in wonder at the heaps of the dead. Here and there they recognized by his armour a Knight of the Round Table. Then they saw a horse that they knew, standing sorrowfully by the dead body of his master, and they recognized Wing Mane and knew it must be the body of Sir Gawain.

Sir Lancelot raised a great tomb of stones for Sir Gawain; for two days and three nights he stayed on his knees by the tomb, weeping and praying for Sir Gawain's soul. On the third day he called all his followers together.

'My fair lords,' he said, 'I thank all of you for your coming into this country but we come too late. For this I will grieve all my life, but against Death may no man rebel. Yet, since it is so, I will myself ride and seek news of my lord King Arthur and of my Lady Guinevere; for their bodies are not on this field of Camlann and they may yet be alive.'

'My lord Sir Lancelot,' said Sir Bors, 'you will find few friends now in this realm.'

But for all that Sir Lancelot sent Sir Bors and all his companions home and rode alone, seeking news. It would have gone hard with him if he had not found the Lady Luned.

'Well,' said Luned, 'as for Arthur the King no mortal man knows if he is alive or dead. But as for Guinevere the Queen I took her to safety myself on Merlin's instructions.' Then she told Lancelot where to find the Queen. 'But whether she will welcome you,' added Luned, 'God knows, for I do not.'

Lancelot found Guinevere in a convent nearby. It was a shock for him because she was dressed not as a queen but as a nun. It was a shock for her, an even greater one, to see a man she had never expected to see again on this earth. She fainted three times. Then she called the nuns of the convent together and this is what she said to Sir Lancelot in their presence:

'Through this man and me have all these wars been fought, and all those noble knights been slain. Therefore, Sir Lancelot,

I beg you with all my heart for all the love that ever was between us, never more to look upon my face but to go back to your own land for my sake. For through you and me is the flower of knights that was the fellowship of the Round Table destroyed.'

'Nay,' said Sir Lancelot, 'that I will never do. For I will never be false to you. The same destiny that you have chosen I will choose; for I take record of God that in you I had all my earthly joy. But since that joy is ended, I will go now to a hermit, grey or white, that will receive me; and live there as a hermit myself for God's sake. Wherefore, Lady, I pray you kiss me once and then never no more.'

'Nay, Sir Lancelot,' said the Queen, trembling, 'for the love of my noble Lord King Arthur that shall I never do.'

Then Sir Lancelot and Queen Guinevere said a last farewell. There was never a man so hard-hearted that would not have wept his heart out to see their sorrow. Sir Lancelot rode on his way till he found a hermitage, and there a grey hermit welcomed him, throwing his one arm around him. Because of this one arm Sir Lancelot recognized that it was Sir Bedevere. Sir Bedevere told him the true story of the Morte Arthur; and so for seven years the two knights dwelt together in that hermitage, praying for their dead companions and weeping for their own sins and for the sorrows of the realm of Logres.

At the end of seven years Sir Lancelot dreamt that Queen Guinevere was dead. He set out walking to the convent with Sir Bedevere, and when they finally reached the convent they found that she had died only half an hour before. Sir Lancelot did not weep when he saw her face but he heaved a great sigh. So they buried her, wrapped in cered cloth of Raines from the top to the toe. When she was put into the Earth, then at last Sir Lancelot cried a great cry.

'I remember her beauty and her nobleness, that was both with her King and with her,' he cried. 'And when I remember how by my fault and my pride they were both laid low, that pair that were peerless of all living, when I remember their kindness and my unkindness, my heart sinks low.'

After that Sir Lancelot was never well again but lay grovelling on the tomb of Queen Guinevere. Sometimes he fell into a broken sleep, but mostly he prayed day and night, till he dried and dwined away.

Sir Bors and his kin came back to Logres searching for Sir Lancelot. But when at last they came to his bed they found him lying there smiling sweetly, stark dead.

'Alas,' said Sir Lionel, 'for this was the most noble knight that ever lived, the most courteous too and the most forgiving to his enemies, the mightiest knight of his hands that this world has ever known and the most loved.'

They lit a hundred torches and escorted his body to his own castle of Joyous Garde. There they buried him, with his shield and his sword and his helm beside him. Sir Bedevere said that for all Sir Lancelot was a sinful man, he had seen the angels heave him up to Heaven, and they believed Sir Bedevere because he was now a holy man and a hermit. Then, leaving him to watch the tomb, they rode sorrowfully on their own way.

THE END.

King Arthur and his Kingdom

King Arthur lived most of his life in the castle-city of Camelot, in the realm of Logres which covered the Seven Kingdoms. We do not know where these seven kingdoms were. We do not know where Camelot was, nor how far the realm of Logres extended, nor where was Lyonesse; and we have no idea at all where Annwen, the Glass Island, that men called Avalon, could be found. There are lands and islands nowadays called Cornwall and the Orkneys and Ireland. But perhaps men have only named them in memory of the kingdoms their far-away ancestors once visited and knew. All we know for sure is that one day King Arthur will come again.